PENGUI

KING SOLOMON'S MINES

BY SIR HENRY RIDER HAGGARD

SIR HENRY RIDER HAGGARD (1856–1925). Public servant, reformer, commissioner, agriculturist and well-known story teller, Rider Haggard was the author of thirty-four adventure novels of which *King Solomon's Mines*, *She* and *Allan Quatermain* are now best remembered.

Henry Rider Haggard was born in Bradenham in Norfolk in 1856. He was the sixth son of a lawyer and was educated in Ipswich. In 1875 his father procured for him the post of junior secretary to the Governor of Natal, Sir Henry Bulwer. He set sail for South Africa and spent six years there, fascinated by its landscape, wildlife, tribal society and mysterious past. He returned to England in 1880 and was called to the Bar to Lincoln's Inn four years later. His first and perhaps most celebrated novel, *King Solomon's Mines*, is set in Africa and was published soon after he had qualified in 1885. It was so successful that Haggard was able to move back to Norfolk, where he could concentrate on his writing. He produced a whole series of spellbinding and extravagant romances set in far-flung corners of the world: Iceland, Constantinople, Mexico, Ancient Egypt and, of course, Africa. Both *She* and *Allan Quatermain* were published in 1887, and by 1890, at the age of thirty-four, Haggard had become both an enormously successful writer and a household name. He used his position well and did much to further causes, accepting an honorary post and giving countless after-dinner speeches. He was great friends with fellow writer Rudyard Kipling and with the anthropologist and scholar Andrew Lang, to whom *She* is inscribed.

A private man, Haggard was deeply shattered by the death of his son in 1891, and for many months afterwards was rarely to be seen outside his Norfolk home. After an unsuccessful stand for Parliament in 1894 Haggard threw ... ng and writing once more. One ... t extensively was the state of

British agriculture and his *A Farmer's Year* (1898) and *Rural England* (1902) made a substantial contribution to alleviating the plight of the farmer and small-holder of the time. Throughout his life Haggard continued to travel widely, visiting exotic places that helped fuel his imagination for new stories. He was knighted in 1912 and died in 1925.

Written in the same period as *She*, *Allan Quatermain* and *Jess*, *King Solomon's Mines* is one of Haggard's most exciting adventure stories. Its African setting is vividly described and shows his love for fascination with that continent.

PENGUIN POPULAR CLASSICS

KING SOLOMON'S MINES

H. RIDER HAGGARD

PENGUIN BOOKS

PENGUIN BOOKS

Published by the Penguin Group
Penguin Books Ltd, 80 Strand, London WC2R ORL, England
Penguin Putnam Inc., 375 Hudson Street, New York, New York 10014, USA
Penguin Books Australia Ltd, Ringwood, Victoria, Australia
Penguin Books Canada Ltd, 10 Alcorn Avenue, Toronto, Ontario, Canada M4V 3B2
Penguin Books India (P) Ltd, 11 Community Centre, Panchsheel Park,
New Delhi – 110 017, India
Penguin Books (NZ) Ltd, Cnr Rosedale and Airborne Roads, Albany, Auckland,
New Zealand
Penguin Books (South Africa) (Pty) Ltd, 24 Sturdee Avenue, Rosebank 2196, South Africa

Penguin Books Ltd, Registered Offices: 80 Strand, London WC2R ORL, England

www.penguin.com

First published 1885
Published in Penguin Popular Classics 1994
002

Printed in Great Britain by Clays Ltd, St Ives plc

ISBN-13: 978-0-14119-778-4

www.greenpenguin.co.uk

ALWAYS LEARNING   **PEARSON**

Dedication

THIS FAITHFUL BUT UNPRETENDING RECORD

OF A REMARKABLE ADVENTURE

IS HEREBY RESPECTFULLY DEDICATED

BY THE NARRATOR

ALLAN QUATERMAIN

TO ALL THE BIG AND LITTLE BOYS

WHO READ IT

AUTHOR'S NOTE

THE author ventures to take this opportunity to thank his readers for the kind reception they have accorded to the successive editions of this tale during the last twelve years. He hopes that in its present form it will fall into the hands of an even wider public, and that it may in years to come continue to afford amusement to those who are still young enough at heart to love a story of treasure, war, and wild adventure.

DITCHINGHAM,
 11th March 1898.

POST SCRIPTUM

NOW, in 1905, I can only add how glad I am that my romance should continue to please so many readers. Imagination has been verified by fact; the King Solomon's Mines I dreamed of have been discovered, and are putting out their gold once more, and, according to the latest reports, their diamonds also; the Kukuanas or, rather, the Matabele, have been tamed by the white man's bullets, but still there seem to be many who find pleasure in these simple pages. That they may continue so to do, even to the third and fourth generation, or perhaps longer still, would, I am sure, be the hope of our old and departed friend, ALLAN QUATERMAIN.

H. RIDER HAGGARD.

DITCHINGHAM,
 15th July 1905.

INTRODUCTION

Now that this book is printed, and about to be given to the world, a sense of its shortcomings, both in style and contents, weighs very heavily upon me. As regards the latter, I can only say that it does not pretend to be a full account of everything we did and saw. There are many things connected with our journey into Kukuanaland that I should have liked to dwell upon at length, which, as it is, have been scarcely alluded to. Amongst these are the curious legends which I collected about the chain armour that saved us from destruction in the great battle of Loo, and also about the "Silent Ones" or Colossi at the mouth of the stalactite cave. Again, if I had given way to my own impulses, I should have wished to go into the differences, some of which are to my mind very suggestive, between the Zulu and Kukuana dialects. Also a few pages might have been given up profitably to the consideration of the indigenous flora and fauna of Kukuanaland.* Then there remains the most interesting subject—that, as it is, has only been touched on incidentally—of the magnificent system of military organization in force in that country, which, in my opinion, is much superior to that inaugurated by Chaka in Zululand, inasmuch as it permits of even more rapid mobilization, and does not necessitate the employment of the pernicious system of forced celibacy. Lastly, I have scarcely spoken of the domestic and family customs of the Kukuanas, many of which are exceedingly quaint, or of their proficiency in the art of smelting and welding metals. This science they carry to considerable perfection, of which a good example is to be seen in their " tollas," or heavy throwing knives, the backs of these weapons being made of hammered iron, and the edges of beautiful steel welded with great skill on to the iron frames. The fact of the matter is, I thought, with Sir Henry Curtis and Captain Good, that the best plan would be to tell my story in a plain, straightforward manner, and to leave these matters to be dealt with subsequently in whatever way ultimately may appear to be desirable. In the meanwhile I shall, of course, be delighted to

* I discovered eight varieties of antelope, with which I was previously totally unacquainted, and many new species of plants, for the most part of the bulbous tribe.—A. Q.

give all information in my power to anybody interested in such things.

And now it only remains for me to offer apologies for my blunt way of writing. I can but say in excuse of it that I am more accustomed to handle a rifle than a pen, and cannot make any pretence to the grand literary flights and flourishes which I see in novels—for sometimes I like to read a novel. I suppose they—the flights and flourishes—are desirable, and I regret not being able to supply them ; but at the same time I cannot help thinking that simple things are always the most impressive, and that books are easier to understand when they are written in plain language, though perhaps I have no right to set up an opinion on such a matter. " A sharp spear," runs the Kukuana saying, " needs no polish " ; and on the same principle I venture to hope that a true story, however strange it may be, does not require to be decked out in fine words.

ALLAN QUATERMAIN

CONTENTS

KING SOLOMON'S MINES

CHAPTER I

I MEET SIR HENRY CURTIS

IT is a curious thing that at my age—fifty-five last birthday—I should find myself taking up a pen to try to write a history. I wonder what sort of a history it will be when I have finished it, if ever I come to the end of the trip! I have done a good many things in my life, which seems a long one to me, owing to my having begun work so young, perhaps. At an age when other boys are at school I was earning my living as a trader in the old Colony. I have been trading, hunting, fighting, or mining ever since. And yet it is only eight months ago that I made my pile. It is a big pile now that I have got it —I don't yet know how big—but I do not think I would go through the last fifteen or sixteen months again for it; no, not if I knew that I should come out safe at the end, pile and all. But then I am a timid man, and dislike violence; moreover, I am fairly sick of adventure. I wonder why I am going to write this book: it is not in my line. I am not a literary man,

though very devoted to the Old Testament and
also to the " Ingoldsby Legends." Let me try
to set down my reasons, just to see if I have any.

First reason : Because Sir Henry Curtis and
Captain John Good asked me.

Second reason : Because I am laid up here at
Durban with the pain in my left leg. Ever since
that confounded lion got hold of me I have been
liable to this trouble, and being rather bad just
now, it makes me limp more than ever. There
must be some poison in a lion's teeth, otherwise
how is it that when your wounds are healed
they break out again, generally, mark you, at
the same time of year that you got your mauling ?
It is a hard thing when one has shot sixty-five
lions and more, as I have in the course of my life,
that the sixty-sixth should chew your leg like a
quid of tobacco. It breaks the routine of the
thing, and putting other considerations aside, I
am an orderly man and don't like that. This is
by the way.

Third reason : Because I want my boy Harry,
who is over there at the hospital in London
studying to become a doctor, to have something
to amuse him and keep him out of mischief for
a week or so. Hospital work must sometimes
pall and grow rather dull, for even of cutting
up dead bodies there may come satiety, and as
this history will not be dull, whatever else it may
be, it will put a little life into things for a day
or two while Harry is reading it.

Fourth reason and last : Because I am going
to tell the strangest story that I know of. It
may seem a queer thing to say, especially considering that there is no woman in it—except
Foulata. Stop, though ! there is Gagaoola, if

she was a woman and not a fiend. But she was a hundred at least, and therefore not marriageable, so I don't count her. At any rate, I can safely say that there is not a *petticoat* in the whole history.

Well, I had better come to the yoke. It is a stiff place, and I feel as though I were bogged up to the axle. But " *sutjes, sutjes*," as the Boers say—I am sure I don't know how they spell it —softly does it. A strong team will come through at last, that is, if they are not too poor. You can never do anything with poor oxen. Now to begin.

I, Allan Quatermain, of Durban, Natal, Gentleman, make oath and say—That's how I began my deposition before the magistrate about poor Khiva's and Ventvögel's sad deaths ; but somehow it doesn't seem quite the right way to begin a book. And, besides, am I a gentleman ? What is a gentleman ? I don't quite know, and yet I have had to do with niggers—no, I will scratch out that word " niggers," for I do not like it. I've known natives who *are*, and so you will say, Harry, my boy, before you have done with this tale, and I have known mean whites with lots of money and fresh out from home, too, who *are not*.

At any rate, I was born a gentleman, though I have been nothing but a poor travelling trader and hunter all my life. Whether I have remained so I know not, you must judge of that. Heaven knows I've tried. I have killed many men in my time, yet I have never slain wantonly or stained my hand in innocent blood, but only in self-defence. The Almighty gave us our lives and I suppose He meant us to defend them, at

least I have always acted on that, and I hope
it will not be brought up against me when my
clock strikes. There, there, it is a cruel and
wicked world, and for a timid man I have been
mixed up in a deal of slaughter. I cannot tell
the rights of it, but at any rate I have never
stolen, though once I cheated a Kafir out of a
herd of cattle. But then he had done me a dirty
turn, and it has troubled me ever since into the
bargain.

Well, it is eighteen months or so ago since first
I met Sir Henry Curtis and Captain Good. It
was in this way. I had been up elephant hunting
beyond Bamangwato, and had met with bad luck.
Everything went wrong that trip, and to top up
with I got the fever badly. So soon as I was well
enough I trekked down to the Diamond Fields,
sold such ivory as I had, together with my
wagon and oxen, discharged my hunters, and took
the postcart to the Cape. After spending a week
in Cape Town, finding that they overcharged me
at the hotel, and having seen everything there
was to see, including the botanical gardens,
which seem to me likely to confer a great benefit
on the country, and the new Houses of Parliament,
which I expect will do nothing of the sort, I
determined to go back to Natal by the *Dunkeld*,
then lying at the docks waiting for the *Edinburgh
Castle* due in from England. I took my berth
and went aboard, and that afternoon the Natal
passengers from the *Edinburgh Castle* transhipped
and we weighed and put out to sea.

Among these passengers who came on board
were two who excited my curiosity. One, a
gentleman of about thirty, was perhaps the
biggest-chested and longest-armed man I ever

saw. He had yellow hair, a thick yellow beard, clear-cut features, and large grey eyes set deep in his head. I never saw a finer-looking man, and somehow he reminded me of an ancient Dane. Not that I know much of ancient Danes, though I knew a modern Dane who did me out of ten pounds ; but I remember once seeing a picture of some of those gentry, who, I take it, were a kind of white Zulus. They were drinking out of big horns, and their long hair hung down their backs. As I looked at my friend standing there by the companion-ladder, I thought that if he only let his hair grow a little, put one of those chain shirts on to his great shoulders, and took hold of a battle-axe and a horn mug, he might have sat as a model for that picture. And by the way it is a curious thing, and just shows how the blood will out, I discovered afterwards that Sir Henry Curtis, for that was the big man's name, is of Danish blood.* He also reminded me strongly of somebody else, but at the time I could not remember who it was.

The other man who stood talking to Sir Henry was short, stout, and dark, and of quite a different cut. I suspected at once that he was a naval officer ; I don't know why, but it is difficult to mistake a navy man. I have gone shooting trips with several of them in the course of my life, and they have always proved themselves the best and bravest and nicest fellows I ever met, though sadly given, some of them, to the use of profane language. I asked a page or two back, what is a

* Mr. Quatermain's ideas about ancient Danes seem to be rather confused ; we have always understood that they were dark-haired people. Probably he was thinking of Saxons.— *Editor.*

gentleman ?   I'll answer the question now : a
Royal Naval officer is, in a general sort of way,
though of course there may be a black sheep
among them here and there.   I fancy it is just
the wide seas and the breath of God's winds that
wash their hearts and blow the bitterness out of
their minds and make them what men ought to
be.

Well, to return, I was right again ; I ascertained
that the dark man *was* a naval officer, a lieutenant
of thirty-one, who, after seventeen years' service,
had been turned out of her Majesty's employ
with the barren honour of a commander's rank,
because it was impossible that he should be
promoted.   This is what people who serve the
Queen have to expect : to be shot out into the
cold world to find a living just when they are
beginning to really understand their work, and
to reach the prime of life.   I suppose they don't
mind it, but for my own part I had rather earn
my bread as a hunter.   One's halfpence are as
scarce perhaps, but you do not get so many
kicks.

The officer's name I found out—by referring to
the passengers' list—was Good—Captain John
Good.   He was broad, of medium height, dark,
stout, and rather a curious man to look at.   He
was so very neat and so very clean-shaved, and
he always wore an eye-glass in his right eye.   It
seemed to grow there, for it had no string, and
he never took it out except to wipe it.   At first
I thought he used to sleep with it, but afterwards
I found that this was a mistake.   He put it in
his trousers pocket when he went to bed, together
with his false teeth, of which he had two beautiful
sets that, my own being none of the best, have

often caused me to break the tenth commandment. But I am anticipating.

Soon after we had got under way evening closed in, and brought with it very dirty weather. A keen breeze sprung up off land, and a kind of aggravated Scotch mist soon drove everybody from the deck. As for the *Dunkeld*, she is a flat-bottomed punt, and going up light as she was, she rolled very heavily. It almost seemed as though she would go right over, but she never did. It was quite impossible to walk about, so I stood near the engines where it was warm, and amused myself with watching the pendulum, which was fixed opposite to me, swinging slowly backwards and forwards as the vessel rolled, and marking the angle she touched at each lurch.

" That pendulum's wrong ; it is not properly weighted," suddenly said a somewhat testy voice at my shoulder. Looking round I saw the naval officer whom I had noticed when the passengers came aboard.

" Indeed, now what makes you think so ? " I asked.

" Think so. I don't think at all. Why there " —as she righted herself after a roll—" if the ship had really rolled to the degree that thing pointed to then she would never have rolled again, that's all. But it is just like these merchant skippers, they always are so confoundedly careless."

Just then the dinner bell rung, and I was not sorry, for it is a dreadful thing to have to listen to an officer of the Royal Navy when he gets on to that subject. I only know one worse thing, and it is to hear a merchant skipper express his candid opinion of officers of the Royal Navy.

Captain Good and I went down to dinner together, and there we found Sir Henry Curtis already seated. He and Captain Good were placed together, and I sat opposite to them. The captain and I soon fell into talk about shooting and what not; he asking me many questions, and I answering them as well as I could. Presently he got on to elephants.

"Ah, sir," called out somebody who was sitting near me, "you've reached the right man for that; Hunter Quatermain should be able to tell you about elephants if anybody can."

Sir Henry, who had been sitting quite quiet listening to our talk, started visibly.

"Excuse me, sir," he said, leaning forward across the table, and speaking in a low deep voice, a very suitable voice, it seemed to me, to come out of those great lungs. "Excuse me, sir, but is your name Allan Quatermain?"

I said that it was.

The big man made no further remark, but I heard him mutter "fortunate" into his beard.

Presently dinner came to an end, and as we were leaving the saloon Sir Henry strolled up and asked me if I would come into his cabin to smoke a pipe. I accepted, and he led the way to the *Dunkeld* deck cabin, and a very good cabin it is. It had been two cabins, but when Sir Garnet or one of those big swells went down the coast in the *Dunkeld*, they knocked away the partition and have never put it up again. There was a sofa in the cabin, and a little table in front of it. Sir Henry sent the steward for a bottle of whisky, and the three of us sat down and lit our pipes.

"Mr. Quatermain," said Sir Henry Curtis,

when the steward had brought the whisky and
lit the lamp, " the year before last about this
time you were, I believe, at a place called Bamangwato, to the north of the Transvaal."

" I was," I answered, rather surprised that
this gentleman should be so well acquainted with
my movements, which were not, so far as I was
aware, considered of general interest.

" You were trading there, were you not ? " put
in Captain Good, in his quick way.

" I was. I took up a wagon-load of goods,
made a camp outside the settlement, and stopped
till I had sold them."

Sir Henry was sitting opposite to me in a
Madeira chair, his arms leaning on the table.
He now looked up, fixing his large grey eyes
full upon my face. There was a curious anxiety
in them I thought.

" Did you happen to meet a man called Neville
there ? "

" Oh, yes ; he outspanned alongside of me for
a fortnight to rest his oxen before going on to the
interior. I had a letter from a lawyer a few
months back, asking me if I knew what had
become of him, which I answered to the best
of my ability at the time."

" Yes," said Sir Henry, " your letter was forwarded to me. You said in it that the gentleman
called Neville left Bamangwato at the beginning
of May in a wagon with a driver, a voorlooper,
and a Kafir hunter called Jim, announcing his
intention of trekking if possible as far as Inyati,
the extreme trading post in the Matabele country,
where he would sell his wagon and proceed on
foot. You also said that he did sell his wagon,
for six months afterwards you saw the wagon

in the possession of a Portuguese trader, who
told you that he had bought it at Inyati from
a white man whose name he had forgotten, and
that he believed the white man with the native
servant had started off for the interior on a
shooting trip."

" Yes."

Then came a pause.

" Mr. Quatermain," said Sir Henry suddenly,
" I suppose you know or can guess nothing more
of the reasons of my—of Mr. Neville's journey to
the northward, or as to what point that journey
was directed ? "

" I heard something," I answered, and stopped.
The subject was one which I did not care to
discuss.

Sir Henry and Captain Good looked at each
other, and Captain Good nodded.

" Mr. Quatermain," went on the former, " I
am going to tell you a story, and ask your
advice, and perhaps your assistance. The agent
who forwarded me your letter told me that I might
rely upon it implicitly, as you were," he said,
" well known and universally respected in Natal,
and especially noted for your discretion."

I bowed and drank some whisky and water to
hide my confusion, for I am a modest man—and
Sir Henry went on.

" Mr. Neville was my brother."

" Oh," I said, starting, for now I knew who
Sir Henry had reminded me of when first I saw
him. His brother was a much smaller man
and had a dark beard, but now that I thought
of it, he possessed eyes of the same shade of grey
and with the same keen look in them ; the
features too were not unlike.

" He was," went on Sir Henry, " my only and younger brother, and till five years ago I do not suppose that we were ever a month away from each other. But just about five years ago a misfortune befell us, as sometimes does happen in families. We quarrelled bitterly, and I behaved unjustly to my brother in my anger."

Here Captain Good nodded his head vigorously to himself. The ship gave a big roll just then so that the looking-glass, which was fixed opposite us to starboard, was for a moment nearly over our heads, and as I was sitting with my hands in my pockets and staring upwards, I could see him nodding like anything.

" As I daresay you know," went on Sir Henry, " if a man dies intestate, and has no property but land, real property it is called in England, it all descends to his eldest son. It so happened that just at the time when we quarrelled our father died intestate. He had put off making his will until it was too late. The result was that my brother, who had not been brought up to any profession, was left without a penny. Of course it would have been my duty to provide for him, but at the time the quarrel between us was so bitter that I did not—to my shame I say it (and he sighed deeply)—offer to do anything. It was not that I grudged him justice, but I waited for him to make advances, and he made none. I am sorry to trouble you with all this, Mr. Quatermain, but I must to make things clear, eh, Good ? "

" Quite so, quite so," said the captain. " Mr. Quatermain will, I am sure, keep this history to himself."

" Of course," said I, for I rather pride myself on my discretion, for which, as Sir Henry had heard, I have some repute.

" Well," went on Sir Henry, " my brother had a few hundred pounds to his account at the time. Without saying anything to me he drew out this paltry sum, and, having adopted the name of Neville, started off for South Africa in the wild hope of making a fortune. This I learned afterwards. Some three years passed, and I heard nothing of my brother, though I wrote several times. Doubtless the letters never reached him. But as time went on I grew more and more troubled about him. I found out, Mr. Quatermain, that blood is thicker than water."

" That's true," said I, thinking of my boy Harry.

" I found out, Mr. Quatermain, that I would have given half my fortune to know that my brother George, the only relation I possess, was safe and well, and that I should see him again."

" But you never did, Curtis," jerked out Captain Good, glancing at the big man's face.

" Well, Mr. Quatermain, as time went on I became more and more anxious to find out if my brother was alive or dead, and if alive to get him home again. I set inquiries on foot, and your letter was one of the results. So far as it went it was satisfactory, for it showed that till lately George was alive, but it did not go far enough. So, to cut a long story short, I made up my mind to come out and look for him myself, and Captain Good was so kind as to come with me."

"Yes," said the captain; "nothing else to do, you see. Turned out by my Lords of the Admiralty to starve on half-pay. And now, perhaps, sir, you will tell us what you know or have heard of the gentleman called Neville."

CHAPTER II

THE LEGEND OF SOLOMON'S MINES

"WHAT was it that you heard about my brother's journey at Bamangwato?" said Sir Henry, as I paused to fill my pipe before answering Captain Good.

"I heard this," I answered, "and I have never mentioned it to a soul till to-day. I heard that he was starting for Solomon's Mines."

"Solomon's Mines?" ejaculated both my hearers at once. "Where are they?"

"I don't know," I said; "I know where they are said to be. Once I saw the peaks of the mountains that border them, but there were a hundred and thirty miles of desert between me and them, and I am not aware that any white man ever got across it save one. But perhaps the best thing I can do is to tell you the legend of Solomon's Mines as I know it, you passing your word not to reveal anything I tell you without my permission. Do you agree to that? I have my reasons for asking it."

Sir Henry nodded, and Captain Good replied, "Certainly, certainly."

"Well," I began, "as you may guess, generally speaking, elephant hunters are a rough set of men who do not trouble themselves with much beyond the facts of life and the ways of Kafirs.

But here and there you meet a man who takes the trouble to collect traditions from the natives, and tries to make out a little piece of the history of this dark land. It was such a man as this who first told me the legend of Solomon's Mines, now a matter of nearly thirty years ago. That was when I was on my first elephant hunt in the Matabele country. His name was Evans, and he was killed the following year, poor fellow, by a wounded buffalo, and lies buried near the Zambesi Falls. I was telling Evans one night, I remember, of some wonderful workings I had found whilst hunting koodoo and eland in what is now the Lydenburg district of the Transvaal. I see they have come across these workings again lately in prospecting for gold, but I knew of them years ago. There is a great wide wagon road cut out of the solid rock, and leading to the mouth of the working or gallery. Inside the mouth of this gallery are stacks of gold quartz piled up ready for roasting, which shows that the workers, whoever they are, must have left in a hurry. Also, about twenty paces in, the gallery is built across, and a beautiful bit of masonry it is.

"'Ay,' said Evans, 'but I will spin you a queerer yarn than that;' and he went on to tell me how he had found in the far interior a ruined city, which he believed to be the Ophir of the Bible, and, by the way, other more learned men have said the same long since poor Evans's time. I was, I remember, listening open-eared to all these wonders, for I was young at the time, and this story of an ancient civilization and of treasures which those old Jewish or Phœnician adventurers used to extract from a country long since lapsed into the darkest barbarism took a great hold upon my imagination, when suddenly he said to me, ' Lad, did you ever hear of the Suliman Mountains up to the north-west of the Mashukulumbwe country ? ' I told him I never had. ' Ah, well,' he said, ' that is where Solomon really had his mines, his diamond mines, I mean.'

" ' How do you know that ? ' I asked.

" ' Know it ! why what is " Suliman " but a corruption of Solomon ?* And, besides, an old Isanusi or witch doctoress up in the Manica country told me all about it. She said that the people who lived across those mountains were a " branch " of the Zulus, speaking a dialect of Zulu, but finer and bigger men even ; that there lived among them great wizards, who had learned their art from white men when " all the world was dark," and who had the secret of a wonderful mine of " bright stones." '

" Well, I laughed at this story at the time, though it interested me, for the Diamond Fields were not discovered then, but poor Evans went off and was killed, and for twenty years I never thought any more of the matter. However, just twenty years afterwards—and that is a long time, gentlemen ; an elephant hunter does not often live for twenty years at his business —I heard something more definite about Suliman's Mountains and the country which lies behind them. I was up beyond the Manica country, at a place called Sitanda's Kraal, and a miserable place it was, for a man could get nothing to eat, and there was but little game about. I had an attack of fever, and was in

---

* Suliman is the Arabic form of Solomon.—*Editor*.

a bad way generally, when one day a Portugee
arrived with a single companion—a half-breed.
Now I know your low-class Delagoa Portugee
well. There is no greater devil unhung in a
general way, battening as he does upon human
agony and flesh in the shape of slaves. But this
was quite a different type of man to the mean
fellows whom I have been accustomed to meet ;
indeed, in appearance he reminded me more
of the polite doms I have read about, for he was
tall and thin, with large dark eyes and curling
grey mustachios. We talked together a little,
for he could speak broken English, and I understood a little Portugee, and he told me that his
name was José Silvestre, and that he had a place
near Delagoa Bay. When he went on next day
with his half-breed companion, he said ' Good-
bye,' taking off his hat quite in the old style.

"' Good-bye, señor,' he said ; ' if ever we meet
again I shall be the richest man in the world,
and I will remember you.' I laughed a little—
I was too weak to laugh much—and watched
him strike out for the great desert to the west,
wondering if he was mad, or what he thought
he was going to find there.

" A week passed, and I got the better of my
fever. One evening I was sitting on the ground
in front of the little tent I had with me, chewing
the last leg of a miserable fowl I had bought
from a native for a bit of cloth worth twenty
fowls, and staring at the hot red sun sinking
down over the desert, when suddenly I saw a
figure, apparently that of a European, for it
wore a coat, on the slope of the rising ground
opposite to me, about three hundred yards
away. The figure crept along on its hands and

knees, then it got up and staggered forward a few yards on its legs, only to fall and crawl again. Seeing that it must be somebody in distress, I sent one of my hunters to help him, and presently he arrived, and whom do you suppose it turned out to be ? "

" José Silvestre, of course," said Captain Good.

" Yes, José Silvestre, or rather his skeleton and a little skin. His face was bright yellow with bilious fever, and his large dark eyes stood nearly out of his head, for all the flesh had gone. There was nothing but yellow parchment-like skin, white hair, and the gaunt bones sticking up beneath.

" ' Water ! for the sake of Christ, water ! ' he moaned, and I saw that his lips were cracked, and his tongue, which protruded between them, was swollen and blackish.

" I gave him water with a little milk in it, and he drank it in great gulps, two quarts or so, without stopping. I would not let him have any more. Then the fever took him again, and he fell down and began to rave about Suliman's Mountains, and the diamonds, and the desert. I carried him into the tent and did what I could for him, which was little enough ; but I saw how it must end. About eleven o'clock he grew quieter and I lay down for a little rest and went to sleep. At dawn I woke again, and in the half light saw Silvestre sitting up, a strange, gaunt form, and gazing out towards the desert. Presently the first ray of the sun shot right across the wide plain before us till it reached the far-away crest of one of the tallest of the Suliman Mountains more than a hundred miles away.

There it is ! ' cried the dying man in

Portuguese, and pointing with his long, thin arm, ' but I shall never reach it, never. No one will ever reach it ! '

" Suddenly he paused, and seemed to take a resolution. ' Friend,' he said, turning towards me, ' are you there ? My eyes grow dark.'

" ' Yes,' I said ; ' yes, lie down now, and rest.'

" ' Ay,' he answered, ' I shall rest soon, I have time to rest—all eternity. Listen, I am dying ! You have been good to me. I will give you the writing. Perhaps you will get there if you can live to pass the desert, which has killed my poor servant and me.'

" Then he groped in his shirt and brought out what I thought was a Boer tobacco pouch made of the skin of the Swart-vet-pens or sable antelope. It was fastened with a little strip of hide, what we call a rimpi, and this he tried to loose, but could not. He handed it to me. ' Untie it,' he said. I did so, and extracted a bit of torn yellow linen, on which something was written in rusty letters. Inside this rag was a paper.

" Then he went on feebly, for he was growing weak : ' The paper has all that is on the linen. It took me years to read. Listen : my ancestor, a political refugee from Lisbon, and one of the first Portuguese who landed on these shores, wrote that when he was dying on those mountains which no white foot ever pressed before or since. His name was José da Silvestra, and he lived three hundred years ago. His slave, who waited for him on this side of the mountains, found him dead, and brought the writing home to Delagoa. It has been in the family ever since, but none have cared to read it, till at last

I did. And I have lost my life over it, but another may succeed, and become the richest man in the world—the richest man in the world. Only give it to no one, señor ; go yourself ! ' Then he began to wander again, and in an hour it was all over.

" God rest him ! he died very quietly, and I buried him deep, with big boulders on his breast ; so I do not think that the jackals can have dug him up. And then I came away."

" Ay, but the document ? " said Sir Henry, in a tone of deep interest.

" Yes, the document ; what was in it ? " added the captain.

" Well, gentlemen, if you like I will tell you. I have never showed it to anybody yet except to a drunken old Portuguese trader who translated it for me, and had forgotten all about it by the next morning. The original rag is at my home in Durban, together with poor Dom José's translation, but I have the English rendering in my pocket-book, and a facsimile of the map, if it can be called a map. Here it is."

" I, José da Silvestra, who am now dying of hunger in the little cave where no snow is on the north side of the nipple of the southernmost of the two mountains I have named Sheba's Breasts, write this in the year 1590 with a cleft bone upon a remnant of my raiment, my blood being the ink. If my slave should find it when he comes, and should bring it to Delagoa, let my friend (name illegible) bring the matter to the knowledge of the king, that he may send an army which, if they live through the desert and the mountains, and can overcome the brave Kukuanes and their devilish arts, to which end

many priests should be brought, will make him
the richest king since Solomon.   With my own

Sketch Map of the Route to King Solomon's Mines.

eyes have I seen the countless diamonds stored
in Solomon's treasure chamber behind the white

Death; but through the treachery of Gagool the witch-finder I might bring nought away, scarcely my life. Let him who comes follow the map, and climb the snow of Sheba's left breast till he reaches the nipple, on the north side of which is the great road Solomon made, from whence three days' journey to the King's Palace. Let him kill Gagool. Pray for my soul. Farewell.

JOSÉ DA SILVESTRA."*

* Eu José da Silvestra que estou morrendo de fome ná pequena cova onde não ha neve ao lado norte do bico mais ao sul das duas montanhas que chamei seio de Sheba; escrevo isto no anno 1590; escrevo isto com um pedaço d' ôsso n' um farrapo de minha roupa e com sangue meu por tinta; se o meu escravo dér com isto quando venha ao levar para Lourenzo Marquez, que o meu amigo —— leve a cousa ao conhecimento d' El Rei, para que possa mandar um exercito que, se desfiler pelo deserto e pelas montanhas e mesmo sobrepujar os bravos Kukuanes e suas artes diabolicas, pelo que se deviam trazer muitos padres Fara o Rei mais rico depois de Salomão. Com meus proprios olhos vé os di amantes sem conto guardados nas camaras do thesouro de Salomão a traz da morte branca, mas pela traição de Gagoa a feiticeira achadora, nada poderia levar, e apenas a minha vida. Quem vier siga o mappa e trepe pela neve de Sheba peito à esquerda até chegar ao bico, do lado norte do qual está a grande estrada do Solomão por elle feita, donde ha tre dias de jornada até ao Palacio do Rei. Mate Gagoal. Reze por minha alma. Adeos.

JOSÉ DA SILVESTRA.

When I had finished reading the above, and shown the copy of the map, drawn by the dying hand of the old Dom with his blood for ink, there followed a silence of astonishment.

"Well," said Captain Good, "I have been round the world twice, and put in at most ports, but may I be hung for a mutineer if ever I heard a yarn like this out of a story book, or in it either, for the matter of that."

"It's a queer tale, Mr. Quatermain," said Sir

Henry. "I suppose you are not hoaxing us? It is, I know, sometimes thought allowable to take in a greenhorn."

"If you think that, Sir Henry," I said, much put out, and pocketing my paper, for I do not like to be thought one of those silly fellows who consider it witty to tell lies, and who are for ever boasting to newcomers of extraordinary hunting adventures which never happened, "why, there is an end of the matter," and I rose to go.

Sir Henry laid his large hand upon my shoulder. "Sit down, Mr. Quatermain," he said, "I beg your pardon; I see very well you do not wish to deceive us, but the story sounded so strange that I could hardly believe it."

"You shall see the original map and writing when we reach Durban," I answered, somewhat mollified, for really when I came to consider the question it was scarcely wonderful that he should doubt my good faith. "But I have not told you about your brother. I knew the man Jim who was with him. He was a Bechuana by birth, a good hunter, and for a native a very clever man. That morning on which Mr. Neville was starting I saw Jim standing by my wagon and cutting up tobacco on the disselboom.

"'Jim,' said I, 'where are you off to this trip? Is it elephants?'

"'No, Baas,' he answered, 'we are after something worth much more than ivory.'

"'And what might that be?' I said, for I was curious. 'Is it gold?'

"'No, Baas, something worth more than gold,' and he grinned.

" I asked no more questions, for I did not like to lower my dignity by seeming inquisitive, but I was puzzled. Presently Jim finished cutting his tobacco.

" ' Baas,' said he.

" I took no notice.

" ' Baas,' said he again.

" ' Eh, boy, what is it ? ' I asked.

" ' Baas, we are going after diamonds.'

" ' Diamonds ! why, then, you are steering in the wrong direction ; you should head for the Fields.'

" ' Baas, have you ever heard of Suliman's Berg ? '—that is, Solomon's Mountains, Sir Henry.

" ' Ay ! '

" ' Have you ever heard of the diamonds there ? ''

" ' I have heard a foolish story, Jim.'

" ' It is no story, Baas. I once knew a woman who came from there, and reached Natal with her child, she told me :—she is dead now.'

" ' Your master will feed the aasvögels '— that is, vultures—' Jim, if he tries to reach Suliman's country, and so will you if they can get any pickings off your worthless old carcass,' said I.

" He grinned. ' Mayhap, Baas. Man must die ; I'd rather like to try a new country myself ; the elephants are getting worked out about here.'

" ' Ah ! my boy,' I said, ' you wait till the " pale old man " gets a grip of your yellow throat, and then we shall hear what sort of a tune you sing.'

" Half an hour after that I saw Neville's wagon move off. Presently Jim came back running. 'Good-bye, Baas,' he said. 'I didn't like to start without bidding you good-bye, for I daresay you are right, and that we shall never trek south again.'

"'Is your master really going to Suliman's Berg, Jim, or are you lying?'

"'No,' he answered, 'he is going. He told me he was bound to make his fortune somehow, or try to; so he might as well have a fling for the diamonds.'

"'Oh!' I said; 'wait a bit, Jim; will you take a note to your master, Jim, and promise not to give it to him till you reach Inyati?' which was some hundred miles off.

"'Yes, Baas.'

"So I took a scrap of paper, and wrote on it, 'Let him who comes . . . . climb the snow of Sheba's left breast, till he reaches the nipple, on the north side of which is Solomon's great road.'

"'Now, Jim,' I said, 'when you give this to your master, tell him he had better follow the advice on it implicitly. You are not to give it to him now, because I don't want him back asking me questions which I won't answer. Now be off, you idle fellow, the wagon is nearly out of sight.'

"Jim took the note and went, and that is all I know about your brother, Sir Henry; but I am much afraid——"

"Mr. Quatermain," said Sir Henry, "I am going to look for my brother; I am going to trace him to Suliman's Mountains and over them if necessary, till I find him, or until I know that he is dead. Will you come with me?"

I am, as I think I have said, a cautious man, indeed a timid one, and this suggestion frightened me. It seemed to me that to undertake such a journey would be to go to certain death, and putting other considerations aside, as I had a son to support, I could not afford to die just then.

"No, thank you, Sir Henry, I think I had rather not," I answered. "I am too old for wild-goose chases of that sort, and we should only end up like my poor friend Silvestre. I have a son dependent on me, so I cannot afford to risk my life."

Both Sir Henry and Captain Good looked very disappointed.

"Mr. Quatermain," said the former, "I am well off, and I am bent upon this business. You may put the remuneration for your services at whatever figure you like in reason, and it shall be paid over to you before we start. Moreover, I will arrange in the event of anything untoward happening to us or to you, that your son shall be suitably provided for. You will see from this offer how necessary I think your presence. Also if by chance we should reach this place and find diamonds, they shall belong to you and Good equally. I do not want them. But of course that promise is worth nothing at all, though the same thing would apply to any ivory we might get. You may pretty well make your own terms with me, Mr. Quatermain; and of course I shall pay all expenses."

"Sir Henry," said I, "this is the most liberal proposal I ever had, and one not to be sneezed at by a poor hunter and trader. But the job is the biggest I have come across, and I must take time to think over it. I will give you my answer before we get to Durban."

"Very good," answered Sir Henry, and then I said good-night and turned in, and dreamt about poor long-dead Silvestre and the diamonds.

CHAPTER III

UMBOPA ENTERS OUR SERVICE

IT takes from four to five days, according to the speed of the vessel and the state of the weather, to run up from the Cape to Durban. Sometimes, if the landing is bad at East London, where they have not yet made that wonderful harbour they talk so much of, and sink such a mint of money in, a ship is delayed for twenty-four hours before the cargo boats can get out to take off the goods. But on this occasion we had not to wait at all, for there were no breakers on the bar to speak of, and the tugs came out at once with the long strings of ugly flat-bottomed boats behind them, into which the packages were bundled with a crash. It did not matter what they might be, over they went slap bang ; whether they contained china or woollen goods they met with the same treatment. I saw one case holding four dozen champagne smashed all to bits, and there was the champagne fizzing and boiling about in the bottom of the dirty cargo boat. It was a wicked waste, and evidently so the Kafirs in the boats thought, for they found a couple of unbroken bottles, and knocking the necks off drank the contents. But they had not allowed for the expansion caused by the fizz in the wine, and, feeling themselves swelling, rolled about in the bottom of the boat, calling out that the good liquor was " tagati "—that is, bewitched. I spoke to them from the vessel and told them it was the white man's strongest medicine, and that they were as good as dead men. Those Kafirs went to the shore in a very great fright, and I do not think that they will touch champagne again.

Well, all the time that we were running up to Natal I was thinking over Sir Henry Curtis's offer. We did not speak any more on the subject for a day or two, though I told them many hunting yarns, all true ones. There is no need to tell lies about hunting, for so many curious things happen within the knowledge of a man whose business it is to hunt ; but this is by the way.

At last, one beautiful evening in January, which is our hottest month, we steamed past the coast of Natal expecting to make Durban Point by sunset. It is a lovely coast all along from East London, with its red sandhills and wide sweeps of vivid green, dotted here and there with Kafir kraals, and bordered by a ribbon of white surf, which spouts up in pillars of foam where it hits the rocks. But just before you come to Durban there is a peculiar richness about the landscape. There are the sheer kloofs cut in the hills by the rushing rains of centuries, down which the rivers sparkle ; there is the deepest green of the bush, growing as God planted it, and the other greens of the mealie gardens and the sugar patches, while here and there a white house, smiling out at the placid sea, puts a finish and gives an air of homeliness to the scene. For to my mind, however

beautiful a view may be, it requires the presence
of man to make it complete, but perhaps that is
because I have lived so much in the wilderness,
and therefore know the value of civilization,
though to be sure it drives away the game.   The
Garden of Eden, no doubt, was fair before man
was, but I always think it must have been fairer
when Eve was walking about it.

To return, we had miscalculated a little, and
the sun was well down before we dropped anchor
off the Point, and heard the gun which told the
good folks of Durban that the English mail was
in.   It was too late to think of getting over the
bar that night, so we went comfortably to dinner,
after seeing the mails carried off in the life-
boat.

When we came up again the moon was out, and
shining so brightly over sea and shore that she
almost paled the quick large flashes from the
lighthouse.   From the shore floated sweet spicy
odours that always remind me of hymns and
missionaries, and in the windows of the houses on
the Berea sparkled a hundred lights.   From a
large brig lying near came the music of the sailors
as they worked at getting the anchor up in order
to be ready for the wind.   Altogether it was a
perfect night, such a night as you sometimes get
in Southern Africa, and it threw a garment of peace
over everybody as the moon threw a garment of
silver over everything.   Even the great bull-dog,
belonging to a sporting passenger, seemed to
yield to its gentle influences, and forgetting
his yearning to come to close quarters with the
baboon in a cage on the fo'c'sle, snored happily
in the door of the cabin, dreaming no doubt that
he had finished him, and happy in his dream.

We three—that is, Sir Henry Curtis, Captain Good, and myself—went and sat by the wheel, and were quiet for a while.

"Well, Mr. Quatermain," said Sir Henry presently, "have you been thinking about my proposals?"

"Ay," echoed Captain Good, "what do you think of them, Mr. Quatermain? I hope that you are going to give us the pleasure of your company so far as Solomon's Mines, or wherever the gentleman you knew as Neville may have got to."

I rose and knocked out my pipe before I answered. I had not made up my mind, and wanted an additional moment to complete it. Before the burning tobacco had fallen into the sea it was completed; just that little extra second did the trick. It is often the way when you have been bothering a long time over a thing.

"Yes, gentlemen," I said, sitting down again, "I will go, and by your leave I will tell you why, and on what conditions. First for the terms which I ask.

"1. You are to pay all expenses, and any ivory or other valuables we may get is to be divided between Captain Good and myself.

"2. That you pay me £500 for my services on the trip before we start, I undertaking to serve you faithfully till you choose to abandon the enterprise, or till we succeed, or disaster overtakes us.

"3. That before we trek you execute a deed agreeing, in the event of my death or disablement, to pay my boy Harry, who is studying medicine over there in London, at Guy's Hospital, a sum of £200 a year for five years, by which time he ought to be able to earn a living for himself if he is worth his salt. That is all, I think, and I daresay you will say quite enough too."

" No," answered Sir Henry, " I accept them gladly. I am bent upon this project, and would pay more than that for your help, considering the peculiar and exclusive knowledge which you possess."

" Pity I did not ask it, then, but I won't go back on my word. And now that I have got my terms I will tell you my reasons for making up my mind to go. First of all, gentlemen, I have been observing you both for the last few days, and if you will not think me impertinent I may say that I like you, and I believe that we shall come up well to the yoke together. That is something, let me tell you, when one has a long journey like this before one.

" And now as to the journey itself, I tell you flatly, Sir Henry and Captain Good, that I do not think it probable we can come out of it alive, that is, if we attempt to cross the Suliman Mountains. What was the fate of the old Dom da Silvestra three hundred years ago ? What was the fate of his descendant twenty years ago ? What has been your brother's fate ? I tell you frankly, gentlemen, that as their fates were so I believe ours will be."

I paused to watch the effect of my words. Captain Good looked a little uncomfortable, but Sir Henry's face did not change. " We must take our chance," he said.

" You may perhaps wonder," I went on, " why, if I think this, I, who am, as I told you, a timid man, should undertake such a journey. It is for two reasons. First I am a fatalist, and believe that my time is appointed to come quite without reference to my own movements and will, and that if I am to go to Suliman's Mountains to be killed, I shall go there and shall be killed. God Almighty, no doubt, knows His mind about me, so I need not trouble on that point. Secondly, I am a poor man. For nearly forty years I have hunted and traded, but I have never made more than a living. Well, gentlemen, I don't know if you are aware that the average life of an elephant hunter from the time he takes to the trade is between four to five years. So you see I have lived through about seven generations of my class, and I should think that my time cannot be far off anyway. Now, if anything were to happen to me in the ordinary course of business, by the time my debts are paid there would be nothing left to support my son Harry whilst he was getting in the way of earning a living, whereas now he will be provided for for five years. There is the whole affair in a nutshell."

" Mr. Quatermain," said Sir Henry, who had been giving me his most serious attention, " your motives for undertaking an enterprise which you believe can only end in disaster reflect a great deal of credit on you. Whether or not you are right, of course time and the event alone can show. But whether you are right or wrong, I may as well tell you at once that I am going through with it to the end, sweet or bitter. If we are to be knocked on the head, all I have to say is, that I hope we get a little shooting first, eh, Good ? "

" Yes, yes," put in the captain. " We have all three of us been accustomed to face danger, and to hold our lives in our hands in various ways, so it is no good turning back now. And now I vote we go down to the saloon and take an observation just for luck, you know." And we did—through the bottom of a tumbler.

Next day we went ashore, and I put up Sir Henry and Captain Good at the little shanty I have built on the Berea, and which I call my home. There are only three rooms and a kitchen in it, and it is constructed of green brick with a galvanized iron roof, but there is a good garden with the best loquot trees in it that I know, and some nice young mangoes, of which I hope great things. The curator of the botanical gardens gave them to me. It is looked after by an old hunter of mine named Jack, whose thigh was so badly broken by a buffalo cow in Sikukuni's country that he will never hunt again. But he can potter about and garden, being a Griqua by birth. You will never persuade a Zulu to take much interest in gardening. It is a peaceful art, and peaceful arts are not in his line.

Sir Henry and Good slept in a tent pitched in my little grove of orange trees at the end of the garden, for there was no room for them in the house, and what with the smell of the bloom, and the sight of the green and golden fruit—in Durban you will see all three on the tree together—I daresay it is a pleasant place enough, for we have few mosquitos here on the Berea, unless there happens to come an unusually heavy rain.

Well, to get on—for unless I do, Harry, you will be tired of my story before we ever fetch up at Suliman's Mountains—having once made up my mind to go I set about making the necessary preparations. First I secured the deed from Sir Henry, providing for you, my boy, in case of accidents. There was some difficulty about its legal execution, as Sir Henry was a stranger here

and the property to be charged is over the water ;
but it was ultimately got over with the help of a
lawyer, who charged £20 for the job—a price
that I thought outrageous. Then I pocketed
my cheque for £500.

Having paid this tribute to my bump of caution,
I bought a wagon and a span of oxen on Sir
Henry's behalf, and beauties they were. It was
a twenty-two-foot wagon with iron axles, very
strong, very light, and built throughout of stink
wood ; not quite a new one, having been to the
diamond fields and back, but in my opinion, all
the better for that, for I could see that the wood
was well seasoned. If anything is going to give
in a wagon, or if there is green wood in it, it will
show out on the first trip. This particular vehicle
was what we call a " half-tented " wagon, that
is to say, only covered in over the after twelve
feet, leaving all the front part free for the neces-
saries we had to carry with us. In this after part
were a hide " cartle," or bed, on which two people
could sleep, also racks for rifles, and many other
little conveniences. I gave £125 for it, and
think that it was cheap at the price.

Then I bought a beautiful team of twenty salted
Zulu oxen, which I had kept my eye on for a year
or two. Sixteen oxen are the usual number for
a team, but I took four extra to allow for casual-
ties. These Zulu cattle are small and light, not
more than half the size of the Africander oxen,
which are generally used for transport purposes ;
but they will live where the Africanders would
starve, and with a moderate load can make five
miles a day better going, being quicker and not so
liable to become footsore. What is more, this
lot were thoroughly " salted," that is, they had

worked all over South Africa, and so had become proof, comparatively speaking, against red water, which so frequently destroys whole teams of oxen when they get on to strange " veldt " or grass country.   As for " lung sick," which is a dreadful form of pneumonia, very prevalent in this country, they had all been inoculated against it. This is done by cutting a slit in the tail of an ox, and binding in a piece of the diseased lung of an animal which has died of the sickness.   The result is that the ox sickens, takes the disease in a mild form, which causes its tail to drop off, as a rule about a foot from the root, and becomes proof against future attacks.   It seems cruel to rob the animal of his tail, especially in a country where there are so many flies, but it is better to sacrifice the tail and keep the ox than to lose both tail and ox, for a tail without an ox is not much good, except to dust with.   Still it does look odd to trek along behind twenty stumps, where there ought to be tails.   It seems as though Nature had made a trifling mistake, and stuck the stern ornaments of a lot of prize bull-dogs on to the rumps of the oxen.

Next came the question of provisioning and medicines, one which required the most careful consideration, for what we had to do was to avoid lumbering the wagon, and yet to take everything absolutely necessary.   Fortunately, it turned out that Good is a bit of a doctor, having at some period in his previous career managed to pass through a course of medical and surgical instruction, which he has more or less kept up.   He is not, of course, qualified, but he knows more about it than many a man who can write M.D. after his name, as we found out afterwards, and he had a splendid travelling medicine chest and a set of instruments. Whilst we were at Durban he cut off a Kafir's big toe in a way which it was a pleasure to see. But he was quite nonplussed when the Kafir, who had sat stolidly watching the operation, asked him to put on another, saying that a " white one " would do at a pinch.

There remained, when these questions were satisfactorily settled, two further important points for consideration, namely, that of arms and that of servants. As to the arms I cannot do better than put down a list of those which we finally decided on from among the ample store that Sir Henry had brought with him from England, and those which I owned. I copy it from my pocket-book, where I made the entry at the time.

" Three heavy breech-loading double-eight elephant guns, weighing about fifteen pounds each, to carry a charge of eleven drachms of black powder." Two of these were by a well-known London firm, most excellent makers, but I do not know by whom mine, which is not so highly finished, was made. I have used it on several trips, and shot a good many elephants with it, and it has always proved a most superior weapon, thoroughly to be relied on.

" Three double-500 Expresses, constructed to stand a charge of six drachms," sweet weapons, and admirable for medium-sized game, such as eland or sable antelope, or for men, especially in an open country and with the semi-hollow bullet.

" One double No. 12 central-fire Keeper's shot-gun, full choke both barrels." This gun proved of the greatest service to us afterwards in shooting game for the pot.

Three Winchester repeating rifles (not carbines), spare guns.

" Three single-action Colt's revolvers, with the heavier, or American pattern of cartridge."

This was our total armament, and doubtless the reader will observe that the weapons of each class were of the same make and calibre, so that the cartridges were interchangeable, a very important point. I make no apology for detailing it at length, for every experienced hunter will know how vital a proper supply of guns and ammunition is to the success of an expedition.

Now as to the men who were to go with us. After much consultation we decided that their number should be limited to five, namely, a driver, a leader, and three servants.

The driver and leader I found without much difficulty, two Zulus, named respectively Goza and Tom ; but to get the servants proved a more difficult matter. It was necessary that they should be thoroughly trustworthy and brave men, as in a business of this sort our lives might depend upon their conduct. At last I secured two, one a Hottentot called Ventvögel or " wind-bird," and one a little Zulu named Khiva, who had the merit of speaking English perfectly. Ventvögel I had known before ; he was one of the most perfect " spoorers," that is, game trackers, I ever had to do with, and tough as whipcord. He never seemed to tire. But he had one failing, so common with his race, drink. Put him within reach of a bottle of grog and you could not trust him. However, as we were going beyond the region of grog-shops this little weakness of his did not so much matter.

Having secured these two men I looked in vain

for a third to suit my purpose, so we determined
to start without one, trusting to luck to find a
suitable man on our way up country. But, as
it happened, on the evening before the day we
had fixed for our departure the Zulu Khiva informed me that a Kafir was waiting to see me.
Accordingly, when we had done dinner, for we
were at table at the time, I told Khiva to bring
him in. Presently a tall, handsome-looking man,
somewhere about thirty years of age, and very
light-coloured for a Zulu, entered, and lifting
his knob-stick by way of salute, squatted himself
down in the corner on his haunches, and sat silent.
I did not take any notice of him for a while, for
it is a great mistake to do so. If you rush into
conversation at once a Zulu is apt to think you a
person of little dignity or consideration. I
observed, however, that he was a " Keshla " or
ringed man, that is, he wore on his head the black
ring, made of a species of gum polished with fat
and worked up in the hair, which is usually
assumed by Zulus on attaining a certain age or
dignity. Also it struck me that his face was
familiar to me.

" Well," I said at last, " what is your name ? "

" Umbopa," answered the man in a slow, deep
voice.

" I have seen your face before."

" Yes ; the Inkoosi, the chief, my father, saw
my face at the place of the Little Hand "—that
is, Isandhlwana—" on the day before the battle."

Then I remembered. I was one of Lord Chelms-
ford's guides in that unlucky Zulu War, and took
part in the battle, which I had the good fortune
to survive. I will say nothing about it here,
indeed the subject is painful to me. On the day

before it happened, however, I fell into conversation with this man, who held some small command among the native auxiliaries, and he had expressed to me his doubts of the safety of the camp. At the time I told him to hold his tongue, and leave such matters to wiser heads ; but afterwards I thought of his words.

" I remember," I said ; " what is it you want ? "

" It is this, ' Macumazahn.' " That is my Kafir name, and means the man who gets up in the middle of the night, or, in vulgar English, he who keeps his eyes open. " I hear that you go on a great expedition far into the North with the white chiefs from over the water. Is it a true word ? "

" It is."

" I hear that you go even to the Lukanga River, a moon's journey beyond the Manica country. Is this so also, Macumazahn ? "

" Why do you ask whither we go ? What is it to you ? " I answered suspiciously, for the objects of our journey had been kept a dead secret.

" It is this, O white men, that if indeed you travel so far I would travel with you."

There was a certain assumption of dignity in the man's mode of speech, and especially in his use of the words " O white men," instead of " O Inkosis," or chiefs, which struck me.

" You forget yourself a little," I said. " Your words run out unawares. That is not the way to speak. What is your name, and where is your kraal ? Tell us, that we may know with whom we have to deal."

" My name is Umbopa. I am of the Zulu people, yet not of them. The house of my tribe is in the far North ; it was left behind when the

Zulus came down here a ' thousand years ago,'
long before Chaka reigned in Zululand. I have
no kraal. I have wandered for many years. I
came from the North as a child to Zululand. I
was Cetewayo's man in the Nkomabakosi Regiment, serving there under the Captain, Umslopo-
gaasi of the Axe, who taught my hands to fight.
Afterwards I ran away from Zululand and came
to Natal because I wanted to see the white man's
ways. Then I fought against Cetewayo in the
war. Since then I have been working in Natal.
Now I am tired, and would go North again. Here
is not my place. I want no money, but I am a
brave man, and am worth my place and meat.
I have spoken."

'I was rather puzzled by this man and his way
of speech. It was evident to me from his manner
that in the main he was telling the truth, but
somehow he was different from the ordinary run
of Zulus, and I rather mistrusted his offer to come
without pay. Being in a difficulty, I translated
his words to Sir Henry and Good, and asked
them their opinion.

Sir Henry told me to ask him to stand up.
Umbopa did so, at the same time slipping off the
long military great coat which he wore, and
revealing himself naked except for the moocha
round his centre and a necklace of lions' claws.
Certainly he was a magnificent-looking man ; I
never saw a finer native. Standing about six
foot three high he was broad in proportion, and
very shapely. In that light, too, his skin looked
scarcely more than dark, except here and there
where deep black scars marked old assegai wounds.
Sir Henry walked up to him and looked into his
proud, handsome face.

" They make a good pair, don't they ? " said Good ; " one as big as the other."

" I like your looks, Mr. Umbopa, and I will take you as my servant," said Sir Henry in English.

Umbopa evidently understood him, for he answered in Zulu, " It is well ; " and then added, with a glance at the white man's great stature and breadth, " We are men, thou and I."

CHAPTER IV

AN ELEPHANT HUNT

NOW I do not propose to narrate at full length all the incidents of our long travel up to Sitanda's Kraal, near the junction of the Lukanga and Kalukwe Rivers, a journey of more than a thousand miles from Durban, the last three hundred or so of which we had to make on foot, owing to the frequent presence of the dreadful " tsetse " fly, whose bite is fatal to all animals except donkeys and men.

We left Durban at the end of January, and it was in the second week of May that we camped near Sitanda's Kraal. Our adventures on the way were many and various, but as they were of the sort which befall every African hunter—with one exception to be presently detailed—I shall not set them down here, lest I should render this history too wearisome.

At Inyati, the outlying trading station in the Matabele country, of which Lobengula (a great scoundrel) is king, with many regrets we parted from our comfortable wagon. Only twelve oxen remained to us out of the beautiful span of twenty which I had bought at Durban. One we lost from the bite of a cobra, three had perished from " poverty " and the want of water, one strayed, and the other three died from eating the poisonous

herb called " tulip." Five more sickened from
this cause, but we managed to cure them with doses
of an infusion made by boiling down the tulip
leaves. If administered in time this is a very
effective antidote.

The wagon and oxen we left in the immediate
charge of Goza and Tom, our driver and leader,
both of them trustworthy boys, requesting a
worthy Scotch missionary who lived in this distant
place to keep an eye to it. Then, accompanied by
Umbopa, Khiva, Ventvögel, and half a dozen
bearers whom we hired on the spot, we started off
on foot upon our wild quest. I remember we were
all a little silent on the occasion of this departure, and I think that each of us was wondering
if we should ever see our wagon again ; for my
part I never expected to do so. For a while we
tramped on in silence, till Umbopa, who was
marching in front, broke into a Zulu chant about
how some brave men, tired of life and the tameness
of things, started off into a great wilderness to
find new things, or die, and how, lo and behold !
when they had travelled far into the wilderness,
they found that it was not a wilderness at all, but
a beautiful place full of young wives and fat cattle,
of game to hunt and enemies to kill.

Then we all laughed and took it for a good omen.
Umbopa was a cheerful savage, in a dignified sort
of way, when he was not suffering from one of his
fits of brooding, and he had a wonderful knack
of keeping up our spirits. We all grew very fond
of him.

And now for the one adventure to which I am
going to treat myself, for I do dearly love a
hunting yarn.

About a fortnight's march from Inyati we came

across a peculiarly beautiful bit of well-watered
woodland country. The kloofs in the hills were
covered with dense bush, " idoro " bush as the
natives call it, and in some places, with the " wacht-
een-beche," or " wait-a-little thorn," and there
were great quantities of the lovely " machabell "
tree, laden with refreshing yellow fruit having
enormous stones. This tree is the elephant's
favourite food, and there were not wanting signs
that the great brutes had been about, for not only
was their spoor frequent, but in many places the
trees were broken down and even uprooted. The
elephant is a destructive feeder.

One evening, after a long day's march, we came
to a spot of great loveliness. At the foot of a
bush-clad hill lay a dry river-bed, in which,
however, were to be found pools of crystal water
all trodden round with the hoof-prints of game.
Facing this hill was a park-like plain, where grew
clumps of flat-topped mimosa, varied with
occasional glossy-leaved machabells, and all
round stretched the sea of pathless, silent
bush.

As we emerged into this river-bed path suddenly
we started a troop of tall giraffes, who galloped,
or rather sailed off, in their strange gait, their
tails screwed up over their backs, and their hoofs
rattling like castanets. They were about three
hundred yards from us, and therefore practically
out of shot, but Good, who was walking ahead
and had an express loaded with solid ball in his
hand, could not resist temptation. Lifting his
gun, he let drive at the last, a young cow. By
some extraordinary chance the ball struck it
full on the back of the neck, shattering the spinal
column, and that giraffe went rolling head over

heels just like a rabbit. I never saw a more
curious thing.

" Curse it ! " said Good—for I am sorry to say
he had a habit of using strong language when
excited—contracted, no doubt, in the course of
his nautical career ; " curse it ! I've killed him."

" *Ou*, Bougwan," ejaculated the Kafirs ; " *ou !
ou !* "

They called Good " Bougwan," or Glass Eye,
because of his eye-glass.

" Oh, ' Bougwan ' ! " re-echoed Sir Henry and
I, and from that day Good's reputation as a
marvellous shot was established, at any rate
among the Kafirs. Really he was a bad one, but
whenever he missed we overlooked it for the sake
of that giraffe.

Having set some of the " boys " to cut off the
best of the giraffe meat, we went to work to build
a " scherm " near one of the pools and about
a hundred yards to the right of it. This is done
by cutting a quantity of thorn bushes and piling
them in the shape of a circular hedge. Then the
space enclosed is smoothed, and dry tambouki
grass, if obtainable, is made into a bed in the
centre, and a fire or fires lighted.

By the time the " scherm " was finished the
moon peeped up, and our dinner of giraffe steaks
and roasted marrow bones was ready. How we
enjoyed those marrow-bones, though it was rather
a job to crack them ! I know of no greater
luxury than giraffe marrow, unless it is elephant's
heart, and we had that on the morrow. We ate
our simple meal by the light of the moon, pausing
at times to thank Good for his wonderful shot ;
then we began to smoke and yarn, and a curious
picture we must have made squatting there

round the fire. I, with my short grizzled hair
sticking up straight, and Sir Henry with his
yellow locks, which were getting rather long,
were rather a contrast, especially as I am thin,
and short and dark, weighing only nine stone and
a half, and Sir Henry is tall, and broad, and fair,
and weighs fifteen. But perhaps the most
curious-looking of the three, taking all the circumstances of the case into consideration, was Captain
John Good, R.N. There he sat upon a leather
bag, looking just as though he had come in
from a comfortable day's shooting in a civilized
country, absolutely clean, tidy, and well dressed.
He wore a shooting suit of brown tweed, with a
hat to match, and neat gaiters. As usual, he
was beautifully shaved, his eye-glass and his
false teeth appeared to be in perfect order, and
altogether the neatest man I ever had to do with
in the wilderness. He even sported a collar,
of which he had a supply, made of white gutta-
percha.

"You see, they weigh so little," he said to
me innocently, when I expressed my astonishment at the fact ; "and I always like to turn
out like a gentleman." Ah ! if he could have
foreseen the future and the raiment prepared
for him.

Well, there we three sat yarning away in the
beautiful moonlight, and watching the Kafirs
a few yards off sucking their intoxicating
" daccha " from a pipe of which the mouthpiece
was made of the horn of an eland, till one by one
they rolled themselves up in their blankets and
went to sleep by the fire, that is, all except
Umbopa, who sat a little apart, his chin resting
on his hand, and thinking deeply. I noticed

that he never mixed much with the other Kafirs.

Presently from the depths of the bush behind us, came a loud " *woof, woof !* " That's a lion," said I, and we started up to listen. Hardly had we done so, when from the pool, about a hundred yards off, we heard the strident trumpeting of an elephant. " *Unkungunklovo ! Indlovu !* " " Elephant ! Elephant ! " whispered the Kafirs ; and a few minutes afterwards we saw a succession of vast shadowy forms moving slowly from the direction of the water towards the bush.

Up jumped Good, burning for slaughter, and thinking, perhaps, that it was as easy to kill elephant as he had found it to shoot a giraffe, but I caught him by the arm and pulled him down.

" It's no good," I whispered, " let them go."

" It seems that we are in a paradise of game. I vote we stop here a day or two, and have a go at them," said Sir Henry presently.

I was rather surprised, for hitherto Sir Henry had always been for pushing on as fast as possible, more especially since we ascertained at Inyati that about two years ago an Englishman of the name of Neville *had* sold his wagon there, and gone on up country. But I suppose his hunter instincts got the better of him for a while.

Good jumped at the idea, for he was longing to have a shot at those elephants ; and so, to speak the truth, did I, for it went against my conscience to let such a herd as that escape without a pull at them.

" All right, my hearties," said I. " I think we want a little recreation. And now let's turn in,

for we ought to be off by dawn, and then perhaps
we may catch them feeding before they move
on.''

The others agreed, and we proceeded to make
our preparations. Good took off his clothes, shook
them, put his eye-glass and his false teeth into
his trousers pocket, and folding each article neatly,
placed it out of the dew under a corner of his
mackintosh sheet. Sir Henry and I contented
ourselves with rougher arrangements, and soon
were curled up in our blankets, and dropping
off into the dreamless sleep that rewards the
traveller.

Going, going, go—What was that ?

Suddenly from the direction of the water came
sounds of violent scuffling, and next instant there
broke upon our ears a succession of the most
awful roars. There was no mistaking their
origin ; only a lion could make such a noise as
that. We all jumped up and looked towards
the water, in the direction of which we saw a
confused mass, yellow and black in colour,
staggering and struggling towards us. We seized
our rifles, and slipping on our veldtschoons, that
is shoes made of untanned hide, ran out of the
scherm towards it. By this time the mass had
fallen, and was rolling over and over on the
ground, and when we reached the spot it struggled
no longer, but lay quite still.

Now we saw what it was. On the grass there
lay a sable antelope bull—the most beautiful of
all the African antelopes—quite dead, and
transfixed by its great curved horns was a
magnificent black-maned lion, also dead. Evidently what had happened was this. The
sable antelope had come down to drink at the pool

where the lion—no doubt the same which we had heard—was lying in wait. While the antelope drank, the lion had sprung upon him, to be received upon the sharp curved horns and transfixed. Once before I saw a similar thing happen. Then the lion, unable to free himself, had torn and bitten at the back and neck of the bull, which, maddened with fear and pain, had rushed on until it dropped dead.

As soon as we had examined the dead beasts sufficiently we called the Kafirs, and between us managed to drag their carcasses up to the scherm. After that we went in and lay down, to wake no more till dawn.

With the first light we were up and making ready for the fray. We took with us the three eight-bore rifles, a good supply of ammunition, and our large water-bottles, filled with weak cold tea, which I have always found the best stuff to shoot on. After swallowing a little breakfast we started, Umbopa, Khiva, and Ventvögel accompanying us. The other Kafirs we left with instructions to skin the lion and the sable antelope and to cut up the latter.

We had no difficulty in finding the broad elephant trail, which Ventvögel, after examination, pronounced to have been made by between twenty and thirty elephants, most of them full-grown bulls. But the herd had moved on some way during the night, and it was nine o'clock, and already very hot, before, from the broken trees, bruised leaves and bark, and smoking droppings, we knew that we could not be far off them.

Presently we caught sight of the herd, which numbered, as Ventvögel had said, between twenty and thirty, standing in a hollow, having finished their morning meal, and flapping their great ears. It was a splendid sight, for they were only about two hundred yards from us. Taking a handful of dry grass, I threw it into the air to see how the wind was; for if once they winded us I knew they would be off before we could get a shot. Finding that, if anything, it blew from the elephants to us, we crept on stealthily, and thanks to the cover managed to get within forty yards or so of the great brutes. Just in front of us and broadside on, stood three splendid bulls, one of them with enormous tusks. I whispered to the others that I would take the middle one; Sir Henry covering the elephant to the left, and Good the bull with the big tusks.

" Now," I whispered.

Boom! boom! boom! went the three heavy rifles, and down came Sir Henry's elephant, dead as a hammer, shot right through the heart. Mine fell on to its knees, and I thought that he was going to die, but in another moment he was up and off, tearing along straight past me. As he went I gave him the second barrel in the ribs, and this brought him down in good earnest. Hastily slipping in two fresh cartridges I ran close up to him and a ball through the brain put an end to the poor brute's struggles. Then I turned to see how Good had fared with the big bull, which I had heard screaming with rage and pain as I gave mine its quietus. On reaching the captain I found him in a great state of excitement. It appeared that on receiving the bullet the bull had turned and come straight for his assailant, who had barely time to get out of his way, and then charged blindly on past him, in the direction

of our encampment. Meanwhile the herd
had crashed off in wild alarm in the other
direction.

For a while we doubted whether to go after
the wounded bull or to follow the herd, and
finally deciding for the latter alternative, departed,
thinking that we had seen the last of those big
tusks. I have often wished since that we had.
It was easy work to follow the elephants, for
they had left a trail like a carriage road behind
them, crushing down the thick bush in their
furious flight as though it were tambouki
grass.

But to come up with them was another matter,
and we had struggled on under a broiling sun for
over two hours before we found them. With
the exception of one bull, they were standing
together, and I could see, from their unquiet way
and the manner in which they kept lifting their
trunks to test the air, that they were on the look-
out for mischief. The solitary bull stood fifty
yards or so to this side of the herd, over which he
was evidently keeping sentry, and about sixty
yards from us. Thinking that he would see or
wind us, and that it would probably start them
off again if we tried to get nearer, especially
as the ground was rather open, we all aimed at
this bull, and at my whispered word, we fired.
The three shots took effect, and down he went,
dead. Again the herd started, but unfortunately
for them about a hundred yards further on was
a nullah, or dried water track, with steep banks,
a place very much resembling the one where
the Prince Imperial was killed in Zululand. Into
this the elephants plunged, and when we reached
the edge we found them struggling in wild con-

fusion to get up the other bank, filling the air with their screams, and trumpeting as they pushed one another aside in their selfish panic, just like so many human beings. Now was our opportunity, and firing away as quickly as we could load, we killed five of the poor beasts, and no doubt should have bagged the whole herd, had they not suddenly given up their attempts to climb the bank and rushed headlong down the nullah. We were too tired to follow them, and perhaps also a little sick of slaughter, eight elephants being a pretty good bag for one day.

So after we were rested a little, and the Kafirs had cut out the hearts of two of the dead elephants for supper, we started homewards, very well pleased with ourselves, having made up our minds to send the bearers on the morrow to chop out the tusks.

Shortly after we re-passed the spot where Good had wounded the patriarchal bull we came across a herd of eland, but did not shoot at them, as we had plenty of meat. They trotted past us, and then stopped behind a little patch of bush about a hundred yards away, wheeling round to look at us. As Good was anxious to get a near view of them, never having seen an eland close, he handed his rifle to Umbopa, and, followed by Khiva, strolled up to the patch of bush. We sat down and waited for him, not sorry of the excuse for a little rest.

The sun was just going down in its reddest glory, and Sir Henry and I were admiring the lovely scene, when suddenly we heard an elephant scream, and saw its huge and rushing form with uplifted trunk and tail silhouetted against the

great red globe of the sun. Next second we saw
something else, and that was Good and Khiva
tearing back towards us with the wounded bull
—for it was he—charging after them. For a
moment we did not dare to fire—though at that
distance it would have been of little use if we had
done so—for fear of hitting one of them, and the
next a dreadful thing happened—Good fell a
victim to his passion for civilized dress. Had
he consented to discard his trousers and gaiters
like the rest of us, and to hunt in a flannel shirt
and a pair of veldtschoons, it would have been
all right. But as it was, his trousers cumbered
him in that desperate race, and presently, when
he was about sixty yards from us, his boot,
polished by the dry grass, slipped, and down
he went on his face right in front of the
elephant.

We gave a gasp, for we knew that he must die,
and ran as hard as we could towards him. In
three seconds it had ended, but not as we thought.
Khiva, the Zulu boy, saw his master fall, and brave
lad as he was, had turned and flung his assegai
straight into the elephant's face. It stuck in
his trunk.

With a scream of pain, the brute seized the
poor Zulu, hurled him to the earth, and placing
one huge foot on to his body about the middle,
twined its trunk round his upper part and *tore
him in two*.

We rushed up mad with horror, and fired again
and again, till presently the elephant fell upon
the fragments of the Zulu.

As for Good, he rose and wrung his hands over
the brave man who had given his life to save him,
and, though I am an old hand, I felt a lump

grow in my throat. Umbopa stood contemplating the huge dead elephant and the mangled remains of poor Khiva.

"Ah, well," he said presently, "he is dead, but he died like a man!"

CHAPTER V

OUR MARCH INTO THE DESERT

WE had killed nine elephants, and it took us two days to cut out the tusks, and having brought them into camp, to bury them carefully in the sand under a large tree, which made a conspicuous mark for miles round. It was a wonderfully fine lot of ivory. I never saw a better, averaging as it did between forty and fifty pounds a tusk. The tusks of the great bull that killed poor Khiva scaled one hundred and seventy pounds the pair, so nearly as we could judge.

As for Khiva himself, we buried what remained of him in an ant-bear hole, together with an assegai to protect himself with on his journey to a better world. On the third day we marched again, hoping that we might live to return to dig up our buried ivory, and in due course, after a long and wearisome tramp, and many adventures which I have not space to detail, we reached Sitanda's Kraal, near the Lukanga River, the real starting-point of our expedition. Very well do I recollect our arrival at that place. To the right was a scattered native settlement with a few stone cattle kraals and some cultivated lands down by the water, where these savages grew their scanty supply of grain, and beyond it stretched great tracts of waving " veldt " covered with tall grass, over which herds of the smaller game were wandering. To the left lay the vast desert. This spot appears to be the outpost of the fertile country, and it would be difficult to say to what natural causes such an abrupt change in the character of the soil is due. But so it is.

Just below our encampment flowed a little stream, on the farther side of which is a stony slope, the same down which, twenty years before, I had seen poor Silvestre creeping back after his attempt to reach Solomon's Mines, and beyond that slope begins the waterless desert, covered with a species of karoo scrub.

It was evening when we pitched our camp, and the great ball of the sun was sinking into the desert, sending glorious rays of many-coloured light flying over all its vast expanse. Leaving Good to superintend the arrangement of our little camp, I took Sir Henry with me, and walking to the top of the slope opposite, we gazed across the desert. The air was very clear, and far, far away I could distinguish the faint blue outlines here and there capped with white of the Suliman Berg.

" There," I said, " there is the wall round Solomon's Mines, but God knows if we shall ever climb it."

" My brother should be there, and if he is, I shall reach him somehow," said Sir Henry, in that tone of quiet confidence which marked the man.

" I hope so," I answered, and turned to go back to the camp, when I saw that we were not alone. Behind us, also gazing earnestly towards the far-off mountains, stood the great Kafir Umbopa.

The Zulu spoke when he saw that I had observed him, addressing Sir Henry, to whom he had attached himself.

" Is it to that land that thou wouldst journey, Incubu ? " (a native word meaning, I believe, an elephant, and the name given to Sir Henry by the Kafirs) he said, pointing towards the mountains with his broad assegai.

I asked him sharply what he meant by addressing his master in that familiar way. It is very well for natives to have a name for one among themselves, but it is not decent that they should call a white man by their heathenish appellations to his face. The Zulu laughed a quiet little laugh which angered me.

" How dost thou know that I am not the equal of the Inkosi whom I serve ! " he said. " He is of a royal house, no doubt ; one can see it in his size and by his mien ; so, mayhap, am I. At least I am as great a man. Be my mouth, O Macumazahn, and say my words to the Inkoos Incubu, my master, for I would speak to him and to thee."

I was angry with the man, for I am not accustomed to be talked to in that way by Kafirs, but somehow he impressed me, and besides I was curious to know what he had to say. So I translated, expressing my opinion at the same time that he was an impudent fellow, and that his swagger was outrageous.

" Yes, Umbopa," answered Sir Henry, " I would journey there."

" The desert is wide and there is no water in it, the mountains are high and covered with snow, and man cannot say what lies beyond them behind the place where the sun sets ; how shalt thou come thither, Incubu, and wherefore dost thou go ? "

I translated again.

" Tell him," answered Sir Henry, " that I go because I believe that a man of my blood, my brother, has gone there before me, and I journey to seek him."

" That is so, Incubu ; a Hottentot I met on the road told me that a white man went out into the desert two years ago towards those mountains with one servant, a hunter. They never came back."

" How do you know it was my brother ? " asked Sir Henry.

" Nay, I know not. But the Hottentot, when I asked what the white man was like, said that he had thy eyes and a black beard. He said, too, that the name of the hunter with him was Jim ; that he was a Bechuana hunter and wore clothes."

" There is no doubt about it," said I ; " I knew Jim well."

Sir Henry nodded. " I was sure of it," he said. " If George set his mind upon a thing he generally did it. It was always so from his boyhood. If he meant to cross the Suliman Berg he has crossed it, unless some accident overtook him, and we must look for him on the other side."

Umbopa understood English, though he rarely spoke it.

" It is a far journey, Incubu," he put in, and I translated his remark.

" Yes," answered Sir Henry, " it is far. But there is no journey upon this earth that a man may not make if he sets his heart to it. There is nothing, Umbopa, that he cannot do, there

are no mountains he may not climb, there are
no deserts he cannot cross, save a mountain and
a desert of which you are spared the knowledge,
if love leads him and he holds his life in his hand
counting it as nothing, ready to keep it or lose
it as Heaven may order."

I translated.

" Great words, my father," answered the Zulu
—I always called him a Zulu, though he was
not really one—" great swelling words fit to fill
the mouth of a man. Thou art right, my father
Incubu. Listen! what is life? It is a
feather, it is the seed of the grass, blown
hither and thither, sometimes multiplying itself
and dying in the act, sometimes carried away
into the heavens. But if the seed be good and
heavy it may perchance travel a little way on
the road it wills. It is well to try and journey
one's road and to fight with the air. Man must
die. At the worst he can but die a little sooner.
I will go with thee across the desert and over
the mountains, unless perchance I fall to the
ground on the way, my father."

He paused a while, and then went on with
one of those strange bursts of rhetorical eloquence
that Zulus sometimes indulge in, which to my
mind, full though they are of vain repetitions,
show that the race is by no means devoid of
poetic instinct and of intellectual power.

" What is life? Tell me, O white men, who
are wise, who know the secrets of the world, and
the world of stars, and the world that lies above
and around the stars; who flash your words
from afar without a voice; tell me, white men,
the secret of our life—whither it goes and whence
it comes!

"You cannot answer me; you know not. Listen, I will answer. Out of the dark we came, into the dark we go. Like a storm-driven bird at night we fly out of the Nowhere; for a moment our wings are seen in the light of the fire, and, lo! we are gone again into the Nowhere. Life is nothing. Life is all. It is the Hand with which we hold off Death. It is the glow-worm that shines in the night-time and is black in the morning; it is the white breath of the oxen in winter; it is the little shadow that runs across the grass and loses itself at sunset."

"You are a strange man," said Sir Henry, when he had ceased.

Umbopa laughed. "It seems to me that we are much alike, Incubu. Perhaps I seek a brother over the mountains."

I looked at him suspiciously. "What dost thou mean?" I asked; "what dost thou know of those mountains?"

"A little; a very little. There is a strange land yonder, a land of witchcraft and beautiful things; a land of brave people, and of trees, and streams, and snow peaks, and a great white road. I have heard of it. But what is the good of talking? It grows dark. Those who live to see will see."

Again I looked at him doubtfully. The man knew too much.

"You not need fear me, Macumazahn," he said, interpreting my look. "I dig no holes for you to fall in. I make no plots. If ever we cross those mountains behind the sun I will tell what I know. But Death sits upon them. Be wise and turn back. Go and hunt elephants, my masters. I have spoken."

And without another word he lifted his spear in salutation, and returned towards the camp, where shortly afterwards we found him cleaning a gun like any other Kafir.

" That is an odd man," said Sir Henry.

" Yes," answered I, " too odd by half. I don't like his little ways. He knows something, and will not speak out. But I suppose it is no use quarrelling with him. We are in for a curious trip, and a mysterious Zulu won't make much difference one way or another."

Next day we made our arrangements for starting. Of course it was impossible to drag our heavy elephant rifles and other kit with us across the desert, so dismissing our bearers we made an arrangement with an old native who had a kraal close by to take care of them till we returned. It went to my heart to leave such things as those sweet tools to the tender mercies of an old thief of a savage whose greedy eyes I could see gloating over them. But I took some precautions.

First of all I loaded all the rifles, placing them at full cock, and informed him that if he touched them they would go off. He tried the experiment instantly with my eight-bore, and it did go off, and blew a hole right through one of his oxen, which was just then being driven up to the kraal, to say nothing of knocking him head over heels with the recoil. He got up considerably startled, and not at all pleased at the loss of the ox, which he had the impudence to ask me to pay for, and nothing would induce him to touch the guns again.

" Put the live devils out of the way up there in the thatch," he said, " or they will kill us all."

Then I told him that, when we came back, if one of those things was missing I would kill him and all his people by witchcraft ; and if we died and he tried to steal the rifles I would come and haunt him and turn his cattle mad and his milk sour till life was a weariness, and would make the devils in the guns come out and talk to him in a way he did not like, and generally gave him a good idea of judgment to come. After that he swore he would look after them as though they were his father's spirit. He was a very superstitious old Kafir and a great villain.

Having thus disposed of our superfluous gear we arranged the kit we five—Sir Henry, Good, myself, Umbopa, and the Hottentot Ventvögel —were to take with us on our journey. It was small enough, but do what we would we could not get its weight down under about forty pounds a man. This is what it consisted of :—

The three express rifles and two hundred rounds of ammunition.

The two Winchester repeating rifles (for Umbopa and Ventvögel), with two hundred rounds of cartridge.

Three " Colt " revolvers and sixty rounds of cartridge.

Five Cochrane's water-bottles, each holding four pints.

Five blankets.

Twenty-five pounds' weight of biltong—*i.e.* sun-dried game flesh.

Ten pounds' weight of best mixed beads for gifts.

A selection of medicine, including an ounce of quinine, and one or two small surgical instruments.

Our knives, a few sundries, such as a compass, matches, a pocket filter, tobacco, a trowel, a bottle of brandy, and the clothes we stood in.

This was our total equipment, a small one indeed for such a venture, but we dared not attempt to carry more. Indeed, that load was a heavy one per man with which to travel across the burning desert, for in such places every additional ounce tells. But try as we would we could not see our way to reducing it. There was nothing taken but what was absolutely necessary.

With great difficulty, and by the promise of a present of a good hunting-knife each, I succeeded in persuading three wretched natives from the village to come with us for the first stage, twenty miles, and to carry a large gourd holding a gallon of water apiece. My object was to enable us to refill our water bottles after the first night's march, for we determined to start in the cool of the evening. I gave out to these natives that we were going to shoot ostriches, with which the desert abounded. They jabbered and shrugged their shoulders, saying that we were mad and should perish of thirst, which I must say seemed probable ; but being desirous of obtaining the knives, which were almost unknown treasures up there, they consented to come, having probably reflected that, after all, our subsequent extinction would be no affair of theirs.

All next day we rested and slept, and at sunset ate a hearty meal of fresh beef washed down with tea, the last, as Good sadly remarked, we were likely to drink for many a long day. Then, having made our final preparations, we lay down and waited for the moon to rise. At last about nine o'clock up she came in all her glory, flooding the wild country with light, and throwing a silver sheen on the expanse of rolling desert before us, which looked as solemn and quiet and as alien to man as the star-studded firmament above. We rose up, and in a few minutes were ready, and yet we hesitated a little, as human nature is prone to hesitate on the threshold of an irrevocable step. We three white men stood by ourselves. Umbopa, assegai in hand and a rifle across his shoulders, looked out fixedly across the desert a few paces ahead of us ; while the hired natives, with the gourds of water, and Ventvögel, were gathered in a little knot behind.

" Gentlemen," said Sir Henry presently, in his deep voice, " we are going on about as strange a journey as men can make in this world. It is very doubtful if we can succeed in it. But we are three men who will stand together for good or for evil to the last. And now before we start let us for a moment pray to the Power who shapes the destinies of men, and who ages since has marked out our paths, that it may please Him to direct our steps in accordance with His will."

Taking off his hat, for the space of a minute or so, he covered his face with his hands, and Good and I did likewise.

I do not say that I am a first-rate praying man, few hunters are, and as for Sir Henry I never heard him speak like that before, and only once since, though deep down in his heart I believe that he is very religious. Good too is pious, though apt to swear. Anyhow I do not remember, excepting on one single occasion, ever putting in a better prayer in my life than I did during that minute, and somehow I felt the happier for it. Our future was so completely unknown, and I think the unknown and the awful always bring a man nearer to his Maker.

" And now," said Sir Henry, " *trek !* "

So we started.

We had nothing to guide ourselves by except the distant mountains and old José da Silvestra's chart, which, considering that it was drawn by a dying and half-distraught man on a fragment of linen three centuries ago, was not a very satisfactory sort of thing to work with. Still, such as it was, our sole hope of success depended upon it. If we failed in finding that pool of bad water which the old Dom marked as being situated in the middle of the desert, about sixty miles from our starting-point, and as far from the mountains, in all probability we must perish miserably of thirst. And to my mind the chances of our finding it in that great sea of sand and karoo scrub seemed almost infinitesimal Even supposing that da Silvestra had marked the pool right, what was there to prevent its having been dried up by the sun generations ago, or trampled in by game, or filled with the drifting sand ?

On we tramped silently as shades through the night and in the heavy sand. The karoo bushes caught our feet and retarded us, and the sand worked into our veldtschoons and Good's shooting boots, so that every few miles we had to stop and empty them ; but still the night kept fairly cool, though the atmosphere was thick and heavy, giving a sort of creamy feel to the air, and we made fair progress. It was very

silent and lonely there in the desert, oppressively
so indeed. Good felt this, and once began to
whistle " The Girl I left behind me," but the notes
sounded lugubrious in that vast place, and he
gave it up.

Shortly afterwards a little incident occurred
which, though it startled us at the time, gave
rise to a laugh. Good was leading, as the holder
of the compass, which, being a sailor, of course
he understood thoroughly, and we were toiling
along in single file behind him, when suddenly
we heard the sound of an exclamation, and he
vanished. Next second there arose all around
us a most extraordinary hubbub, snorts, groans,
and wild sounds of rushing feet. In the faint
light, too, we could descry dim galloping forms
half hidden by wreaths of sand. The natives
threw down their loads and prepared to bolt,
but remembering that there was nowhere to run
to, they cast themselves upon the ground and
howled out that it was the devil. As for Sir
Henry and myself we stood amazed ; nor was
our amazement lessened when we perceived the
form of Good careering off in the direction of
the mountains, apparently mounted on the back
of a horse and halloaing wildly. In another
second he threw up his arms, and we heard him
come to the earth with a thud.

Then I saw what had happened ; we had
stumbled upon a herd of sleeping quagga, on
to the back of one of which Good actually
had fallen, and the brute naturally enough got
up and made off with him. Calling out to the
others that it was all right, I ran towards Good,
much afraid lest he should be hurt, but to my
great relief I found him sitting in the sand, his

eye-glass still fixed firmly in his eye, rather
shaken and very much frightened, but not in
any way injured.

After this we travelled on without any further
misadventure till about one o'clock, when we
called a halt, and having drunk a little water,
not much, for water was precious, and rested
for half an hour, we started again.

On, on we went, till at last the east began to
blush like the cheek of a girl. Then there came
faint rays of primrose light, that changed presently to golden bars, through which the dawn
glided out across the desert. The stars grew
pale and paler still till at last they vanished ;
the golden moon waxed wan, and her mountain
ridges stood out against her sickly face like the
bones on the cheek of a dying man. Then came
spear upon spear of light flashing far away across
the boundless wilderness, piercing and firing the
veils of mist, till the desert was draped in a
tremulous golden glow, and it was day.

Still we did not halt, though by this time we
should have been glad enough to do so, for we
knew that when once the sun was fully up it
would be almost impossible for us to travel.
At length, about an hour later, we spied a little
pile of boulders rising out of the plain, and to
this we dragged ourselves. As luck would have
it, here we found an overhanging slab of rock
carpeted beneath with smooth sand, which
afforded a most grateful shelter from the heat.
Underneath this we crept, and each of us having
drunk some water and eaten a bit of biltong,
we lay down and soon were sound asleep.

It was three o'clock in the afternoon before
we woke, to find our bearers preparing to return.

They had seen enough of the desert already, and no number of knives would have tempted them to come a step farther. So we took a hearty drink, and having emptied our water-bottles, filled them up again from the gourds that they had brought with them, and then watched them depart on their twenty miles' tramp home.

At half-past four we also started. It was lonely and desolate work, for, with the exception of a few ostriches, there was not a single living creature to be seen on all the vast expanse of sandy plain. Evidently it was too dry for game, and with the exception of a deadly-looking cobra or two we saw no reptiles. One insect, however, we found abundant, and that was the common or house fly. There they came, " not as single spies, but in battalions," as I think the Old Testament* says somewhere. He is an extraordinary animal is the house fly. Go where you will you find him, and so it must have been always. I have seen him enclosed in amber, which is, I was told, quite half a million years old, looking exactly like his descendant of to-day, and I have little doubt but that when the last man lies dying on the earth he will be buzzing round—if this event should happen to occur in summer—watching for an opportunity to settle on his nose.

At sunset we halted, waiting for the moon to rise. At last she came up, beautiful and serene as ever, and, with one halt about two

---

* Readers must beware of accepting Mr. Quatermain's references as accurate, as, it has been found, some are prone to do. Although his reading evidently was limited, the impression produced by it upon his mind was mixed. Thus to him the Old Testament and Shakespeare were interchangeable authorities.—*Editor*.

o'clock in the morning, we trudged on wearily through the night, till at last the welcome sun put a period to our labours. We drank a little and flung ourselves down on the sand, thoroughly tired out, and soon were all asleep. There was no need to set a watch, for we had nothing to fear from anybody or anything in that vast untenanted plain. Our only enemies were heat, thirst, and flies, but far rather would I have faced any danger from man and beast than that awful trinity. This time we were not so lucky as to find a sheltering rock to guard us from the glare of the sun, with the result that about seven o'clock we woke up experiencing the exact sensations one would attribute to a beefsteak on a gridiron. We were literally being baked through and through. The burning sun seemed to be sucking our very blood out of us. We sat up and gasped.

" Phew," said I, grabbing at the halo of flies, which buzzed cheerfully round my head. The heat did not affect *them*.

" My word ! " said Sir Henry.

" It *is* hot ! " echoed Good.

It was hot indeed, and there was not a bit of shelter to be found. Look where we would there was no rock or tree, nothing but an unending glare, rendered dazzling by the heated air that danced over the surface of the desert as it dances over a red-hot stove.

"What is to be done ? " asked Sir Henry: " we can't stand this for long."

We looked at each other blankly.

" I have it," said Good, " we must dig a hole, get in it, and cover ourselves with the karoo bushes."

It did not seem a very promising suggestion, but at least it was better than nothing, so we set to work, and, with the trowel we had brought with us and the help of our hands, in about an hour we succeeded in delving out a patch of ground some ten feet long by twelve wide to the depth of two feet. Then we cut a quantity of low scrub with our hunting-knives, and creeping into the hole, pulled it over us all, with the exception of Ventvögel, on whom, being a Hottentot, the heat had no particular effect. This gave us some slight shelter from the burning rays of the sun, but the atmosphere in that amateur grave can be better imagined than described. The Black Hole of Calcutta must have been a fool to it ; indeed, to this moment I do not know how we lived through the day. There we lay panting, and every now and again moistening our lips from our scanty supply of water. Had we followed our inclination we should have finished all we possessed in the first two hours, but we were forced to exercise the most rigid care, for if our water failed us we knew that very soon we must perish miserably.

But everything has an end, if only you live long enough to see it, and somehow that miserable day wore on towards evening. About three o'clock in the afternoon we determined that we could bear it no longer. It would be better to die walking than to be killed slowly by heat and thirst in this dreadful hole. So taking each of us a little drink from our fast diminishing supply of water, now warmed to about the same temperature as a man's blood, we staggered forward.

We had then covered some fifty miles of

wilderness. If the reader will refer to the rough copy and translation of old da Silvestra's map, he will see that the desert is marked as measuring forty leagues across, and the " pan bad water," is set down as being about in the middle of it. Now forty leagues is one hundred and twenty miles, consequently we ought at the most to be within twelve or fifteen miles of the water if any should really exist.

Through the afternoon we crept slowly and painfully along, scarcely doing more than a mile and a half an hour. At sunset we rested again, waiting for the moon, and after drinking a little managed to get some sleep.

Before we lay down, Umbopa pointed out to us a slight and indistinct hillock on the flat surface of the plain about eight miles away. At the distance it looked like an ant-hill, and as I was dropping off to sleep I fell to wondering what it could be.

With the moon we marched again, feeling dreadfully exhausted, and suffering tortures from thirst and prickly heat. Nobody who has not felt it can know what we went through. We walked no longer, we staggered, now and again falling from exhaustion, and being obliged to call a halt every hour or so. We had scarcely energy left in us to speak. Up to this Good had chatted and joked, for he is a merry fellow ; but now he had not a joke in him.

At last, about two o'clock, utterly worn out in body and mind, we came to the foot of the queer hill, or sand koppie, which at first sight resembled a gigantic ant-heap about a hundred feet high, and covering at the base nearly two acres of ground.

Here we halted, and driven to it by our desperate thirst, sucked down our last drops of water. We had but half a pint a head, and each of us could have drunk a gallon.

Then we lay down. Just as I was dropping off to sleep I heard Umbopa remark to himself in Zulu—

"If we cannot find water we shall all be dead before the moon rises to-morrow."

I shuddered, hot as it was. The near prospect of such an awful death is not pleasant, but even the thought of it could not keep me from sleeping.

CHAPTER VI

WATER ! WATER !

IN two hours' time, that is, about four o'clock, I woke up. So soon as the first heavy demand of bodily fatigue had been satisfied, the torturing thirst from which I was suffering asserted itself. I could sleep no more. I had been dreaming that I was bathing in a running stream, with green banks and trees upon them, and I awoke to find myself in this arid wilderness, and to remember, as Umbopa had said, that if we did not find water this day we must perish miserably. No human creature could live without water in that heat. I sat up and rubbed my grimy face with my dry and horny hands. My lips and eyelids were stuck together, and it was only after some rubbing and with an effort that I was able to open them. It was not far from dawn, but there was none of the bright feel of dawn in the air, which was thick with a hot murkiness I cannot describe. The others were still sleeping. Presently it began to grow light enough to read, so I drew out a little pocket copy of the " Ingoldsby Legends " I had brought with me, and read " The Jackdaw of Rheims." When I got to where

> " A nice little boy held a golden ewer,
> Embossed, and filled with water as pure
> As any that flows between Rheims and Namur,"

literally I smacked my cracked lips, or rather tried to smack them. The mere thought of that pure water made me mad. If the Cardinal had been there with his bell, book, and candle, I would have whipped in and drank his water up, yes, even if he had filled it already with the suds of soap worthy of washing the hands of the Pope, and I knew that the whole concentrated curse of the Catholic Church should fall upon me for so doing. I almost think that I must have been a little light-headed with thirst and weariness and the want of food ; for I fell to thinking how astonished the Cardinal and his nice little boy and the jackdaw would have looked to see a burnt-up, brown-eyed, grizzly-haired little elephant hunter suddenly bound in and put his dirty face into the basin, and swallow every drop of the precious water. The idea amused me so much that I laughed or rather cackled aloud, which woke the others, and they began to rub *their* dirty faces and get *their* gummed-up lips and eyelids apart.

As soon as we were all well awake we began to discuss the situation, which was serious enough. Not a drop of water was left. We turned the water-bottles upside down, and licked the tops, but it was a failure, they were dry as a bone. Good, who had charge of the bottle of brandy, got it out and looked at it longingly ; but Sir Henry promptly took it away from him, for to drink raw spirit would only have been to precipitate the end.

" If we do not find water we shall die," he said.

" If we can trust to the old Dom's map there should be some about," I said ; but nobody seemed to derive much satisfaction from this remark. It was so evident that no great faith could be put in the map. Now it was gradually growing light, and as we sat staring blankly at each other, I observed the Hottentot Ventvögel rise and begin to walk about with his eyes on the ground. Presently he stopped short, and uttering a guttural exclamation, pointed to the earth.

" What is it ? " we exclaimed ; and simultaneously we rose and went to where he was standing staring at the ground.

" Well," I said, " it is pretty fresh springbok spoor ; what of it ? "

" Springbucks do not go far from water," he answered in Dutch.

" No," I answered, " I forgot ; and thank God for it."

This little discovery put new life into us ; it is wonderful, when a man is in a desperate position, how he catches at the slightest hope, and feels almost happy in it. On a dark night a single star is better than nothing.

Meanwhile Ventvögel was lifting his snub nose, and sniffing the hot air for all the world like an old Impala ram who scents danger. Presently he spoke again.

" I *smell* water," he said.

Then we felt quite jubilant, for we knew what a wonderful instinct these wild-bred men possess.

Just at that moment the sun came up gloriously and revealed so grand a sight to our astonished eyes that for a moment or two we even forgot our thirst.

For there, not more than forty or fifty miles from us, glittering like silver in the early rays of the morning sun, soared Sheba's Breasts, and

stretching away for hundreds of miles on each
side of them was the great Suliman Berg. Now
that, sitting here, I attempt to describe the
extraordinary grandeur and beauty of that sight,
language seems to fail me. I am impotent even
before its memory. Straight before us, rose two
enormous mountains, the like of which are not,
I believe, to be seen in Africa, if indeed there are
any such other in the world, measuring each of
them at least fifteen thousand feet in height,
standing not more than a dozen miles apart,
linked together by a precipitous cliff of rock,
and towering in awful white solemnity straight
into the sky. These mountains placed thus,
like the pillars of a gigantic gateway, are shaped
after the fashion of a woman's breasts, and at
times the mists and shadows beneath them take
the form of a recumbent woman, veiled mysteri-
ously in sleep. Their bases swell gently from
the plain, looking at that distance perfectly
round and smooth ; and on the top of each is a
vast hillock covered with snow, exactly corresponding to the nipple on the female breast.
The stretch of cliff that connects them appear
to be some thousand feet in height, and perfectly
precipitous, and on each side of them, so far as
the eye can reach, extend similar lines of cliff,
broken only here and there by flat table-topped
mountains, something like the world-famed one
at Cape Town ; a formation, by the way, very
common in Africa.

To describe the comprehensive grandeur of
that view is beyond my powers. There was
something so inexpressibly solemn and overpowering about those huge volcanoes—for doubtless they are extinct volcanoes—that it quite took

our breath away. For a while the morning
lights played upon the snow and the brown
swelling masses beneath, and then, as though
to veil the majestic sight from our curious eyes,
strange mists and clouds gathered and increased
around the mountains, till presently we could
only trace their pure and gigantic outlines,
showing ghostlike through the fleecy envelope.
Indeed, as we afterwards discovered, usually
they were wrapped in this gauzy mist, which
doubtless accounted for our not having made
them out more clearly before.

Sheba's Breasts had scarcely vanished into
cloud-clad privacy, before our thirst—literally
a burning question—reasserted itself.

It was all very well for Ventvögel to say that
he smelt water, but look which way we would
we could see no signs of it. So far as the eye
might reach there was nothing but arid sweltering
sand and karoo scrub. We walked round the
hillock and gazed about anxiously on the other
side, but it was the same story, not a drop of
water could be seen ; there was no indication of
a pan, a pool, or a spring.

" You are a fool," I said angrily to Ventvögel ;
" there is no water."

But still he lifted his ugly snub nose and
sniffed.

" I smell it, Baas," he answered ; " it is somewhere in the air."

" Yes," I said, " no doubt it is in the clouds,
and about two months hence it will fall and wash
our bones."

Sir Henry stroked his yellow beard thoughtfully. " Perhaps it is on the top of the hill,"
he suggested.

" Rot," said Good ; " whoever heard of water being found at the top of a hill ! "

" Let us go and look," I put in, and hopelessly enough we scrambled up the sandy sides of the hillock, Umbopa leading. Presently he stopped as though he was petrified.

" *Nanzia manzie !* " that is, " Here is water," he cried with a loud voice.

We rushed up to him, and there, sure enough, in a deep cut or indentation on the very top of the sand koppie, was an undoubted pool of water. How it came to be in such a strange place we did not stop to inquire, nor did we hesitate at its black and unpleasant appearance. It was water, or a good imitation of it, and that was enough for us. We gave a bound and a rush, and in another second we were all down on our stomachs sucking up the uninviting fluid as though it were nectar fit for the gods. Heavens, how we did drink ! Then when we had done drinking we tore off our clothes and sat down in the pool, absorbing the moisture through our parched skins. You, Harry my boy, who have only to turn on a couple of taps to summon " hot " and " cold " from an unseen vasty boiler, can have little idea of the luxury of that muddy wallow in brackish tepid water.

After a while we rose from it, refreshed indeed, and fell to on our " biltong," of which we had scarcely been able to touch a mouthful for twenty-four hours, and ate our fill. Then we smoked a pipe, and lay down by the side of that blessed pool, under the overhanging shadow of its bank, and slept till mid-day.

All that day we rested there by the water, thanking our stars that we had been lucky enough

to find it, bad as it was, and not forgetting to
render a due share of gratitude to the shade of
the long-departed da Silvestra, who set its position down so accurately on the tail of his shirt.
The wonderful thing to us was that the pan
should have lasted so long, and the only way in
which I can account for this is on the supposition
that it is fed by some spring deep down in the
sand.

Having filled both ourselves and our water-
bottles as full as possible, in far better spirits we
started off again with the moon. That night
we covered nearly five-and-twenty miles, but,
needless to say, found no more water, though
we were lucky enough on the following day to
get a little shade behind some ant-heaps. When
the sun rose, and, for a while, cleared away the
mysterious mists, Suliman's Berg with the two
majestic Breasts, now only about twenty miles
off, seemed to be towering right above us, and
looked grander than ever. At the approach
of evening we marched again, and, to cut a long
story short, by daylight next morning found ourselves upon the lowest slopes of Sheba's left
breast, for which we had been steadily steering.
By this time our water was exhausted once more,
and we were suffering severely from thirst, nor
indeed could we see any chance of relieving it
till we reached the snow line far above us. After
resting an hour or two, driven to it by our torturing thirst, we went on toiling painfully in
the burning heat up the lava slopes, for we found
that the huge base of the mountain was composed entirely of lava beds belched from the
bowels of the earth in some far past age.

By eleven o'clock we were utterly exhausted,

and, generally speaking, in a very bad state indeed. The lava clinker, over which we must drag our- selves, though smooth compared with some clinker I have heard of, such as that on the Island of Ascension, for instance, was yet rough enough to make our feet very sore, and this, together with our other miseries, had pretty well finished us. A few hundred yards above us were some large lumps of lava, and towards these we steered with the intention of lying down beneath their shade. We reached them, and to our surprise. so far as we had a capacity for surprise left in us, on a little plateau or ridge close by we saw that the clinker was covered with a dense green growth. Evidently soil formed of decomposed lava had rested there, and in due course had become the receptacle of seeds deposited by birds. But we did not take much further interest in the green growth, for one cannot live on grass like Nebuchadnezzar. That requires a special dispensation of Providence and peculiar digestive organs. So we sat down under the rocks and groaned, and for one I wished heartily that we had never started on this fool's errand. As we were sitting there I saw Umbopa get up and hobble towards the patch of green, and a few minutes afterwards, to my great astonishment, I per- ceived that usually very dignified individual dancing and shouting like a maniac, waving some- thing green as he did so. Off we all scrambled towards him as fast as our wearied limbs would carry us, hoping that he had found water.

"What is it, Umbopa, son of a fool?" I shouted in Zulu.

"It is food and water, Macumazahn," and again he waved the green thing.

Then I saw what he had found. It was a melon. We had hit upon a patch of wild melons, thousands of them, and dead ripe.

" Melons ! " I yelled to Good, who was next to me ; and in another second his false teeth were fixed in one of them.

I think we ate about six each before we had done, and poor fruit as they were, I doubt if I ever thought anything nicer.

But melons are not very nutritious, and when we had satisfied our thirst with their pulpy substance, and put a stock to cool by the simple process of cutting them in two and setting them on end in the hot sun to grow cold by evaporation, we began to feel exceedingly hungry. We had still some biltong left, but our stomachs turned from biltong, and besides we were obliged to be very sparing of it, for we could not say when we should find more food. Just at this moment a lucky thing chanced. Looking across the desert I saw a flock of about ten large birds flying straight towards us.

" *Skit, Baas, skit !* " " Shoot, master, shoot ! " whispered the Hottentot, throwing himself on his face, an example which we all followed.

Then I saw that the birds were a flock of *pauw* or bustards, and that they would pass within fifty yards of my head. Taking one of the repeating Winchesters I waited till they were nearly over us, and then jumped to my feet. On seeing me the *pauw* bunched up together, as I expected that they would, and I fired two shots straight into the thick of them, and, as luck would have it, brought one down, a fine fellow, that weighed about twenty pounds. In half an hour we had a fire made of dry melon

stalks, and he was toasting over it, and we made
such a feed as we had not tasted for a week. We
ate that *pauw ;* nothing was left of him but his
leg-bones and his beak, and felt not a little
the better afterwards.

That night we went on again with the moon,
carrying as many melons as we could with us.
As we ascended we found the air grow cooler and
cooler, which was a great relief to us, and at
dawn, so far as we could judge, we were not more
than half a dozen miles from the snow line.
Here we found more melons, and so had no
longer any anxiety about water, for we knew
that we should soon get plenty of snow. But
the ascent had now become very precipitous,
and we made but slow progress, not more than
a mile an hour. Also that night we ate our last
morsel of biltong. As yet, with the exception
of the *pauw*, we had seen no living thing on the
mountain, nor had we come across a single
spring or stream of water, which struck us as
very odd, considering the snow above us, which
must, we thought, melt sometimes. But as we
afterwards discovered, owing to a cause which is
quite beyond my power to explain, all the streams
flowed upon the north side of the mountains.

Now we began to grow very anxious about
food. We had escaped death by thirst, but it
seemed probable that it was only to die of hunger.
The events of the next three miserable days are
best described by copying the entries made at
the time in my note-book.

" 21st May.—Started 11 a.m., finding the
atmosphere quite cold enough to travel by day,
and carrying some water-melons with us.
Struggled on all day, but found no more melons,

having evidently passed out of their district.
Saw no game of any sort. Halted for the night.
at sundown, having had no food for many hours.
Suffered much during the night from cold.

" 22nd.—Started at sunrise again, feeling very
faint and weak. Only made about five miles all
day ; found some patches of snow, of which we
ate, but nothing else. Camped at night under
the edge of a great plateau. Cold bitter. Drank
a little brandy each, and huddled ourselves
together, each wrapped up in his blanket to keep
ourselves alive. Are now suffering frightfully
from starvation and weariness. Thought that
Ventvögel would have died during the night.

" 23rd.—Struggled forward once more as soon
as the sun was well up, and had thawed our limbs
a little. We are now in a dreadful plight, and
I fear that unless we get food this will be our last
day's journey. But little brandy left. Good,
Sir Henry, and Umbopa bear up wonderfully,
but Ventvögel is in a very bad way. Like most
Hottentots, he cannot stand cold. Pangs of
hunger not so bad, but have a sort of numb
feeling about the stomach. Others say the
same. We are now on a level with the precipitous chain, or wall of lava, linking the two
Breasts, and the view is glorious. Behind us
the glowing desert rolls away to the horizon,
and before us lie mile upon mile of smooth hard
snow almost level, but swelling gently upwards,
out of the centre of which the nipple of the
mountain, that appears to be some miles in
circumference, rises about four thousand feet
into the sky. Not a living thing is to be seen.
God help us, I fear that our time is come."

And now I will drop the journal, partly because it is not very interesting reading, and also because what follows requires telling rather more fully.

All that day—the 23rd May—we struggled slowly up the incline of snow, lying down from time to time to rest. A strange gaunt crew we must have looked, while, laden as we were, we dragged our weary feet over the dazzling plain, glaring round us with hungry eyes. Not that there was much use in glaring, for we could see nothing to eat. We did not accomplish more than seven miles that day. Just before sunset we found ourselves exactly under the nipple of Sheba's left breast, which towered thousands of feet into the air, a vast smooth hillock of frozen snow. Weak as we were, we could not but appreciate the wonderful scene, made even more splendid by the flying rays of sunlight from the setting sun, which here and there stained the snow blood-red, and crowned the great dome above us with a diadem of glory.

"I say," gasped Good, presently, "we ought to be somewhere near that cave the old gentleman wrote about."

"Yes," said I, "if there is a cave."

"Come, Quatermain," groaned Sir Henry, "don't talk like that ; I have every faith in the Dom ; remember the water ! We shall find the place soon."

"If we don't find it before dark we are dead men, that is all about it," was my consolatory reply.

For the next ten minutes we trudged in silence, when suddenly Umbopa, who was marching along beside me, wrapped in his blanket, and with a leather belt strapped so tightly round his

stomach, to "make his hunger small," as he
said, that his waist looked like a girl's, caught
me by the arm.

"Look!" he said, pointing towards the
springing slope of the nipple.

I followed his glance, and some two hundred
yards from us perceived what appeared to be a
hole in the snow.

"It is the cave," said Umbopa.

We made the best of our way to the spot, and
found sure enough that the hole was the mouth
of a cave, no doubt the same as that of which
da Silvestra wrote. We were not too soon, for
just as we reached shelter the sun went down
with startling rapidity, leaving the world nearly
dark. In these latitudes there is but little
twilight. So we crept into the cave, which did
not appear to be very big, and huddling ourselves
together for warmth, swallowed what remained
of our brandy—barely a mouthful each—and
tried to forget our miseries in sleep. But the
cold was too intense to allow us to do so, for I
am convinced that at this great altitude the ther-
mometer cannot have marked less than fourteen
or fifteen degrees below freezing-point. What
such a temperature meant to us, enervated as we
were by hardship, want of food, and the great
heat of the desert, the reader may imagine better
than I can describe. Suffice it to say that it
was something as near death from exposure as I
have ever felt. There we sat hour after hour
through the still and bitter night, feeling the
frost wander round and nip us now in the finger,
now in the foot, now in the face. In vain did
we huddle closer and closer; there was no
warmth in our miserable starved carcasses.

Sometimes one of us would drop into an uneasy
slumber for a few minutes, but we could not sleep
much, and perhaps it was fortunate, for if we
had I doubt if we should ever have woke again.
I believe it was only by the force of will that we
kept ourselves alive at all.

Not very long before dawn I heard the Hottentot Ventvögel, whose teeth had been chattering
all night like castanets, give a deep sigh. Then
his teeth stopped chattering. I did not think
anything of it at the time, concluding that he
had gone to sleep. His back was resting against
mine, and it seemed to grow colder and colder,
till at last it felt like ice.

At length the air began to grow grey with
light, then golden arrows sped across the snow,
and at last the glorious sun peeped above the
lava wall and looked in upon our half-frozen
forms, and also upon Ventvögel, sitting there
amongst us *stone dead*. No wonder his back
felt cold, poor fellow. He had died when I heard
him sigh, and was now frozen almost stiff.
Shocked beyond measure we dragged ourselves
from the corpse—how strange is that horror we
mortals have of tne companionship of a dead
body—and left it sitting there, its arms clasped
about its knees.

By this time the sunlight was pouring its cold
rays, for here they were cold, straight into the
mouth of the cave. Suddenly I heard an exclamation of fear from someone, and turned my
head.

And this is what I saw. Sitting at the end of
the cavern—it was not more than twenty feet
long—was another form, of which the head
rested on its chest and the long arms hung down.

I stared at it, and saw that this too was a *dead man*, and, what was more, a white man.

The others saw also, and the sight proved too much for our shattered nerves. One and all we scrambled out of the cave as fast as our half-frozen limbs would allow.

CHAPTER VII

SOLOMON'S ROAD

OUTSIDE the cavern we halted, feeling rather foolish.

"I am going back," said Sir Henry.

"Why?" asked Good.

"Because it has struck me that—what we saw—may be my brother."

This was a new idea, and we re-entered the place to put it to the proof. After the bright light outside, our eyes, weak as they were with staring at the snow, could not pierce the gloom of the cave for a while. Presently, however, they grew accustomed to the semi-darkness, and we advanced towards the dead man.

Sir Henry knelt down and peered into his face.

"Thank God," he said, with a sigh of relief, "it is *not* my brother."

Then I drew near and looked. The body was that of a tall man in middle life with aquiline features, grizzled hair, and a long black moustache. The skin was perfectly yellow, and stretched tightly over the bones. Its clothing, with the exception of what seemed to be the remains of a woollen pair of hose, had been removed, leaving the skeleton-like frame naked. Round the neck of the corpse, which was frozen perfectly stiff, hung a yellow ivory crucifix.

" Who on earth can it be ? " said I.

" Can't you guess ? " asked Good.

I shook my head.

" Why, the old Dom, José da Silvestra, of course—who else ? "

" Impossible," I gasped, " he died three hundred years ago."

" And what is there to prevent him lasting for three thousand years in this atmosphere, I should like to know ? " asked Good. " If only the temperature is sufficiently low, flesh and blood will keep fresh as New Zealand mutton for ever, and Heaven knows it is cold enough here. The sun never gets in here ; no animal comes here to tear or destroy. No doubt his slave, of whom he speaks on the writing, took off his clothes and left him. He could not have buried him alone. Look ! " he went on stooping down to pick up a queerly-shaped bone scraped at the end into a sharp point, " here is the ' cleft bone ' that Silvestra used to draw the map with."

We gazed for a moment astonished, forgetting our own miseries in this extraordinary and, as it seemed to us, semi-miraculous sight.

" Ay," said Sir Henry, " and this is where he got his ink from," and he pointed to a small wound on the dead Dom's left arm. " Did ever man see such a thing before ! "

There was no longer any doubt about the matter, which for my own part I confess perfectly appalled me. There he sat, the dead man, whose directions, written some ten generations ago, had led us to this spot. Here in my own hand was the rude pen with which he had written them, and about his neck hung the crucifix that his dying lips had kissed. Gazing at him, my imagination could reconstruct the last scene of the drama, the traveller dying of cold and starvation, yet striving to convey to the world the great secret which he had discovered :— the awful loneliness of his death, of which the evidence sat before us. It even seemed to me that I could trace on his strongly-marked features a likeness to those of my poor friend Silvestre his descendant, who had died twenty years before in my arms, but perhaps that was fancy. At any rate, there he sat, a sad memento of the fate that so often overtakes those who would penetrate into the unknown ; and there doubtless he will still sit, crowned with the dread majesty of death, for centuries yet unborn, to startle the eyes of wanderers like ourselves, if ever any such should come again to invade his loneliness. The thing overpowered us, already nearly done to death as we were with cold and hunger.

" Let us go," said Sir Henry in a low voice ; " stay, we will give him a companion," and lifting up the dead body of the Hottentot Ventvögel, he placed it near to that of the old Dom. Then he stopped, and with a jerk broke the rotten string of the crucifix which hung round da Silvestra's neck, for his fingers were too cold to attempt to unfasten it. I believe that he still has it. I took the bone pen, and it is before me as I write—sometimes I sign my name with it.

Then leaving these two, the proud white man of a past age, and the poor Hottentot, to keep their eternal vigil in the midst of the eternal snows, we crept out of the cave into the welcome sunshine and resumed our path. wondering in our hearts how many hours it would be before we were even as they are.

When we had walked about half a mile we came to the edge of the plateau, for the nipple of the mountain does not rise out of its exact centre, though from the desert side it seemed to do so. What lay before us we could not see, for the landscape was wreathed in billows of morning fog. Presently, however, the higher layers of mist cleared a little, and revealed, at the end of a long slope of snow, a patch of green grass, some five hundred yards beneath us, through which a stream was running. Nor was this all. By the stream, basking in the bright sun, stood and lay a group of from ten to fifteen *large antelopes*—at that distance we could not see of what species.

The sight filled us with an unreasoning joy. There was food in plenty if only we could get it. But the question was how to get it. The beasts were fully six hundred yards off, a very long shot, and one not to be depended on when our lives hung on the result.

Rapidly we discussed the advisability of trying to stalk the game, but in the end reluctantly dismissed it. To begin with, the wind was not favourable, and further, we must certainly be perceived, however careful we were, against the blinding background of snow, which we should be obliged to traverse.

" Well, we must have a try from where we are," said Sir Henry. " Which shall it be, Quatermain, the repeating rifles or the expresses ? "

Here again was a question. The Winchester repeaters—of which we had two, Umbopa carrying poor Ventvögel's as well as his own—were

sighted up to a thousand yards, whereas the
expresses were only sighted to three hundred
and fifty, beyond which distance shooting with
them was more or less guesswork. On the
other hand, if they did hit, the express bullets,
being "expanding," were much more likely to
bring the game down. It was a knotty point,
but I made up my mind that we must risk it
and use the expresses.

"Let each of us take the buck opposite to
him. Aim well at the point in his shoulder and
high up," said I; "and, Umbopa, do you give
the word, so that we may all fire together."

Then came a pause, each of us aiming his level
best, as indeed a man is likely to do when he
knows that life itself depends upon the shot.

"Fire!" said Umbopa in Zulu, and at almost
the same instant the three rifles rang out loudly;
three clouds of smoke hung for a moment before
us, and a hundred echoes went flying over the
silent snow. Presently the smoke cleared, and
revealed—oh, joy!—a great buck lying on its
back and kicking furiously in its death agony.
We gave a yell of triumph—we were saved—
we should not starve. Weak as we were, we
rushed down the intervening slope of snow,
and in ten minutes from the time of shooting,
that animal's heart and liver were lying before
us. But now a new difficulty arose—we had
no fuel, and therefore could make no fire to
cook them. We gazed at each other in dismay.

"Starving men should not be fanciful," said
Good; "we must eat raw meat."

There was no other way out of the dilemma,
and our gnawing hunger made the proposition
less distasteful than it would otherwise have

been. So we took the heart and liver and buried
them for a few minutes in a patch of snow to
cool them. Then we washed them in the ice-
cold water of the stream, and lastly ate them
greedily. It sounds horrible enough, but
honestly, I never tasted anything so good as that
raw meat. In a quarter of an hour we were
changed men. Our life and vigour came back
to us, our feeble pulses grew strong again, and the
blood went coursing through our veins. But
mindful of the results of over-feeding on starving
stomachs, we were careful not to eat too much,
stopping whilst we were still hungry.

"Thank Heaven!" said Sir Henry; "that
brute has saved our lives. What is it, Quatermain?"

I rose and went to look at the antelope, for
I was not certain. It was about the size of a
donkey, with large curved horns. I had never
seen one like it before, the species was new to
me. It was brown in colour, with faint red
stripes, and grew a thick coat. I afterwards
discovered that the natives of that wonderful
country call these bucks "*Inco.*" They are
very rare, and only found at a great altitude
where no other game will live. This animal
was fairly shot high up in the shoulder, though
whose bullet brought it down we could not, of
course, discover. I believe that Good, mindful
of his marvellous shot at the giraffe, secretly
set it down to his own prowess, and we did not
contradict him.

We had been so busy satisfying our starving
stomachs that hitherto we had not found time
to look about us. But now, having set Umbopa
to cut off as much of the best meat as we were

likely to be able to carry, we began to inspect
our surroundings. The mist had cleared away,
for it was eight o'clock, and the sun sucked it
up, so we were able to take in all the country
before us at a glance. I know not how to describe
the glorious panorama which unfolded itself to
our gaze. I have never seen anything like it
before, nor shall, I suppose, again.

Behind and over us towered Sheba's snowy
Breasts, and below, some five thousand feet
beneath where we stood, lay league on league of
the most lovely champaign country. Here were
dense patches of lofty forest, there a great river
wound its silvery way. To the left stretched
a vast expanse of rich undulating veldt or grass
land, on which we could just make out countless
herds of game or cattle ; at that distance we
could not tell which. This expanse appeared
to be ringed in by a wall of distant mountains.
To the right the country was more or less moun-
tainous ; that is, solitary hills stood up from
its level, with stretches of cultivated land between,
amongst which we could see groups of dome-
shaped huts. The landscape lay before us as
a map, in which rivers flashed like silver snakes,
and Alp-like peaks crowned with wildly twisted
snow wreaths rose in grandeur, whilst over all
was the glad sunlight, and the breath of Nature's
happy life.

Two curious things struck us as we gazed.
First, that the country before us must lie at
least three thousand feet higher than the desert
we had crossed, and secondly, that all the rivers
flowed from south to north. As we had painful
reason to know, there was no water upon the
southern side of the vast range on which we

stood, but on the northern face were many streams, most of which appeared to unite with the great river we could see winding away farther than we could follow it.

We sat down for a while and gazed in silence at this wonderful view. Presently Sir Henry spoke.

"Isn't there something on the map about Solomon's Great Road ? " he said.

I nodded, my eyes still gazing out over the far country.

" Well, look ; there it is ! " and he pointed a little to our right.

Good and I looked accordingly, and there, winding away towards the plain, was what appeared to be a wide turnpike road. We had not seen it at first because, on reaching the plain, it turned behind some broken country. We did not say anything, at least, not much ; we were beginning to lose the sense of wonder. Somehow it did not seem particularly unnatural that we should find a sort of Roman road in this strange land. We accepted the fact, that was all.

" Well," said Good, " it must be quite near us if we cut off to the right. Hadn't we better be making a start ? "

This was sound advice, and as soon as we had washed our faces and hands in the stream we acted on it. For a mile or more we made our way over boulders and across patches of snow, till suddenly, on reaching the top of the little rise we found the road at our feet. It was a splendid road cut out of the solid rock, at least fifty feet wide, and apparently well kept ; but the odd thing about it was that it seemed to

begin there. We walked down and stood on it,
but one single hundred paces behind us, in the
direction of Sheba's Breasts, it vanished, the
entire surface of the mountain being strewn with
boulders interspersed with patches of snow.

" What do you make of this, Quatermain ? "
asked Sir Henry.

I shook my head. I could make nothing of it.

" I have it," said Good ; " the road no doubt
ran right over the range and across the desert
on the other side, but the sand there has covered
it up, and above us it has been obliterated by
some volcanic eruption of molten lava."

This seemed a good suggestion ; at any rate,
we accepted it, and proceeded down the mountain.
It proved a very different business travelling
along down hill on that magnificent pathway
with full stomachs to what it was travelling
uphill over the snow quite starved and almost
frozen. Indeed, had it not been for melancholy
recollections of poor Ventvögel's sad fate, and of
that grim cave where he kept company with the
old Dom, we should have felt positively cheerful,
notwithstanding the sense of unknown dangers
before us. Every mile we walked the atmosphere
grew softer and balmier, and the country before
us shone with a yet more luminous beauty. As
for the road itself, I never saw such an engineering
work, though Sir Henry said that the great
road over the St. Gothard in Switzerland is very
like it. No difficulty had been too great for the
Old World engineer who designed it. At one
place we came to a ravine three hundred feet
broad and at least a hundred deep. This vast
gulf was actually filled in with huge blocks of
dressed stone, having arches pierced through

them at the bottom for a waterway, over which
the road went on sublimely. At another place
it was cut in zigzags out of the side of a precipice
five hundred feet deep, and in a third it tunnelled
through the base of an intervening ridge, a space
of thirty yards or more.

Here we noticed the sides of the tunnel were
covered with quaint sculptures, mostly of mailed
figures driving in chariots. One, which was
exceedingly beautiful, represented a whole battle
scene with a convoy of captives being marched
off in the distance.

"Well," said Sir Henry, after inspecting this
ancient work of art, "it is very well to call this
Solomon's Road, but my humble opinion is that
the Egyptians have been here before Solomon's
people ever set a foot on it. If this isn't Egyptian
handiwork, I must say that it is very like it."

By midday we had advanced sufficiently down
the mountain to reach the region where wood was
to be met with. First we came to scattered bushes
which grew more and more frequent, till at last
we found the road winding through a vast grove
of silver trees similar to those which are to be
seen on the slopes of Table Mountain at Cape
Town. I had never before met with them in all
my wanderings except at the Cape, and their
appearance here astonished me greatly.

"Ah!" said Good, surveying these shining-
leaved trees with evident enthusiasm, "here is
lots of wood; let us stop and cook some dinner;
I have about digested that raw liver."

Nobody objected to this, so leaving the road
we made our way to a stream which was babbling
away not far off, and soon had a goodly fire of
dry boughs blazing. Cutting off some substantial

hunks from the flesh of the *inco* which we had brought with us we proceeded to toast them on the end of sharp sticks, as one sees the Kafirs do, and ate them with relish. After filling ourselves, we lit our pipes and gave ourselves up to enjoyment, which, compared with the hardships we had recently undergone, seemed almost heavenly.

The brook, of which the banks were clothed with dense masses of a gigantic species of maidenhair fern interspersed with feathery tufts of wild asparagus, babbled merrily at our side, the soft air murmured through the leaves of the silver trees, doves cooed around, and bright-winged birds flashed like living gems from bough to bough. It was a Paradise.

The magic of the place combined with an overwhelming sense of dangers left behind, and of the Promised Land reached at last, seemed to charm us into silence. Sir Henry and Umbopa sat conversing in a mixture of broken English and kitchen Zulu in a low voice, but earnestly enough, and I lay, with my eyes half shut, upon that fragrant bed of fern and watched them.

Presently I missed Good, and I looked to see what had become of him. Soon I observed him sitting by the bank of the stream, in which he had been bathing. He had nothing on but his flannel shirt, and his natural habits of extreme neatness having reasserted themselves, he was actively employed in making a most elaborate toilet. He had washed his gutta-percha collar, had thoroughly shaken out his trousers, coat and waistcoat, and was now folding them up neatly till he was ready to put them on, shaking his head sadly as he scanned the numerous rents and tears in them, which naturally had resulted from our frightful journey. Then he took his boots, scrubbed them with a handful of fern, and finally rubbed them over with a piece of fat, which he had carefully saved from the *inco* meat, till they looked, comparatively speaking, respectable. Having inspected them judiciously through his eye-glass, he put the boots on and began a fresh operation. From a little bag that he carried he produced a pocket-comb in which was fixed a tiny looking-glass, and in this he surveyed himself. Apparently he was not satisfied, for he proceeded to do his hair with great care. Then came a pause whilst he again contemplated the effect ; still it was not satisfactory. He felt his chin, on which the accumulated scrub of a ten days' beard was flourishing.

" Surely," thought I, " he is not going to try to shave."

But it was so. Taking the piece of fat with which he had greased his boots, Good washed it thoroughly in the stream. Then diving again into the bag he brought out a little pocket razor with a guard to it, such as are bought by people who are afraid of cutting themselves, or by those about to undertake a sea voyage. Then he scrubbed his face and chin vigorously with the fat and began. But evidently it proved a painful process, for he groaned very much over it, and I was convulsed with inward laughter as I watched him struggling with that stubbly beard. It seemed so very odd that a man should take the trouble to shave himself with a piece of fat in such a place and in our circumstances. At last he succeeded in getting the worst of the scrub off the right side of his face and chin, when suddenly

I, who was watching, became aware of a flash of light that passed by his head.

Good sprang up with a profane exclamation (if it had not been a safety razor he would certainly have cut his throat), and so did I, without the exclamation, and this was what I saw. Standing not more than twenty paces from where I was, and ten from Good, were a group of men. They were very tall and copper-coloured, and some of them wore great plumes of black feathers and short cloaks of leopard skins; this was all I noticed at the moment. In front of them stood a youth of about seventeen, his hand still raised and his body bent forward in the attitude of a Grecian statue of a spear-thrower. Evidently the flash of light had been caused by a weapon, and he had hurled it.

As I looked an old soldier-like man stepped forward out of the group, and catching the youth by the arm said something to him. Then they advanced upon us.

Sir Henry, Good, and Umbopa by this time had seized their rifles and lifted them threateningly. The party of natives still came on. It struck me that they could not know what rifles were, or they would not have treated them with such contempt.

" Put down your guns ! " I hallooed to the others, seeing that our only chance of safety lay in conciliation. They obeyed, and walking to the front I addressed the elderly man who had checked the youth.

" Greeting," I said in Zulu, not knowing what language to use. To my surprise I was understood.

" Greeting," answered the man, not, indeed,

in the same tongue, but in a dialect so closely allied to it that neither Umbopa nor myself had any difficulty in understanding it. Indeed, as we afterwards found out, the language spoken by this people is an old-fashioned form of the Zulu tongue, bearing about the same relationship to it that the English of Chaucer does to the English of the nineteenth century.

" Whence come you ? " he went on, " who are you ? and why are the faces of three of you white, and the face of the fourth as the face of our mother's sons ? " and he pointed to Umbopa. I looked at Umbopa as he said it, and it flashed across me that he was right. The face of Umbopa was like the faces of the men before me, and so was his great form like their forms. But I had not time to reflect on this coincidence.

" We are strangers, and come in peace," I answered, speaking very slowly, so that he might understand me, " and this man is our servant."

" Ye lie," he answered ; " no strangers can cross the mountains where all things perish. But what do your lies matter ?—if ye are strangers then ye must die, for no strangers may live in the land of the Kukuanas. It is the king's law. Prepare then to die, O strangers ! "

I was slightly staggered at this, more especially as I saw the hands of some of the men steal down to their sides, where hung on each what looked to me like a large and heavy knife.

" What does that beggar say ? " asked Good.

" He says we are going to be killed," I answered grimly.

" Oh, Lord ! " groaned Good ; and, as was his way when perplexed, he put his hand to his false teeth, dragging the top set down and allowing them to fly back to his jaw with a snap. It was a most fortunate move, for next second the dignified crowd of Kukuanas uttered a simultaneous yell of horror, and bolted back some yards.

" What's up ? " said I.

" It's his teeth," whispered Sir Henry excitedly. " He moved them. Take them out, Good, take them out ! "

He obeyed, slipping the set into the sleeve of his flannel shirt.

In another second curiosity had overcome fear, and the men advanced slowly. Apparently they had now forgotten their amiable intention of killing us.

" How is it, O strangers," asked the old man solemnly, " that this fat man (pointing to Good, who was clad in nothing but boots and a flannel shirt, and had only half finished his shaving) whose body is clothed, and whose legs are bare, who grows hair on one side of his sickly face and not on the other, and who wears one shining and transparent eye, has teeth that move of themselves, coming away from the jaws and returning of their own free will ? "

" Open your mouth," I said to Good, who promptly curled up his lips and grinned at the old gentleman like an angry dog, revealing to his astonished gaze two thin red lines of gum as utterly innocent of ivories as a new-born elephant. The audience gasped.

" Where are his teeth ? " they shouted ; " with our eyes we saw them."

Turning his head slowly and with a gesture of ineffable contempt, Good swept his hand across his mouth. Then he grinned again, and lo, there were two rows of lovely teeth.

Now the young man who had flung the knife threw himself down on the grass and gave vent to a prolonged howl of terror ; and as for the old gentleman, his knees knocked together with fear.

" I see ye are spirits," he said faltering ; " did ever man born of woman have hair on one side of his face and not on the other, or a round and transparent eye, or teeth which moved and melted away and grew again ? Pardon us, O my lords."

Here was luck indeed, and, needless to say, I jumped at the chance.

" It is granted," I said with an imperial smile. " Nay, ye shall know the truth. We come from another world, though we are men such as ye ; we come," I went on, " from the biggest star that shines at night."

" Oh ! oh ! " groaned the chorus of astonished aborigines.

" Yes," I went on, " we do, indeed ; " and again I smiled benignly as I uttered that amazing lie. " We come to stay with you a little while, and to bless you by our sojourn. Ye will see, O friends, that I have prepared myself for this visit by the learning of your language."

" It is so, it is so," said the chorus.

" Only, my lord," put in the old gentleman, " thou hast learnt it very badly."

I cast an indignant glance at him, and he quailed.

" Now, friends," I continued, " ye might think that after so long a journey we should find it in our hearts to avenge such a reception, mayhap to strike cold in death the impious hand that— that, in short—threw a knife at the head of him whose teeth come and go."

"Spare him, my lords," said the old man in supplication; "he is the king's son, and I am his uncle. If anything befalls him his blood will be required at my hands."

"Yes, that is certainly so," put in the young man with great emphasis.

"Ye may perhaps doubt our power to avenge," I went on, heedless of this byplay. "Stay, I will show you. Here, thou dog and slave (addressing Umbopa in a savage tone), give me the magic tube that speaks;" and I tipped a wink towards my express rifle.

Umbopa rose to the occasion, and with something as nearly resembling a grin as I have ever seen on his dignified face, he handed me the gun.

"It is here, O Lord of Lords," he said with a deep obeisance.

Now just before I had asked for the rifle I perceived a little *klipspringer* antelope standing on a mass of rock about seventy yards away, and had determined to risk a shot at it.

"Ye see that buck," I said, pointing the animal out to the party before me. "Tell me, is it possible for a man born of woman to kill it from here with a noise?"

"It is not possible, my lord," answered the old man.

"Yet shall I kill it," I said quietly.

The old man smiled. "That my lord cannot do," he answered.

I raised the rifle and covered the buck. It was a small animal, and one which a man might well be excused for missing, but I knew that it would not do to miss.

I drew a deep breath, and slowly pressed on the trigger. The buck stood still as a stone.

" Bang ! thud ! " The antelope sprang into the air and fell on the rock dead as a door nail.

A groan of terror burst from the group before us.

" If ye want meat," I remarked coolly, " go fetch that buck."

The old man made a sign, and one of his followers departed, and presently returned bearing the *klipspringer*. I noticed, with satisfaction, that I had hit it fairly behind the shoulder. They gathered round the poor creature's body, gazing at the bullet-hole in consternation.

" Ye see," I said, " I do not speak empty words."

There was no answer.

" If ye doubt our power," I went on, " let one of you stand upon that rock that I may make him as this buck."

None of them seemed at all inclined to take the hint, till at last the king's son spoke.

" It is well said. Do thou, my uncle, go stand upon the rock. It is but a buck that the magic has killed. Surely it cannot kill a man."

The old gentleman did not take the suggestion in good part. Indeed, he seemed hurt.

" No ! no ! " he ejaculated hastily, " my old eyes have seen enough. These are wizards, indeed. Let us bring them to the king. Yet if any wish a further proof, let *him* stand upon the rock, that the magic tube may speak with him."

There was a most general and hasty expression of dissent.

" Let not good magic be wasted on our poor bodies," said one, " we are satisfied. All the witchcraft of our people cannot show the like of this."

"It is so," remarked the old gentleman, in a tone of intense relief; "without any doubt it is so. Listen, children of the Stars, children of the shining eye and the movable teeth, who roar out in thunder and slay from afar. I am Infadoos, son of Kafa, once king of the Kukuana people. This youth is Scragga."

"He nearly scragged me," murmured Good.

"Scragga, son of Twala, the great king— Twala, husband of a thousand wives, chief and lord paramount of the Kukuanas, keeper of the great Road, terror of his enemies, student of the Black Arts, leader of an hundred thousand warriors, Twala the One-eyed, the Black, the Terrible."

"So," said I superciliously, "lead us then to Twala. We do not talk with low people and underlings."

"It is well, my lords, we will lead you, but the way is long. We are hunting three days' journey from the place of the king. But let my lords have patience, and we will lead them."

"So be it," I said carelessly; "all time is before us, for we do not die. We are ready, lead on. But, Infadoos, and thou, Scragga, beware! Play us no tricks, set for us no snares, for before your brains of mud have thought of them we shall know and avenge them. The light from the transparent eye of him with the bare legs and the half-haired face shall destroy you, and go through your land; his vanishing teeth shall fix themselves fast in you and eat you up, you and your wives and children; the magic tubes shall talk with you loudly, and make you sieves. Beware!"

This magnificent address did not fail of its effect ¡

indeed, it was hardly needed, so deeply were our
friends already impressed with our powers.

The old man made a deep obeisance, and
murmured the words " *Koom, Koom,*" which I
afterwards discovered was their royal salute,
corresponding to the " *Bayéte* " of the Zulus,
and turning, addressed his followers. They
at once proceeded to lay hold of all our goods and
chattels, in order to bear them for us, excepting
only the guns, which they would on no account
touch. They even seized Good's clothes, that,
as the reader may remember, were neatly folded
up beside him.

He saw and made a dive for them, and a loud
altercation ensued.

" Let not my lord of the transparent Eye
and the melting Teeth touch them," said the
old man. " Surely his slaves shall carry the
things."

" But I want to put 'em on ! " roared Good,
in nervous English.

Umbopa translated.

" Nay, my lord," answered Infadoos, " would
my lord cover up his beautiful white legs (although
he is so dark Good has a singularly white skin)
from the eyes of his servants ? Have we offended
my lord that he should do such a thing ? "

Here I nearly exploded with laughing ; and
meanwhile one of the men started on with the
garments.

" Damn it ! " roared Good, " that black villain
has got my trousers."

" Look here, Good," said Sir Henry, " you have
appeared in this country in a certain character,
and you must live up to it. It will never do for
you to put on trousers again. Henceforth you

must exist in a flannel shirt, a pair of boots, and an eye-glass."

"Yes," I said, "and with whiskers on one side of your face and not on the other. If you change any of these things the people will think that we are impostors. I am very sorry for you, but, seriously, you must do it. If they once begin to suspect us our lives will not be worth a brass farthing."

"Do you really think so?" said Good gloomily.

"I do, indeed. Your 'beautiful white legs' and your eye-glass are now *the* features of our party, and as Sir Henry says, you must live up to them. Be thankful that you have got your boots on, and that the air is warm."

Good sighed, and said no more, but it took him a fortnight to become accustomed to his new and scant attire.

CHAPTER VIII

WE ENTER KUKUANALAND

ALL that afternoon we travelled along the magnificent roadway, which trended steadily in a north-westerly direction. Infadoos and Scragga walked with us, but their followers marched about one hundred paces ahead.

"Infadoos," I said at length, "who made this road?"

"It was made, my lord, of old time, none know how or when, not even the wise woman Gagool, who has lived for generations. We are not old enough to remember its making. None can make such roads now, but the king suffers no grass to grow upon it."

"And whose are the writings on the wall of the caves through which we have passed on the road?" I asked, referring to the Egyptian-like sculptures that we had seen.

"My lord, the hands that made the road wrote the wonderful writings. We know not who wrote them."

"When did the Kukuana people come into this country?"

"My lord, the race came down here like the breath of a storm ten thousand thousand moons ago, from the great lands which lie there beyond," and he pointed to the north. "They could travel no further because of the high mountains which ring in the land, so say the old voices of our fathers that have descended to us the children, and so says Gagool, the wise woman, the smeller out of witches," and again he pointed to the snow-clad peaks. " The country, too, was good, so they settled here and grew strong and powerful, and now our numbers are like the sea sand, and when Twala the king calls up his regiments their plumes cover the plain so far as the eye of man can reach."

" And if the land is walled in with mountains, who is there for the regiments to fight with ? "

" Nay, my lord, the country is open there towards the north, and now and again warriors sweep down upon us in clouds from a land we know not, and we slay them. It is the third part of the life of a man since there was a war. Many thousands died in it, but we destroyed those who came to eat us up. So since then there has been no war."

" Your warriors must grow weary of resting on their spears, Infadoos."

" My lord, there was one war, just after we destroyed the people that came down upon us, but it was a civil war ; dog ate dog."

" How was that ? "

" My lord, the king, my half-brother, had a brother born at the same birth, and of the same woman. It is not our custom, my lord, to suffer twins to live, the weaker must always die. But the mother of the king hid away the feebler child, which was born the last, for her heart yearned over it, and that child is Twala the king. I am his younger brother, born of another wife."

" Well ? "

" My lord, Kafa, our father, died when we came
to manhood, and my brother Imotu was made
king in his place, and for a space reigned and had
a son by his favourite wife. When the babe
was three years old, just after the great war,
during which no man could sow or reap, a famine
came upon the land, and the people murmured
because of the famine, and looked round like
a starved lion for something to rend. Then it
was that Gagool the wise and terrible woman,
who does not die, made a proclamation to the
people. ' The king Imotu is no king.' And at the
time Imotu was sick with a wound, and lay in his
kraal not able to move.

" Then Gagool went into a hut and led out
Twala, my half-brother, and twin brother to the
king, whom she had hidden since he was born
among the caves and rocks, and stripping the
' moocha ' (waist-cloth) off his loins, showed the
people of the Kukuanas the mark of the sacred
snake coiled round his middle, wherewith the
eldest son of the king is marked at birth, and cried
out loud, ' Behold, your king whom I have saved
for you even to this day ! '

" Now the people being mad with hunger, and
altogether bereft of reason and the knowledge of
truth, cried out—' *The king ! The king !* ' but
I knew that it was not so, for Imotu my brother
was the elder of the twins, and our lawful king.
Then just as the tumult was at its height Imotu
the king, though he was very sick, crawled from
his hut holding his wife by the hand, and followed
by his little son Ignosi—that is, by interpretation,
the lightning.

" ' What is this noise ? ' he asked ; ' Why cry
ye *The king ! The king !* '

" Then Twala, his own brother, born of the same
woman, and in the same hour, ran to him, and
taking him by the hair, stabbed him through the
heart with his knife.   And the people being fickle,
and ever ready to worship the rising sun, clapped
their hands and cried, ' *Twala is king!* Now we
know that Twala is king ! ' "

" And what became of his wife and her son
Ignosi ?   Did Twala kill them too ? "

" Nay, my lord.   When she saw that her lord
was dead the queen seized the child with a cry,
and ran away.   Two days afterwards she came
to a kraal very hungry, and none would give her
milk or food, now that her lord the king was dead,
for all men hate the unfortunate.   But at night-
fall a little child, a girl, crept out and brought her
corn to eat, and she blessed the child, and went
on towards the mountains with her boy before the
sun rose again, and there she must have perished,
for none have seen her since, nor the child Ignosi."

" Then if this child Ignosi had lived he would be
the true king of the Kukuana people ? "

" That is so, my lord ; the sacred snake is
round his middle.   If he lives he is king ; but,
alas ! he is long dead."

" See, my lord," and Infadoos pointed to a vast
collection of huts surrounded by a fence, which
was in its turn encircled by a great ditch, that lay
on the plain beneath us.   " That is the kraal
where the wife of Imotu was last seen with the
child Ignosi.   It is there that we shall sleep to-
night, if, indeed," he added doubtfully, " my lords
sleep at all upon this earth."

" When we are among the Kukuanas, my good
friend Infadoos, we do as the Kukuanas do," I said
majestically, and turned round quickly to address

Good, who was tramping along sullenly behind, his mind fully occupied with unsatisfactory attempts to prevent his flannel shirt from flapping in the evening breeze. To my astonishment I butted into Umbopa, who was walking along immediately behind me, and very evidently had been listening with the greatest interest to my conversation with Infadoos. The expression on his face was most curious, and gave me the idea of a man who was struggling with partial success to bring something long ago forgotten back into his mind.

All this while we had been pressing on at a good rate towards the undulating plain beneath us. The mountains we had crossed now loomed high above our heads, and Sheba's Breasts were veiled modestly in diaphanous wreaths of mist. As we went the country grew more and more lovely. The vegetation was luxuriant, without being tropical ; the sun was bright and warm, but not burning ; and a gracious breeze blew softly along the odorous slopes of the mountains. Indeed, this new land was little less than an earthly paradise ; in beauty, in natural wealth, and in climate I have never seen its like. The Transvaal is a fine country, but it is nothing to Kukuanaland.

So soon as we started Infadoos had despatched a runner to warn the people of the kraal, which, by the way, was in his military command, of our arrival. This man had departed at an extraordinary speed, which Infadoos informed me he would keep up all the way, as running was an exercise much practised among his people.

The result of this message now became apparent. When we arrived within two miles of the kraal we could see that company after company of men were issuing from its gates and marching towards us.

Sir Henry laid his hand upon my arm, and remarked that it looked as though we were going to meet with a warm reception. Something in his tone attracted Infadoos' attention.

" Let not my lords be afraid," he said hastily, " for in my breast there dwells no guile. This regiment is one under my command, and comes out by my orders to greet you."

I nodded easily, though I was not quite easy in my mind.

About half a mile from the gates of this kraal is a long stretch of rising ground sloping gently upwards from the road, and here the companies formed up. It was a splendid sight to see them, each company about three hundred strong, charging swiftly up the rise, with flashing spears and waving plumes, to take their appointed place. By the time we reached the slope twelve such companies, or in all three thousand six hundred men, had passed out and taken up their positions along the road.

Presently we came to the first company, and were able to gaze in astonishment on the most magnificent set of warriors that I have ever seen. They were all men of mature age, mostly veterans of about forty, and not one of them was under six feet in height, whilst many stood six feet three or four. They wore upon their heads heavy black plumes of sakaboola feathers, like those which adorned our guides. Round their waists and also beneath the right knees were bound circlets of white ox tails, and in their left hands they carried round shields measuring about twenty inches across. These shields are very curious. The framework is made of an iron plate beaten out thin, over which is stretched milk-white ox-hide. The weapons that each man wore were simple, but most effective, consisting of a short and very heavy two-edged spear with a wooden shaft, the blade being about six inches across at the widest part. These spears are not used for throwing, but like the Zulu *bangwan*, or stabbing assegai, are for close quarters only, when the wound inflicted by them is terrible. In addition to his *bangwan* every man carried three large and heavy knives, each knife weighing about two pounds. One knife was fixed in the ox-tail girdle, and the other two at the back of the round shield. These knives, which are called " *tollas* " by the Kukuanas, take the place of the throwing assegai of the Zulus. The Kukuana warriors can cast them with great accuracy to a distance of fifty yards, and it is their custom on charging to hurl a volley of them at the enemy as they come to close quarters.

Each company remained still as a collection of bronze statues till we were opposite to it, when at a signal given by its commanding officer, who, distinguished by a leopard skin cloak, stood some paces in front, every spear was raised into the air, and from three hundred throats sprang forth with a sudden roar the royal salute of " *Koom.*" Then, so soon as we had passed, the company formed up behind us and followed us towards the kraal, till at last the whole regiment of the " Greys "—so called from their white shields—the crack corps of the Kukuana people, was marching in our rear with a tread that shook the ground.

At length, branching off from Solomon's Great
Road, we came to the wide fosse surrounding the
kraal, which is at least a mile round, and fenced
with a strong palisade of piles formed of the trunks
of trees.   At the gateway this fosse is spanned
by a primitive drawbridge, which was let down by
the guard to allow us to pass in.   The kraal
is exceedingly well laid out.   Through the centre
runs a wide pathway intersected at right angles
by other pathways so arranged as to cut the huts
into square blocks, each block being the quarters
of a company.   The huts are dome-shaped, and
built, like those of the Zulus, of a framework of
wattle, beautifully thatched with grass ; but,
unlike the Zulu huts, they have doorways through
which we could walk.   Also, they are much
larger, and surrounded by a veranda about six
feet wide, beautifully paved with powdered lime
trodden hard.

All along each side of this wide pathway that
pierces the kraal were ranged hundreds of
women, brought out by curiosity to look at us.
These women, for a native race, are exceedingly
handsome.   They are tall and graceful, and their
figures are wonderfully fine.   The hair, though
short, is rather curly than woolly, the features are
frequently aquiline, and the lips are not unpleasantly thick as is the case among African
races.   But what struck us most was their
exceedingly quiet and dignified air.   They were
as well-bred in their way as the habituées of a
fashionable drawing-room, and in this respect
they differ from Zulu women, and their cousins
the Masai who inhabit the district behind Zanzi-
bar.   Their curiosity had brought them out to see
us, but they allowed no rude expressions of

astonishment or savage criticism to pass their
lips as we trudged wearily in front of them. Not
even when old Infadoos with a surreptitious motion
of the hand pointed out the crowning wonder
of poor Good's "beautiful white legs," did
they suffer the feeling of intense admiration
which evidently mastered their minds to find
expression. They fixed their dark eyes upon
this new and snowy loveliness, for, as I think I
have said, Good's skin is exceedingly white, and
that was all. But it was quite enough for Good,
who is modest by nature.

When we reached the centre of the kraal, Infadoos halted at the door of a large hut, which
was surrounded at a distance by a circle of smaller
ones.

"Enter, Sons of the Stars," he said, in a
magniloquent voice, "and deign to rest awhile
in our humble habitations. A little food shall be
brought to you, so that ye shall have no need to
draw your belts tight from hunger ; some honey
and some milk, and an ox or two, and a few
sheep ; not much, my lords, but still a little
food."

"It is good," said I, "Infadoos, we are weary
with travelling through realms of air ; now let us
rest."

Accordingly we entered into the hut, which we
found amply prepared for our comfort. Couches
of tanned skins were spread for us to lie on, and
water was placed for us to wash in.

Presently we heard a shouting outside, and
stepping to the door, saw a line of damsels
bearing milk and roasted mealies, and honey in a
pot. Behind these were some youths driving a
fat young ox. We received the gifts, and then

one of the young men took the knife from his
girdle and dexterously cut the ox's throat.
In ten minutes it was dead, skinned, and jointed.
The best of the meat was then cut off for us, and
the rest, in the name of our party, I presented to
the warriors round us, who took it and distributed
the " white lords' gift."

Umbopa set to work, with the assistance of an
extremely prepossessing young woman, to boil
our portion in a large earthenware pot over a fire
which was built outside the hut, and when it was
nearly ready we sent a message to Infadoos, and
asked him and Scragga, the king's son, to join us.

Presently they came, and sitting down upon
little stools, of which there were several about the
hut, for the Kukuanas do not in general squat
upon their haunches like the Zulus, they helped
us to get through our dinner. The old gentleman
was most affable and polite, but it struck me that
the young one regarded us with doubt. Together
with the rest of the party, he had been overawed
by our white appearance and by our magic pro-
perties ; but it seemed to me that, on discovering
that we ate, drank, and slept like other mortals,
his awe was beginning to wear off, and to be
replaced by a sullen suspicion—which made me
feel rather uncomfortable.

In the course of our meal Sir Henry suggested
to me that it might be well to try to discover if
our hosts knew anything of his brother's fate, or
if they had ever seen or heard of him ; but, on the
whole, I thought that it would be wiser to say
nothing of the matter at this time.

After supper we filled our pipes and lit them ;
a proceeding which filled Infadoos and Scragga
with astonishment. The Kukuanas were evi-

dently unacquainted with the divine uses of tobacco-smoke. The herb is grown among them extensively; but, like the Zulus, they only use it for snuff, and quite failed to identify it in its new form.

Presently I asked Infadoos when we were to proceed on our journey, and was delighted to learn that preparations had been made for us to leave on the following morning, messengers having already left to inform Twala the king of our coming. It appeared that Twala was at his principal place, known as Loo, making ready for the great annual feast which was to be held in the first week of June. At this gathering all the regiments, with the exception of certain detachments left behind for garrison purposes, are brought up and paraded before the king; and the great annual witch-hunt, of which more by-and-by, is held.

We were to start at dawn; and Infadoos, who was to accompany us, expected that we should reach Loo on the night of the second day, unless we were detained by accident or by swollen rivers.

When they had given us this information our visitors bade us good-night; and, having arranged to watch turn and turn about, three of us flung ourselves down and slept the sweet sleep of the weary, whilst the fourth sat up on the look-out for possible treachery.

CHAPTER IX

TWALA THE KING

IT will not be necessary for me to detail at length the incidents of our journey to Loo. It took two full days' travelling along Solomon's Great Road, which pursued its even course right into the heart of Kukuanaland. Suffice it to say that as we went the country seemed to grow richer and richer, and the kraals, with their wide surrounding belts of cultivation, more and more numerous. They were all built upon the same principles as the first camp which we had reached, and were guarded by ample garrisons of troops. Indeed, in Kukuanaland, as among the Germans, the Zulus, and the Masai, every able-bodied man is a soldier, so that the whole force of the nation is available for its wars, offensive or defensive. As we travelled along we were overtaken by thousands of warriors hurrying up to Loo to be present at the great annual review and festival, and more splendid troops I never saw.

At sunset on the second day we stopped to rest awhile upon the summit of some heights over which the road ran, and there on a beautiful and fertile plain before us lay Loo itself. For a native town it is an enormous place, quite five miles round, I should say, with outlying kraals jutting out from it, that serve on grand occasions as cantonments for the regiments, and a curious horse-shoe-shaped hill, with which we were destined to become better acquainted, about two miles to the north. It is beautifully situated, and through the centre of the kraal, dividing it into two portions, runs a river, which appeared to be bridged in several places, the same indeed that we had seen from the slopes of Sheba's Breasts. Sixty or seventy miles away three great snow-capped mountains, placed at the points of a triangle, started out of the level plain. The conformation of these mountains is unlike that of Sheba's Breasts, being sheer and precipitous, instead of smooth and rounded.

Infadoos saw us looking at them, and volunteered a remark.

" The road ends there," he said, pointing to the mountains known among the Kukuanas as the " Three Witches."

" Why does it end ? " I asked.

" Who knows ? " he answered with a shrug ; " the mountains are full of caves, and there is a great pit between them. It is there that the wise men of old time used to go to get whatever it was they came to this country for, and it is there now that our kings are buried in the Place of Death."

" What was it they came for ? " I asked eagerly.

" Nay, I know not. My lords who have dropped from the Stars should know," he answered with a quick look. Evidently he knew more than he chose to say.

" Yes," I went on, " you are right, in the Stars we learn many things. I have heard, for instance, that the wise men of old came to these mountains to get bright stones, pretty playthings, and yellow iron."

"My lord is wise," he answered coldly ; "I am but a child and cannot talk with my lord on such matters. My lord must speak with Gagool the old, at the king's place, who is wise even as my lord," and he went away.

So soon as he was gone I turned to the others, and pointed out the mountains. "There are Solomon's diamond mines," I said.

Umbopa was standing with them, apparently plunged in one of the fits of abstraction which were common to him, and caught my words.

"Yes, Macumazahn," he put in, in Zulu, "the diamonds are surely there, and you shall have them since you white men are so fond of toys and money."

"How dost thou know that, Umbopa?" I asked sharply, for I did not like his mysterious ways.

He laughed. "I dreamed it in the night, white men," and then he too turned upon his heel and went.

"Now what," said Sir Henry, "is our black friend at ? He knows more than he chooses to say, that is clear. By the way, Quatermain, has he heard anything of—of my brother?"

"Nothing ; he has asked everyone he has become friendly with, but they all declare that no white man has ever been seen in the country before."

"Do you suppose that he got here at all?" suggested Good ; "we have only reached the place by a miracle ; is it likely he could have reached it without the map?"

"I don't know," said Sir Henry gloomily, "but somehow I think that I shall find him."

Slowly the sun sank, and then suddenly dark-

ness rushed down on the land like a tangible
thing. There was no breathing-space between
the day and night, no soft transformation scene,
for in these latitudes twilight does not exist.
The change from day to night is as quick and
as absolute as the change from life to death. The
sun sank and the world was wreathed in shadows.
But not for long, for see in the west there is a
glow, then come rays of silver light, and at last
the full and glorious moon lights up the plain and
shoots its gleaming arrows far and wide, filling
the earth with a faint refulgence.

We stood and watched the lovely sight, whilst
the stars grew pale before this chastened majesty,
and felt our hearts lifted up in the presence of a
beauty that I cannot describe. Mine has been a
rough life, but there are a few things I am thankful
to have lived for, and one of them is to have seen
that moon shine on Kukuanaland.

Presently our meditations were broken in upon
by our polite friend Infadoos.

" If my lords are rested we will journey on to
Loo, where a hut is made ready for my lords
to-night. The moon is now bright, so that we
shall not fall by the way."

We assented, and in an hour's time were at the
outskirts of the town, of which the extent, mapped
out as it was by thousands of camp fires, appeared
absolutely endless. Indeed, Good, who is always
fond of a bad joke, christened it " Unlimited Loo."
Soon we came to a moat with a drawbridge, where
we were met by the rattling of arms and the
hoarse challenge of a sentry. Infadoos gave some
password that I could not catch, which was met
with a salute, and we passed on through the
central street of the great grass city. After

nearly half an hour's tramp, past endless lines of
huts, Infadoos halted at last by the gate of a little
group of huts which surrounded a small courtyard
of powdered limestone, and informed us that these
were to be our " poor " quarters.

We entered, and found that a hut had been
assigned to each of us. These huts were superior
to any that we had yet seen, and in each was a
most comfortable bed made of tanned skins,
spread upon mattresses of aromatic grass. Food
too was ready for us, and so soon as we had
washed ourselves with water which stood ready
in earthenware jars, some young women of handsome appearance brought us roasted meats, and
mealie cobs daintily served on wooden platters,
and presented them to us with deep obeisances.

We ate and drank, and then the beds having
been all moved into one hut by our request, a
precaution at which the amiable young ladies
smiled, we flung ourselves down to sleep,
thoroughly wearied with our long journey.

When we woke it was to find the sun high in the
heavens, and the female attendants, who did not
seem to be troubled by any false shame, already
standing inside the hut, having been ordered to
attend and help us to " make ready."

" Make ready, indeed," growled Good ; " when
one has only a flannel shirt and a pair of boots,
that does not take long. I wish you would ask
them for my trousers, Quatermain."

I asked accordingly, but was informed that
these sacred relics had already been taken to the
king, who would see us in the forenoon.

Somewhat to their astonishment and disappointment, having requested the young ladies
to step outside, we proceeded to make the best

toilet that the circumstances admitted of. Good
even went the length of again shaving the right
side of his face ; the left, on which now appeared
a very fair crop of whiskers, we impressed upon
him he must on no account touch. As for ourselves, we were contented with a good wash and
combing our hair. Sir Henry's yellow locks
were now almost upon his shoulders, and he looked
more like an ancient Dane than ever, while my
grizzled scrub was fully an inch long, instead of half
an inch, which in a general way I considered my
maximum length.

By the time that we had eaten our breakfasts,
and smoked a pipe, a message was brought to
us by no less a personage than Infadoos himself
that Twala the king was ready to see us, if we
would be pleased to come.

We remarked in reply that we should prefer
to wait till the sun was a little higher, we were
yet weary with our journey, etc., etc. It is
always well, when dealing with uncivilized people,
not to be in too great a hurry. They are apt
to mistake politeness for awe or servility. So,
although we were quite as anxious to see Twala
as Twala could be to see us, we sat down and
waited for an hour, employing the interval in
preparing such presents as our slender stock
of goods permitted—namely the Winchester
rifle which had been used by poor Ventvögel,
and some beads. The rifle and ammunition
we determined to present to his Royal Highness,
and the beads were for his wives and courtiers.
We had already given a few to Infadoos and
Scragga, and found that they were delighted
with them, never having seen anything like
them before. At length we declared that we

were ready, and guided by Infadoos, started
off to the audience, Umbopa carrying the rifle
and beads.

After walking a few hundred yards we came
to an enclosure, something like that surrounding
the huts which had been allotted to us, only
fifty times as big, for it could not have covered
less than six or seven acres of ground. All
round the outside fence stood a row of huts,
which were the habitations of the king's wives.
Exactly opposite the gateway, on the further
side of the open space, was a very large hut,
built by itself, in which his majesty resided.
All the rest was open ground; that is to say,
it would have been open had it not been filled
by company after company of warriors, who
were mustered there to the number of seven
or eight thousand. These men stood still as
statues as we advanced through them, and it
would be impossible to give an adequate idea
of the grandeur of the spectacle which they
presented, with their waving plumes, their
glancing spears, and iron-backed ox-hide shields.

The space in front of the large hut was empty,
but before it were placed several stools. On
three of these, at a sign from Infadoos, we seated
ourselves, Umbopa standing behind us. As
for Infadoos, he took up a position by the door
of the hut. So we waited for ten minutes or
more in the midst of a dead silence, but conscious
that we were the object of the concentrated
gaze of some eight thousand pairs of eyes. It
was a somewhat trying ordeal, but we carried
it off as best we could. At length the door of
the hut opened, and a gigantic figure, with a
splendid tiger-skin karross flung over its shoulders,

stepped out, followed by the boy Scragga, and
what appeared to us to be a withered-up monkey,
wrapped in a fur cloak. The figure seated itself
upon a stool, Scragga took his stand behind it,
and the withered-up monkey crept on all fours
into the shade of the hut and squatted down.

Still there was silence.

Then the gigantic figure slipped off the karross
and stood up before us, a truly alarming spectacle. It was that of an enormous man with
the most entirely repulsive countenance we had
ever beheld. The man's lips were thick as a
negro's, the nose was flat, he had but one gleaming black eye, for the other was represented
by a hollow in the face, and his whole expression
was cruel and sensual to a degree. From the
large head rose a magnificent plume of white
ostrich feathers, his body was clad in a shirt
of shining chain armour, whilst round the waist
and right knee were the usual garnishes of white
ox-tail. In his right hand was a huge spear,
about the neck a thick torque of gold, and bound
on to the forehead shone dully a single and
enormous uncut diamond.

Still there was silence ; but not for long.
Presently the man, whom we rightly guessed
to be the king, raised the great javelin in his
hand. Instantly eight thousand spears were
lifted in answer, and from eight thousand throats
rang out the royal salute of " *Koom.*" Three
times this was repeated, and each time the earth
shook with the noise, that can only be compared
to the deepest notes of thunder.

" Be humble, O people," piped out a thin
voice which seemed to come from the monkey
in the shade, " it is the king."

" *It is the king,*" boomed out eight thousand throats in answer. " *Be humble, O people, it is the king.*"

Then there was dead silence again—dead silence. Presently, however, it was broken. A soldier on our left dropped his shield, which fell with a clatter on to the limestone flooring.

Twala turned his cold eye in the direction of the noise.

" Come hither, thou," he said in a cold voice.

A fine young man stepped out of the ranks, and stood before him.

" It was thy shield that fell, thou awkward dog. Wilt thou make me a reproach in the eyes of these strangers from the Stars ? What hast thou to say ? "

We saw the poor fellow turn pale under his dusky skin.

" It was by chance, O Calf of the Black Cow," he murmured.

" Then it is a chance for which thou must pay. Thou hast made me foolish ; prepare for death."

" I am the king's ox," was the low answer.

" Scragga," roared the king, " let me see how thou canst use thy spear. Kill me this awkward dog."

Scragga stepped forward with an ill-favoured grin, and lifted his spear. The poor victim covered his eyes with his hand and stood still. As for us, we were petrified with horror.

" Once, twice," he waved the spear and then struck, ah ! right home—the spear stood out a foot behind the soldier's back. He flung up his hands and dropped dead. From the multitude about us rose something like a murmur, it rolled round and round, and died away. The

tragedy was finished; there lay the corpse,
and we had not yet realized that it had been
enacted. Sir Henry sprang up and swore a
great oath, then, overpowered by the sense of
silence, sat down again.

"The thrust was a good one," said the king;
"take him away."

Four men stepped out of the ranks, and lifting
the body of the murdered man, carried it
thence.

"Cover up the blood-stains, cover them up,"
piped out the thin voice that proceeded from
the monkey-like figure; "the king's word is
spoken, the king's doom is done!"

Thereupon a girl came forward from behind
the hut, bearing a jar filled with powdered lime,
which she scattered over the red mark, blotting
it from sight.

Sir Henry meanwhile was boiling with rage
at what had happened; indeed, it was with
difficulty that we could keep him still.

"Sit down, for heaven's sake," I whispered;
"our lives depend on it."

He yielded and remained quiet.

Twala sat silent until the traces of the tragedy
had been removed, then he addressed us.

"White people," he said, "who come hither,
whence I know not, and why I know not,
greeting."

"Greeting, Twala, King of the Kukuanas,"
I answered.

"White people, whence come ye, and what
seek ye?"

"We come from the Stars, ask us not how.
We come to see this land."

"Ye journey from far to see a little thing.

And that man with you," pointing to Umbopa, " does he also come from the Stars ? "

" Even so ; there are people of thy colour in the heavens above ; but ask not of matters too high for thee, Twala the king."

" Ye speak with a loud voice, people of the Stars," Twala answered in a tone which I scarcely liked. " Remember that the stars are far off, and ye are here. How if I make you as him whom they bore away ? "

I laughed out loud, though there was little laughter in my heart.

" O king," I said, " be careful, walk warily over hot stones, lest thou shouldst burn thy feet ; hold the spear by the handle, lest thou shouldst cut thy hands. Touch but one hair of our heads, and destruction shall come upon thee. What, have not these "—pointing to Infadoos and Scragga, who, young villain that he was, was employed in cleaning the blood of the soldier off his spear—" told thee what manner of men we are ? Hast thou seen the like of us ? " and I pointed to Good, feeling quite sure that he had never seen anybody before who looked in the least like *him* as he then appeared.

" It is true, I have not," said the king, surveying Good.

" Have they not told thee how we strike with death from afar ? " I went on.

" They have told me, but I believe them not. Let me see you kill. Kill me a man among those who stand yonder "—and he pointed to the opposite side of the kraal—" and I will believe."

" Nay," I answered ; " we shed no blood of men except in just punishment ; but if thou

wilt see, bid thy servants drive in an ox through
the kraal gates, and before he has run twenty
paces I will strike him dead."

"Nay," laughed the king, "kill me a man
and I will believe."

"Good, O king, so be it," I answered coolly;
"do thou walk across the open space, and before
thy feet reach the gate thou shalt be dead; or
if thou wilt not, send thy son Scragga" (whom
at that moment it would have given me much
pleasure to shoot).

On hearing this suggestion Scragga uttered a
sort of howl, and bolted into the hut.

Twala frowned majestically; the suggestion
did not please him.

"Let a young ox be driven in," he said.

Two men at once departed, running swiftly.

"Now, Sir Henry," said I, "do you shoot.
I want to show this ruffian that I am not the
only magician of the party."

Sir Henry accordingly took the express, and
made ready.

"I hope I shall make a good shot," he
groaned.

"You must," I answered. "If you miss
with the first barrel, let him have the second.
Sight for 150 yards, and wait till the beast turns
broadside on."

Then came a pause, until presently we caught
sight of an ox running straight for the kraal
gate. It came on through the gate, and then,
catching sight of the vast concourse of people,
stopped stupidly, turned round, and bellowed.

"Now's your time," I whispered.

Up went the rifle.

Bang! *thud!* and the ox was kicking on his

back, shot in the ribs. The semi-hollow bullet had done its work well, and a sigh of astonishment went up from the assembled thousands.

I turned round coolly—

" Have I lied, O king ? "

" Nay, white man, it is the truth," was the somewhat awed answer.

" Listen, Twala," I went on. " Thou hast seen. Now know we come in peace, not in war. See," and I held up the Winchester repeater ; " there is a hollow staff that shall enable thee to kill even as we kill, only I lay this charm upon it, thou shalt kill no man with it. If thou liftest it against a man, it shall kill thee. Stay, I will show thee. Bid a soldier step forty paces and place the shaft of a spear in the ground so that the flat blade looks towards us."

In a few seconds it was done.

" Now see, I will break yonder spear."

Taking a careful sight I fired. The bullet struck the flat of the spear, and shattered the blade into fragments.

Again the sigh of astonishment went up.

" Now, Twala, we give this magic tube to thee, and by-and-by I will show thee how to use it ; but beware how thou turnest the magic of the Stars against a man of earth," and I handed him the rifle.

The king took it very gingerly, and laid it down at his feet. As he did so I observed the wizened monkey-like figure creeping from the shadow of the hut. It crept on all fours, but when it reached the place where the king sat it rose upon its feet, and throwing the furry covering from its face, revealed a most extraordinary and weird countenance. Apparently it was that of a woman of great age, so shrunken that in size it seemed no larger than the face of a year-old child, although made up of a number of deep and yellow wrinkles. Set in these wrinkles was a sunken slit, that represented the mouth, beneath which the chin curved outwards to a point. There was no nose to speak of; indeed, the visage might have been taken for that of a sun-dried corpse had it not been for a pair of large black eyes, still full of fire and intelligence, which gleamed and played under the snow-white eye-brows, and the projecting parchment-coloured skull, like jewels in a charnel-house. As for the head itself, it was perfectly bare, and yellow in hue, while its wrinkled scalp moved and contracted like the hood of a cobra.

The figure to which this fearful countenance belonged, a countenance so fearful, indeed, that it caused a shiver of fear to pass through us as we gazed on it, stood still for a moment. Then suddenly it projected a skinny claw armed with nails nearly an inch long, and laying it on the shoulder of Twala the king, began to speak in a thin and piercing voice—

"Listen, O king! Listen, O warriors! Listen, O mountains and plains and rivers, home of the Kukuana race! Listen, O skies and sun, O rain and storm and mist! Listen, O men and women, O youths and maidens, and O ye babes unborn! Listen, all things that live and must die! Listen, all dead things that shall live again—again to die! Listen, the spirit of life is in me, and I prophesy. I prophesy! I prophesy!"

The words died away in a faint wail, and terror seemed to seize upon the hearts of all who heard them, including our own. This old woman was very terrible.

"*Blood! blood! blood!* rivers of blood; blood everywhere. I see it, I smell it, I taste it—it is salt! it runs red upon the ground, it rains down from the skies.

"*Footsteps! footsteps! footsteps!* the tread of the white man coming from afar. It shakes the earth; the earth trembles before her master.

"Blood is good, the red blood is bright; there is no smell like the smell of new-shed blood. The lions shall lap it up and roar, the vultures shall wash their wings in it and shriek with joy.

"I am old! I am old! I have seen much blood; *ha, ha!* but I shall see more ere I die, and be merry. How old am I, think ye! Your fathers knew me, and *their* fathers knew me, and *their* father's fathers. I have seen the white man and know his desires. I am old, but the mountains are older than I. Who made the great road, tell me? Who wrote the pictures on the rocks, tell me? Who reared up the three Silent Ones yonder, that gaze across the pit, tell me?" and she pointed towards the three precipitous mountains which we had noticed on the previous night.

"Ye know not, but I know. It was a white people who were before ye are, who shall be when ye are not, who shall eat you up and destroy you. *Yea! Yea! Yea!*

"And what came they for, the White Ones, the Terrible Ones, the skilled in magic and all learning, the strong, the unswerving? What is that bright stone upon thy forehead, O king? Whose hands made the iron garments upon thy breast, O king? Ye know not, but I know. I the Old One, I the Wise One, I the *Isanust*, the witch doctress!"

Then she turned her bald vulture-head towards us.

"What seek ye, white men of the Stars—ah, yes, of the Stars? Do ye seek a lost one? Ye shall not find him here. He is not here. Never for ages upon ages has a white foot pressed this land; never except once, and he left it but to die. Ye come for bright stones; I know it— I know it; ye shall find them when the blood is dry; but shall ye return whence ye came, or shall ye stop with me? *Ha! ha! ha!*

"And thou, thou with the dark skin and the proud bearing," and she pointed her skinny finger at Umbopa, "who art *thou*, and what seekest *thou*? Not stones that shine, not yellow metal that gleams, these thou leavest to 'white men from the Stars.' Methinks I know thee; methinks I can smell the smell of the blood in thy heart. Strip off the girdle——"

Here the features of this extraordinary creature became convulsed, and she fell to the ground foaming in an epileptic fit, and was carried into the hut.

The king rose up trembling, and waved his hand. Instantly the regiments began to file off, and in ten minutes, save for ourselves, the king, and a few attendants, the great space was left empty.

"White people," he said, "it passes in my mind to kill you. Gagool has spoken strange words. What say ye?"

I laughed. "Be careful, O king, we are not

easy to slay. Thou hast seen the fate of the ox ;
wouldst thou be as the ox is ? "

The king frowned. " It is not well to threaten
a king."

" We threaten not, we speak what is true.
Try to kill us, O king, and learn."

The great savage put his hand to his forehead
and thought.

" Go in peace," he said at length. " To-night
is the great dance. Ye shall see it. Fear not
that I shall set a snare for you. To-morrow I
will think."

" It is well, O king," I answered unconcernedly,
and then, accompanied by Infadoos, we rose and
went back to our kraal.

CHAPTER X

THE WITCH-HUNT

ON reaching our hut I motioned to Infadoos to enter with us.

"Now, Infadoos," I said, "we would speak with thee."

"Let my lords say on."

"It seems to us, Infadoos, that Twala the king is a cruel man."

"It is so, my lords. Alas! the land cries out because of his cruelties. To-night ye shall see. It is the great witch-hunt, and many will be smelt out as wizards and slain. No man's life is safe. If the king covets a man's cattle, or a man's wife, or if he fears a man that he should excite a rebellion against him, then Gagool, whom ye saw, or some of the witch-finding women whom she has taught, will smell that man out as a wizard, and he will be killed. Many must die before the moon grows pale to-night. It is ever so. Perhaps I too shall be killed. As yet I have been spared because I am skilled in war, and beloved by the soldiers; but I know not how long I have to live. The land groans at the cruelties of Twala the king; it is wearied of him and his red ways."

"Then why is it, Infadoos, that the people do not cast him down?"

"Nay, my lords, he is the king, and if he were

killed Scragga would reign in his place, and the
heart of Scragga is blacker than the heart of
Twala his father. If Scragga were king the yoke
upon our neck would be heavier than the yoke
of Twala. If Imotu had never been slain, or if
Ignosi his son had lived, it might have been
otherwise ; but they are both dead."

"How knowest thou that Ignosi is dead ? "
said a voice behind us. We looked round
astonished to see who spoke. It was Umbopa.

"What meanest thou, boy ? " asked Infadoos ;
"who told thee to speak ? "

"Listen, Infadoos," was the answer, "and I
will tell thee a story. Years ago the king Imotu
was killed in this country and his wife fled with
the boy Ignosi. Is it not so ? "

"It is so."

"It was said that the woman and her son died
upon the mountains. Is it not so ? "

"It is even so."

"Well, it came to pass that the mother and
the boy Ignosi did not die. They crossed the
mountains, and were led by a tribe of wandering
desert men across the sands beyond, till at
last they came to water and grass and trees
again."

"How knowest thou this ? "

"Listen. They travelled on and on, many
months' journey, till they reached a land where a
people called the Amazulu, who also are of the
Kukuana stock, live by war, and with them they
tarried many years, till at length the mother
died. Then the son Ignosi became a wanderer
again, and journeyed into a land of wonders,
where white people live, and for many more years
he learned the wisdom of the white people."

" It is a pretty story," said Infadoos incredulously.

" For years he lived there working as a servant and a soldier, but holding in his heart all that his mother had told him of his own place, and casting about in his mind to find how he might get back thither to see his people and his father's house before he died. For long years he lived and waited, and at last the time came, as it ever comes to him who can wait for it, and he met some white men who would seek this unknown land and joined himself to them. The white men started and journeyed on and on, seeking for one who is lost. They crossed the burning desert, they crossed the snow-clad mountains, and reached the land of the Kukuanas, and there they found *thee*, O Infadoos."

" Surely thou art mad to talk thus," said the astonished old soldier.

" Thou thinkest so ; see, I will show thee, O my uncle.

" *I am Ignosi, rightful king of the Kukuanas !* "

Then with a single movement Umbopa slipped off his " moocha " or girdle, and stood naked before us.

" Look," he said ; " what is this ? " and he pointed to the picture of a great snake tattooed in blue round his middle, its tail disappearing into its open mouth just above where the thighs are set into the body.

Infadoos looked, his eyes starting nearly out of his head, and then fell upon his knees.

" *Koom ! Koom !* " he ejaculated ; " it is my brother's son ; it is the king."

" Did I not tell thee so, my uncle ? Rise ; I am not yet the king, but with thy help, and

with the help of these brave white men, who are
my friends, I shall be. Yet the old witch Gagool
was right, the land shall run with blood first,
and hers shall run with it, if she **has** any, for she
killed my father with her words, and drove my
mother forth. And now, Infadoos, choose thou.
Wilt thou put thy hands between my hands and
be my man ? Wilt thou share the dangers that
lie before me, and help me to overthrow this
tyrant and murderer, or wilt thou not ? Choose
thou."

The old man put his hand to his head and
thought. Then he rose, and advancing to where
Umbopa, or rather Ignosi, stood, he knelt before
him and took his hand.

"Ignosi, rightful king of the Kukuanas, I
put my hand between thy hands, and am thy man
till death. When thou wast a babe I dandled
thee upon my knees, now shall my old arm strike
for thee and freedom."

"It is well, Infadoos ; if I conquer, thou shalt
be the greatest man in the kingdom after the king.
If I fail, thou canst only die, and death is not far
off from thee. Rise, my uncle.

"And ye, white men, will ye help me ? What
have I to offer you ! The white stones ! If I
conquer and can find them, ye shall have as many
as ye can carry hence. Will that suffice you ? "

I translated this remark.

"Tell him," answered Sir Henry, "that he
mistakes an Englishman. Wealth is good, and
if it comes in our way we will take it ; but a
gentleman does not sell himself for wealth.
Still, speaking for myself, I say this. I have
always liked Umbopa, and so far as lies in me
will stand by him in this business. It will be

very pleasant to me to try to square matters with that cruel devil Twala. What do you say, Good, and you, Quatermain ? "

" Well," said Good, " to adopt the language of hyperbole, in which all these people seem to indulge, you can tell him that a row is surely good, and warms the cockles of the heart, and that so far as I am concerned I'm his boy. My only stipulation is that he allows me to wear trousers."

I translated the substance of these answers.

" It is well, my friends," said Ignosi, late Umbopa ; " and what sayest thou, Macumazahn, art thou also with me, old hunter, cleverer than a wounded buffalo ? "

I thought awhile and scratched my head.

" Umbopa, or Ignosi," I said, " I don't like revolutions. I am a man of peace, and a bit of a coward "—here Umbopa smiled—" but, on the other hand, I stick to my friends, Ignosi. You have stuck to us and played the part of a man, and I will stick by you. But mind you, I am a trader, and have to make my living, so I accept your offer about those diamonds in case we should ever be in a position to avail ourselves of it. Another thing : we came, as you know, to look for Incubu's (Sir Henry's) lost brother. You must help us to find him."

" That I will do," answered Ignosi. " Stay, Infadoos, by the sign of the snake about my middle, tell me the truth. Has any white man to thy knowledge set his foot within the land ? "

" None, O Ignosi."

" If any white man had been seen or heard of, wouldst thou have known it ? "

" I should certainly have known."

"Thou hearest, Incubu," said Ignosi to Sir Henry; "he has not been here."

"Well, well," said Sir Henry, with a sigh; "there it is; I suppose that he never got so far. Poor fellow, poor fellow! So it has all been for nothing. God's will be done."

"Now for business," I put in, anxious to escape from a painful subject. "It is very well to be a king by right divine, Ignosi, but how dost thou propose to become a king indeed?"

"Nay, I know not. Infadoos, hast thou a plan?"

"Ignosi, Son of the Lightning," answered his uncle, "to-night is the great dance and witch-hunt. Many shall be smelt out and perish, and in the hearts of many others there will be grief and anguish and anger against the king Twala. When the dance is over, then I will speak to some of the great chiefs, who in turn, if I can win them over, will speak to their regiments. I shall speak to the chiefs softly at first, and bring them to see that thou art indeed the king, and I think that by to-morrow's light thou shalt have twenty thousand spears at thy command. And now I must go and think, and hear, and make ready. After the dance is done, if I am yet alive, and we are all alive, I will meet thee here, and we can talk. At the best there must be war."

At this moment our conference was interrupted by the cry that messengers had come from the king. Advancing to the door of the hut we ordered that they should be admitted, and presently three men entered, each bearing a shining shirt of chain armour, and a magnificent battle-axe.

"The gifts of my lord the king to the white

men from the Stars!" said a herald who came
with them.

"We thank the king," I answered; "withdraw."

The men went, and we examined the armour
with great interest. It was the most wonderful
chain work that we had ever seen. A whole coat
fell together so closely that it formed a mass
of links scarcely too big to be covered with both
hands.

"Do you make these things in this country,
Infadoos?" I asked; "they are very beautiful."

"Nay, my lord, they came down to us from our
forefathers. We know not who made them, and
there are but few left.* None but those of
royal blood may be clad in them. They are
magic coats through which no spear can pass,
and those who wear them are well-nigh safe in
the battle. The king is well pleased or much
afraid, or he would not have sent these garments
of steel. Clothe yourselves in them to-night, my
lords."

The rest of that day we spent quietly, resting
and talking over the situation, which was
sufficiently exciting. At last the sun went down,
the thousand watch fires glowed out, and through
the darkness we heard the tramp of many feet
and the clashing of hundreds of spears, as the
regiments passed to their appointed places to
be ready for the great dance. Then the full moon
shone out in splendour, and as we stood watching
her rays, Infadoos arrived, clad in his war dress
and accompanied by a guard of twenty men to

* In the Soudan, swords and coats of mail are still worn by
Arabs, whose ancestors must have stripped them from the
bodies of Crusaders.—*Editor*.

escort us to the dance. As he recommended, we had already donned the shirts of chain armour which the king had sent us, putting them on under our ordinary clothing, and finding to our surprise that they were neither very heavy nor uncomfortable. These steel shirts, which evidently had been made for men of a very large stature, hung somewhat loosely upon Good and myself, but Sir Henry's fitted his magnificent frame like a glove. Then strapping our revolvers round our waists, and taking in our hands the battle-axes which the king had sent with the armour, we started.

On arriving at the great kraal, where we had that morning been received by the king, we found that it was closely packed with some twenty thousand men arranged round it in regiments. These regiments were in turn divided into companies, and between each company ran a little path to allow space for the witch-finders to pass up and down. Anything more imposing than the sight that was presented by this vast and orderly concourse of armed men it is impossible to conceive. There they stood perfectly silent, and the moon poured her light upon the forest of their raised spears, upon their majestic forms, waving plumes, and the harmonious shading of their various-coloured shields. Wherever we looked were line upon line of dim faces surmounted by range upon range of shimmering spears.

"Surely," I said to Infadoos, "the whole army is here?"

"Nay, Macumazahn," he answered, "but a third of it. One third part is present at this dance each year, another third is mustered outside in case there should be trouble when the

killing begins, ten thousand more garrison the
outposts round Loo, and the rest watch at the
kraals in the country. Thou seest it is a great
people."

"They are very silent," said Good; and indeed
the intense stillness among such a vast concourse
of living men was almost overpowering.

"What says Bougwan?" asked Infadoos.

I translated.

"Those over whom the shadow of Death is
hovering are silent," he answered grimly.

"Will many be killed?"

"Very many."

"It seems," I said to the others, "that we
are going to assist at a gladiatorial show arranged
regardless of expense."

Sir Henry shivered, and Good said he wished
that we could get out of it.

"Tell me," I asked Infadoos, "are we in
danger?"

"I know not, my lords, I trust not; but do
not seem afraid. If ye live through the night
all may go well. The soldiers murmur against
the king."

All this while we had been advancing steadily
towards the centre of the open space, in the midst
of which were placed some stools. As we proceeded we perceived another small party coming
from the direction of the royal hut.

"It is the king, Twala, Scragga his son, and
Gagool the old; and see, with them are those
who slay," and Infadoos pointed to a little group
of about a dozen gigantic and savage-looking
men, armed with spears in one hand and heavy
kerries in the other.

The king seated himself upon the centre stool,

Gagool crouched at his feet, and the others stood behind him.

"Greeting, white lords," Twala cried, as we came up; "be seated, waste not precious time—the night is all too short for the deeds that must be done. Ye come in a good hour, and shall see a glorious show. Look round, white lords; look round," and he rolled his one wicked eye from regiment to regiment. "Can the Stars show you such a sight as this? See how they shake in their wickedness, all those who have evil in their hearts and fear the judgment of ' Heaven above.' "

" *Begin! begin!* " piped Gagool, in her thin piercing voice; "the hyænas are hungry, they howl for food. *Begin! begin!* "

Then for a moment there was intense stillness, made horrible by a presage of what was to come.

The king lifted his spear, and suddenly twenty thousand feet were raised, as though they belonged to one man, and brought down with a stamp upon the earth. This was repeated three times, causing the solid ground to shake and tremble. Then from a far point of the circle a solitary voice began a wailing song, of which the refrain ran something as follows :—

" *What is the lot of man born of woman ?* "

Back came the answer rolling out from every throat in that vast company—

" *Death !* "

Gradually, however, the song was taken up by company after company, till the whole armed multitude were singing it, and I could no longer follow the words, except in so far as they appeared to represent various phases of human passions, fears, and joys. Now it seemed to be a love song, now a majestic swelling war chant, and last of all a death dirge ending suddenly in one heart-breaking wail that went echoing and rolling away in a volume of blood-curdling sound.

Again silence fell upon the place, and again it was broken by the king lifting his hand. Instantly we heard a pattering of feet, and from out of the masses of warriors strange and awful figures appeared running towards us. As they drew near we saw that these were women, most of them aged, for their white hair, ornamented with small bladders taken from fish, streamed out behind them. Their faces were painted in stripes of white and yellow; down their backs hung snake-skins, and round their waists rattled circlets of human bones, while each held a small forked wand in her shrivelled hand. In all there were ten of them. When they arrived in front of us they halted, and one of them pointing with her wand towards the crouching figure of Gagool, cried out—

" Mother, old mother, we are here."

" *Good! good! good!* " answered that aged Iniquity. " Are your eyes keen, *Isanusis* [witch doctresses], ye seers in dark places ? "

" Mother, they are keen."

" *Good! good! good!* Are your ears open, *Isanusis*, ye who hear words that come not from the tongue ? "

" Mother, they are open."

" *Good! good! good!* Are your senses awake, *Isanusis*—can ye smell blood, can ye purge the land of the wicked ones who compass evil against the king and against their neighbours ? Are ye ready to do the justice of ' Heaven above,' ye whom I have taught, who have eaten of the

bread of my wisdom, and drunk of the water of
my magic ? "

" Mother, we can."

" Then go ! Tarry not, ye vultures ; see,
the slayers "—pointing to the ominous group of
executioners behind—" make sharp their spears ;
the white men from afar are hungry to see.
Go ! "

With a wild yell Gagool's horrid ministers
broke away in every direction, like fragments
from a shell, the dry bones round their waists
rattling as they ran, and headed for various points
of the dense human circle. We could not watch
them all, so we fixed our eyes upon the *Isanusi*
nearest to us. When she came to within a few
paces of the warriors she halted and began to
dance wildly, turning round and round with an
almost incredible rapidity, and shrieking out
sentences such as " I smell him, the evil-doer ! "
" He is near, he who poisoned his mother ! "
" I hear the thoughts of him who thought evil
of the king ! "

Quicker and quicker she danced, till she lashed
herself into such a fury of excitement that the
foam flew in flecks from her gnashing jaws, till
her eyes seemed to start from her head, and her
flesh to quiver visibly. Suddenly she stopped
dead and stiffened all over, like a pointer dog
when he scents game, and with outstretched
wand she began to creep stealthily towards the
soldiers before her. It seemed to us that as she
came their stoicism gave way, and that they
shrank from her. As for ourselves, we followed
her movements with a horrible fascination.
Presently, still creeping and crouching like a
dog, the *Isanusi* was before them. Then she

halted and pointed and again crept on a pace or two.

Suddenly the end came. With a shriek she sprang in and touched a tall warrior with her forked wand. Instantly two of his comrades, those standing immediately next to him, seized the doomed man, each by one arm, and advanced with him towards the king.

He did not resist, but we saw that he dragged his limbs as though they were paralysed, and that his fingers, from which the spear had fallen, were limp like those of a man newly dead.

As he came, two of the villainous executioners stepped forward to meet him. Presently they met, and the executioners turned round, looking towards the king as though for orders.

" *Kill !* " said the king.

" *Kill !* " squeaked Gagool.

" *Kill !* " re-echoed Scragga, with a hollow chuckle.

Almost before the words were uttered the horrible deed was done. One man had driven his spear into the victim's heart, and to make assurance doubly sure, the other had dashed out his brains with a great club.

" *One,* " counted Twala the king, just like a black Madame Defarge, as Good said, and the body was dragged a few paces away and stretched out.

Hardly was the thing done before another poor wretch was brought up, like an ox to the slaughter. This time we could see, from the leopard-skin cloak, that the man was a person of rank. Again the awful syllables were spoken, and the victim fell dead.

" *Two,* " counted the king.

And so the deadly game went on, till about a hundred bodies were stretched in rows behind us. I have heard of the gladiatorial shows of the Cæsars, and of the Spanish bull-fights, but I take the liberty of doubting if they were either of them half so horrible as this Kukuana witch-hunt. Gladiatorial shows and Spanish bull-fights, at any rate, contributed to the public amusement, which certainly was not the case here. The most confirmed sensation-monger would fight shy of sensation if he knew that it was well on the cards that he would, in his own proper person, be the subject of the next "event."

Once we rose and tried to remonstrate, but were sternly repressed by Twala.

"Let the law take its course, white men. These dogs are magicians and evil-doers; it is well that they should die," was the only answer vouchsafed to us.

About half-past ten there was a pause. The witch finders gathered themselves together, apparently exhausted with their bloody work, and we thought that the performance was done with. But it was not so, for presently, to our surprise, the ancient woman, Gagool, rose from her crouching position, and supporting herself with a stick, staggered off into the open space. It was an extraordinary sight to see this frightful vulture-headed old creature, bent nearly double with extreme age, gather strength by degrees, until at last she rushed about almost as actively as her ill-omened pupils. To and fro she ran, chanting to herself, till suddenly she made a dash at a tall man standing in front of one of the regiments, and touched him. As she did this a sort of groan went up from the regiment which he evidently commanded. But all the same, two of its officers seized him and brought him up for execution. We learned afterwards that he was a man of great wealth and importance, being indeed a cousin of the king's.

He was slain, and the king counted one hundred and three. Then Gagool again sprang to and fro, gradually drawing nearer and nearer to ourselves.

" Hang me if I don't believe she is going to try her games on us," ejaculated Good in horror.

" Nonsense ! " said Sir Henry.

As for myself, when I saw that old fiend dancing nearer and nearer, my heart positively sank into my boots. I glanced behind us at the long rows of corpses, and shivered.

Nearer and nearer waltzed Gagool, looking for all the world like an animated crooked stick, her horrid eyes gleaming and glowing with a most unholy lustre.

Nearer she came, and yet nearer, every creature in that vast assemblage watching her movements with intense anxiety. At last she stood still and pointed.

" Which is it to be ? " asked Sir Henry to himself.

In a moment all doubts were set at rest, for the old hag had rushed in and touched Umbopa, alias Ignosi, on the shoulder.

" I smell him out," she shrieked. " Kill him, kill him, he is full of evil ; kill him, the stranger, before blood flows for him. Slay him, O king."

There was a pause, which I instantly took advantage of.

" O king," I called out, rising from my seat,

" this man is the servant of thy guests, he is their dog ; whosoever sheds the blood of our dog sheds our blood. By the sacred law of hospitality I claim protection for him."

" Gagool, mother of the witch-finders, has smelt him out ; he must die, white men," was the sullen answer.

" Nay, he shall not die," I replied ; " he who tries to touch him shall die indeed."

" Seize him ! " roared Twala to the executioners, who stood around red to the eyes with the blood of their victims.

They advanced towards us, and then hesitated. As for Ignosi, he clutched his spear, and raised it as though determined to sell his life dearly.

" Stand back, ye dogs ! " I shouted, " if ye would see to-morrow's light. Touch one hair of his head and your king dies," and I covered Twala with my revolver. Sir Henry and Good also drew their pistols, Sir Henry pointing his at the leading executioner, who was advancing to carry out the sentence, and Good taking a deliberate aim at Gagool.

Twala winced perceptibly as my barrel came in a line with his broad chest.

" Well," I said, " what is it to be, Twala ? " Then he spoke.

" Put away your magic tubes," he said ; " ye have adjured me in the name of hospitality, and for that reason, but not from fear of what ye can do, I spare him. Go in peace."

" It is well," I answered unconcernedly ; " we are weary of slaughter, and would sleep. Is the dance ended ? "

" It is ended," Twala answered sulkily. " Let these dead dogs," pointing to the long row of corpses, " be flung out to the hyænas and the vultures," and he lifted his spear.

Instantly the regiments began to defile through the kraal gateway in perfect silence, a fatigue party only remaining behind to drag away the corpses of those who had been sacrificed.

Then we rose also, and making our salaam to his majesty, which he hardly deigned to acknowledge, we departed to our huts.

"Well," said Sir Henry, as we sat down, having first lit a lamp of the sort used by the Kukuanas, of which the wick is made from the fibre of a species of palm leaf, and the oil from clarified hippopotamus fat, "well, I feel uncommonly inclined to be sick."

"If I had any doubts about helping Umbopa to rebel against that infernal blackguard," put in Good, "they are gone now. It was as much as I could do to sit still while that slaughter was going on. I tried to keep my eyes shut, but they would open just at the wrong time. I wonder where Infadoos is. Umbopa, my friend, you ought to be grateful to us; your skin came near to having an air-hole made in it."

"I am grateful, Bougwan," was Umbopa's answer, when I had translated, "and I shall not forget. As for Infadoos, he will be here by-and-by. We must wait."

So we lit our pipes and waited.

CHAPTER XI

WE GIVE A SIGN

FOR a long while—two hours, I should think
—we sat there in silence, being too much
overwhelmed by the recollection of the horrors
we had seen to talk. At last, just as we were
thinking of turning in—for the night drew nigh
to dawn—we heard a sound of steps. Then came
the challenge of a sentry posted at the kraal
gate, which apparently was answered, though
not in an audible tone, for the steps still advanced ;
and in another second Infadoos had entered the
hut, followed by some half-dozen stately-looking
chiefs.

" My lords," he said, " I have come according
to my word. My lords and Ignosi, rightful king
of the Kukuanas, I have brought with me these
men," pointing to the row of chiefs, " who are
great men among us, having each one of them the
command of three thousand soldiers, that live
but to do their bidding, under the king's. I have
told them of what I have seen, and what my ears
have heard. Now let them also behold the sacred
snake around thee, and hear thy story, Ignosi,
that they may say whether or no they will make
cause with thee against Twala the king."

By way of answer, Ignosi again stripped off
his girdle and exhibited the snake tattooed about

155

him. Each chief in turn drew near and examined the sign by the dim light of the lamp, and without saying a word passed on to the other side.

Then Ignosi resumed his moocha, and addressing them, repeated the history he had detailed in the morning.

" Now ye have heard, chiefs," said Infadoos, when he had done, " what say ye ; will ye stand by this man and help him to his father's throne, or will ye not ? The land cries out against Twala, and the blood of the people flows like the waters in spring. Ye have seen to-night. Two other chiefs there were with whom I had it in my mind to speak, and where are they now. The hyænas howl over their corpses. Soon shall ye be as they are if ye strike not. Choose then, my brothers."

The eldest of the six men, a short, thick-set warrior, with white hair, stepped forward a pace and answered—

" Thy words are true, Infadoos ; the land cries out. My own brother is among those who died to-night ; but this is a great matter, and the thing is hard to believe. How know we that if we lift our spears it may not be for a cheat and a liar ? It is a great matter, I say, and none can see the end of it. For of this be sure, blood will flow in rivers before the deed is done ; many will still cleave to the king, for men worship the sun that still shines bright in the heavens, rather than that which has not risen. These white men from the stars, their magic is great, and Ignosi is under the cover of their wing. If he be indeed the rightful king, let them give us a sign, and let the people have a sign, that all,

may see. So shall men cleave to us, knowing
that the white man's magic is with them."

" Ye have the sign of the snake," I answered.

" My lord, it is not enough. The snake may
have been placed there since the man's child-
hood. Show us the sign. We will not move without a sign."

The others gave a decided assent, and I turned
in perplexity to Sir Henry and Good, and explained the situation.

" I think that I have it," said Good exultingly ;
" ask them to give us a moment to think."

I did so, and the chiefs withdrew. So soon
as they had gone Good went to the little box
where he kept his medicines, unlocked it, and
took out a note-book, in the fly-leaves of which
was an almanack. " Now look here, you fellows,
isn't to-morrow the 4th of June ? " he said.

We had kept a careful note of the days, so
were able to answer that it was.

" Very good ; then here we have it—' 4 June,
total eclipse of the moon commences at 8.15
Greenwich time, visible in Teneriffe—*South
Africa*, etc.' There's a sign for you. Tell them
we will darken the moon to-morrow night."

The idea was a splendid one ; indeed, the only
weak spot about it was the fear lest Good's
almanack might be incorrect. If we made a
false prophecy on such a subject, our prestige
would be gone for ever, and so would Ignosi's
chance of the throne of the Kukuanas.

" Suppose the almanack is wrong," suggested
Sir Henry to Good, who was busily employed in
working out something on a blank page of the
book.

" I see no reason to suppose anything of the

sort," was his answer. "Eclipses always come up to time; at least that is my experience of them, and it especially states that this one will be visible in South Africa. I have worked out the reckonings as well as I can, without knowing our exact position; and I make out that the eclipse should begin here about ten o'clock to-morrow night, and last till half-past twelve. For an hour and a half or so there should be almost total darkness."

"Well," said Sir Henry, "I suppose we had better risk it."

I acquiesced, though doubtfully, for eclipses are queer cattle to deal with—it might be a cloudy night, for instance—and sent Umbopa to summon the chiefs back. Presently they came, and I addressed them thus—

"Great men of the Kukuanas, and thou, Infadoos, listen. We love not to show our powers, for to do so is to interfere with the course of nature, and plunge the world into fear and confusion. But since this matter is a great one, and as we are angered against the king because of the slaughter we have seen, and because of the act of the *Isanusi* Gagool, who would have put our friend Ignosi to death, we have determined to break the rule, and to give such a sign that all men may see. Come hither;" and I led them to the door of the hut and pointed to the red ball of the fading moon. "What see ye there?"

"We see the dying moon," answered the spokesman of the party.

"It is so. Now tell me, can any mortal man put out that moon before her hour of setting, and bring the curtain of black night down on to the land?"

The chief laughed a little. "No, my lord, that no man can do. The moon is stronger than man who looks on her, nor can she vary in her courses."

"Ye say so. Yet I tell you that to-morrow night, two hours before midnight, will we cause the moon to be eaten up for the space of an hour and half an hour. Yes, deep darkness shall cover the earth, and it shall be for a sign that Ignosi is indeed king of the Kukuanas. If we do this thing will ye be satisfied?"

"Yea, my lords," answered the old chief with a smile, which was reflected on the faces of his companions; "if ye do this thing we will be satisfied indeed."

"It shall be done; we three, Incubu, Bougwan, and Macumazahn, have said it, and it shall be done. Dost thou hear, Infadoos?"

"I hear, my lord, but it is a wonderful thing that ye promise, to put out the moon, the mother of the world, when she is at her full."

"Yet shall we do it, Infadoos."

"It is well, my lords. To-day, two hours after sunset, Twala will send for my lords to witness the girls dance, and one hour after the dance begins the girl whom Twala thinks the fairest shall be killed by Scragga, the king's son, as a sacrifice to the silent Stone Ones, who sit and keep watch by the mountains yonder," and he pointed towards the three strange-looking peaks where Solomon's road was supposed to end. "Then let my lords darken the moon, and save the maiden's life, and the people will believe indeed."

"Ay," said the old chief, still smiling a little, "the people will believe indeed."

"Two miles from Loo," went on Infadoos,

" there is a hill curved like a new moon, a stronghold, where my regiment, and three other regiments which these chiefs command, are stationed. This morning we will make a plan whereby two or three other regiments may be moved there also. Then if in truth my lords can darken the moon, in the darkness I will take my lords by the hand and lead them out of Loo to this place, where they shall be safe, and thence we can make war upon Twala the king."

" It is good," said I. " Now leave us to sleep awhile and to make ready our magic."

Infadoos rose, and, having saluted us, departed with the chiefs.

" My friends," said Ignosi, as soon as they were gone, " can ye do this wonderful thing, or were ye speaking empty words to the men ? "

" We believe that we can do it, Umbopa— Ignosi, I mean."

" It is strange," he answered, " and had ye not been Englishmen I would not have believed it ; but I have learned that English ' gentlemen ' tell no lies. If we live through the matter, be sure that I will repay you."

" Ignosi," said Sir Henry, " promise me one thing."

" I will promise, Incubu, my friend, even before I hear it," answered the big man with a smile. " What is it ? "

" This : that if ever you come to be king of this people you will do away with the smelling out of wizards such as we saw last night ; and that the killing of men without trial shall no longer take place in the land."

Ignosi thought for a moment after I had translated this request, and then answered—

" The ways of black people are not as the ways
of white men, Incubu, nor do we value life so
highly. Yet I will promise it. If it be in my
power to hold them back, the witch-finders shall
hunt no more, nor shall any man die the death
without trial and judgment."

" That's a bargain then," said Sir Henry ;
" and now let us get a little rest."

Thoroughly wearied out, we were soon sound
asleep, and slept till Ignosi woke us about
eleven o'clock. Then we rose, washed, and ate
a hearty breakfast. After that we went outside
the hut and walked about, amusing ourselves
with examining the structure of the Kukuana
huts and observing the customs of the women.

" I hope that eclipse will come off," said Sir
Henry presently.

" If it does not it will soon be all up with us,"
I answered mournfully ; " for so sure as we are
living men some of those chiefs will tell the whole
story to the king, and then there will be another
sort of eclipse, and one that we shall not like."

Returning to the hut we ate some dinner, and
passed the rest of the day in receiving visits of
ceremony and curiosity. At length the sun set,
and we enjoyed a couple of hours of such quiet
as our melancholy forebodings would allow to
us. Finally, about half-past eight, a messenger
came from Twala to bid us to the great annual
" dance of girls " which was about to be celebrated.

Hastily we put on the chain shirts that the
king had sent to us, and taking our rifles and
ammunition with us, so as to have them handy
in case we had to fly, as suggested by Infadoos,
we started boldly enough, though with inward

fear and trembling. The great space in front
of the king's kraal bore a very different appearance
from that which it had presented on the previous
evening. In place of the grim ranks of serried
warriors were company after company of Kukuana
girls, not over-dressed, so far as clothing went,
but each crowned with a wreath of flowers, and
holding a palm leaf in one hand and a white
arum lily in the other. In the centre of the open
moonlit space sat Twala the king, with old Gagool
at his feet, attended by Infadoos, the boy Scragga,
and twelve guards. There were also present
about a score of chiefs, amongst whom I recognized most of our friends of the night before.

Twala greeted us with much apparent cor-
diality, though I saw him fix his one eye viciously
on Umbopa.

"Welcome, white men from the Stars," he
said; "this is another sight from that which
your eyes gazed on by the light of last night's
moon, but it is not so good a sight. Girls are
pleasant, and were it not for such as these,"
and he pointed round him, "we should none of
us be here this day; but men are better. Kisses
and the tender words of women are sweet, but
the sound of the clashing of the spears of warriors,
and the smell of men's blood, are sweeter far!
Would ye have wives from among our people,
white men? If so, choose the fairest here, and
ye shall have them, as many as ye will," and he
paused for an answer.

As the prospect did not seem to be without
attractions for Good, who, like most sailors, is
of a susceptible nature, being elderly and wise,
and foreseeing the endless complications that
anything of the sort would involve, for women

bring trouble so surely as the night follows the
day, I put in a hasty answer—

" Thanks to thee, O king, but we white men
wed only with white women like ourselves. Your
maidens are fair, but they are not for us ! "

The king laughed. " It is well. In our land
there is a proverb which runs, ' Women's eyes are
always bright, whatever the colour,' and another
that says, ' Love her who is present, for be sure
she who is absent is false to thee ; ' but perhaps
these things are not so in the Stars. In a land
where men are white all things are possible. So
be it, white men ; the girls will not go begging !
Welcome again ; and welcome, too, thou black
one ; if Gagool here had won her way, thou
wouldst have been stiff and cold by now. It is
lucky for thee that thou too camest from the
Stars ; ha ! ha ! "

" I can kill thee before thou killest me, O
king," was Ignosi's calm answer, " and thou
shalt be stiff before my limbs cease to
bend."

Twala started. " Thou speakest boldly, boy,"
he replied angrily ; " presume not too far."

" He may well be bold in whose lips are truth.
The truth is a sharp spear which flies home and
misses not. It is a message from the ' Stars,'
O king."

Twala scowled, and his one eye gleamed
fiercely, but he said nothing more.

" Let the dance begin," he cried, and then the
flower-crowned girls sprang forward in companies,
singing a sweet song and waving the delicate
palms and white lilies. On they danced, looking
faint and spiritual in the delicate sad light of
the risen moon ; now whirling round and round,

now meeting in mimic warfare, swaying, eddying here and there, coming forward, falling back in an ordered confusion delightful to witness. At last they paused, and a beautiful young woman sprang out of the ranks and began to pirouette in front of us with a grace and vigour which would have put most ballet girls to shame. At length she retired exhausted, and another took her place, then another and another, but none of them, either in grace, skill, or personal attractions, came up to the first.

When the chosen girls had all danced, the king lifted his hand.

" Which deem ye the fairest, white men ? " he asked.

" The first," said I unthinkingly. Next second I regretted it, for I remembered that Infadoos had told us that the fairest woman must be offered up as a sacrifice.

" Then is my mind as your minds, and my eyes are your eyes. She is the fairest ; and a sorry thing it is for her, for she must die ! "

" *Ay, must die !* " piped out Gagool, casting a glance of her quick eyes in the direction of the poor girl, who, as yet ignorant of the awful fate in store for her, was standing some ten yards off in front of a company of maidens, engaged in nervously picking a flower from her wreath to pieces, petal by petal.

" Why, O king ? " said I, restraining my indignation with difficulty ; " the girl has danced well, and pleased us ; she is fair too ; it would be hard to reward her with death."

Twala laughed as he answered—

" It is our custom, and the figures who sit in stone yonder," and he pointed towards the three

distant peaks, "must have their due. Did I
fail to put the fairest girl to death to-day, misfortune would fall upon me and my house. Thus
runs the prophecy of my people : ' If the king
offer not a sacrifice of a fair girl, on the day of
the dance of maidens, to the Old Ones who sit
and watch on the mountains, then shall he fall,
and his house.' Look ye, white men, my brother
who reigned before me offered not the sacrifice,
because of the tears of the woman, and he fell,
and his house, and I reign in his stead. It is
finished ; she must die ! " Then turning to the
guards—" Bring her hither ; Scragga, make
sharp thy spear."

Two of the men stepped forward, and as they
advanced, the girl, for the first time realizing
her impending fate, screamed aloud and turned
to fly. But the strong hands caught her fast,
and brought her, struggling and weeping, before
us.

" What is thy name, girl ? " piped Gagool.
" What ! wilt thou not answer ? Shall the king's
son do his work at once ? "

At this hint, Scragga, looking more evil than
ever, advanced a step and lifted his great spear,
and at that moment I saw Good's hand creep to
the revolver. The poor girl caught the faint
glint of steel through her tears, and it sobered
her anguish. She ceased struggling, and clasping
her hands convulsively, stood shuddering from
head to foot.

" See," cried Scragga in high glee, " she shrinks
from the sight of my little plaything even before
she has tasted it," and he tapped the broad blade
of his spear.

" If ever I get the chance you shall pay for

that, you young hound!" I heard Good mutter beneath his breath.

"Now that thou art quiet, give us thy name, my dear. Come, speak out, and fear not," said Gagool in mockery.

"Oh, mother," answered the girl, in trembling accents, "my name is Foulata, of the house of Suko. Oh, mother, why must I die? I have done no wrong!"

"Be comforted," went on the old woman in her hateful tone of mockery. "Thou must die, indeed, as a sacrifice to the Old Ones who sit yonder," and she pointed to the peaks; "but it is better to sleep in the night than to toil in the daytime; it is better to die than to live, and thou shalt die by the royal hand of the king's own son."

The girl Foulata wrung her hands in anguish, and cried out aloud, "Oh, cruel! and I so young! What have I done that I should never again see the sun rise out of the night, or the stars come following on his track in the evening, that I may no more gather the flowers when the dew is heavy, or listen to the laughing of the waters? Woe is me, that I shall never see my father's hut again, nor feel my mother's kiss, nor tend the lamb that is sick! Woe is me, that no lover shall put his arm around me and look into my eyes, nor shall men children be born of me! Oh, cruel, cruel!"

And again she wrung her hands and turned her tear-stained, flower-crowned face to heaven, looking so lovely in her despair—for she was indeed a beautiful woman—that assuredly the sight of her would have melted the heart of any less cruel than were the three fiends before us. Prince

Arthur's appeal to the ruffians who came to blind him was not more touching than that of this savage girl.

But it did not move Gagool or Gagool's master, though I saw signs of pity among the guards behind, and on the faces of the chiefs ; and as for Good, he gave a fierce snort of indignation, and made a motion as though to go to her assistance. With all a woman's quickness, the doomed girl interpreted what was passing in his mind, and by a sudden movement flung herself before him, and clasped his " beautiful white legs " with her hands.

" Oh, white father from the Stars ! " she cried, " throw over me the mantle of thy protection ; let me creep into the shadow of thy strength, that I may be saved. Oh, keep me from these cruel men and from the mercies of Gagool ! "

" All right, my hearty, I'll look after you," sang out Good, in nervous Saxon.

" Come, get up, there's a good girl," and he stooped and caught her hand.

Twala turned and motioned to his son, who advanced with his spear lifted.

" Now's your time," whispered Sir Henry to me ; " what are you waiting for ? "

" I am waiting for that eclipse," I answered ; " I have had my eye on the moon for the last half-hour, and I never saw it look healthier."

" Well, you must risk it now, or the girl will be killed. Twala is losing patience."

Recognizing the force of the argument, and having cast one more despairing look at the bright face of the moon, for never did the most ardent astronomer with a theory to prove await a celestial event with such anxiety, I stepped with all the dignity that I could command between the prostrate girl and the advancing spear of Scragga.

"King," I said, "it shall not be; we will not endure this thing; let the girl go in safety."

Twala rose from his seat in wrath and astonishment, and from the chiefs and serried ranks of maidens who had closed in slowly upon us in anticipation of the tragedy came a murmur of amazement.

"*Shall not be!* thou white dog, that yappest at the lion in his cave; *shall not be!* art thou mad? Be careful lest this chicken's fate overtake thee, and those with thee. How canst thou save her or thyself? Who art thou that thou settest thyself between me and my will? Back, I say. Scragga, kill her! Ho! guards, seize these men."

At this cry armed men ran swiftly from behind the hut, where they had evidently been placed beforehand.

Sir Henry, Good, and Umbopa ranged themselves alongside of me, and lifted their rifles.

"Stop!" I shouted boldly, though at the moment my heart was in my boots. "Stop! we, the white men from the Stars, say that it shall not be. Come but one pace nearer, and we will put out the moon, as we who dwell in her House can do, and plunge the land in darkness. Dare to disobey, and ye shall taste of our magic."

My threat produced an effect; the men halted, and Scragga stood still before us, his spear lifted.

"Hear him! hear him!" piped Gagool; "hear the liar who says that he will put out the moon like a lamp. Let him do it, and the girl shall be spared. Yes, let him do it, or die by the girl, he and those with him."

I glanced up at the moon despairingly, and now to my intense joy and relief saw that we—or rather the almanack—had made no mistake. On the edge of the great orb lay a faint rim of shadow, while a smoky hue grew and gathered upon its bright surface.

Then I lifted my hand solemnly towards the sky, an example which Sir Henry and Good followed, and quoted a line or two from the "Ingoldsby Legends" at it in the most impressive tones that I could command. Sir Henry followed suit with a verse out of the Old Testament, whilst Good addressed the Queen of Night in a volume of the most classical bad language which he could think of.

Slowly the penumbra, the shadow of a shadow, crept on over the bright surface, and as it crept I heard deep gasps of fear rising from the multitude around.

"Look, O king!" I cried; "look, Gagool! Look, chiefs and people and women, and see if the white men from the Stars keep their word, or they be but empty liars!

"The moon grows black before your eyes; soon there will be darkness—ay, darkness in the hour of the full moon. Ye have asked for a sign; it is given to you. Grow dark, O Moon! withdraw thy light, thou pure and holy one; bring the proud heart to the dust, and eat up the world with shadows."

A groan of terror burst from the onlookers. Some stood petrified with dread, others threw themselves upon their knees and cried aloud. As for the king, he sat still and turned pale beneath his dusky skin. Only Gagool kept her courage.

"It will pass," she cried; "I have seen the

like before ; no man can put out the moon ; lose
not heart ; sit still—the shadow will pass."

"Wait, and ye shall see," I replied, hopping
with excitement. "O Moon! Moon! Moon!
wherefore art thou so cold and fickle ?" This
appropriate quotation was from the pages of a
popular romance that I chanced to have read
recently, though now I come to think of it, it
was ungrateful of me to abuse the Lady of the
Heavens, who was showing herself to be the truest
of friends to us, however she may have behaved
to the impassioned lover in the novel. Then I
added : "Keep it up, Good, I can't remember
any more poetry. Curse away, there's a good
fellow."

Good responded nobly to this tax upon his
inventive faculties. Never before had I the
faintest conception of the breadth and depth and
height of a naval officer's objurgatory powers.
For ten minutes he went on without stopping,
and he scarcely ever repeated himself.

Meanwhile the dark ring crept on, and that
great assembly fixed their eyes upon the sky
and stared and stared in fascinated silence.
Strange and unholy shadows encroached upon
the moonlight, an ominous quiet filled the place.
Everything grew still as death. Slowly and
in the midst of this most solemn silence the
minutes sped away, and while they sped the full
moon passed deeper and deeper into the shadow
of the earth, as the inky segment of its circle slid
in awful majesty across the lunar craters. The
great pale orb seemed to draw near and to grow
in size. She turned a coppery hue, then that
portion of her surface which was unobscured
as yet grew grey and ashen, and at length, as

totality approached, her mountains and her plains were to be seen glowing luridly through a crimson gloom.

On, yet on, crept the ring of darkness ; it was now more than half across the blood-red orb. The air grew thick, and still more deeply tinged with dusky crimson. On, yet on, till we could scarcely see the fierce faces of the group before us. No sound rose now from the spectators, and Good stopped swearing.

" The moon is dying—the white wizards have killed the moon," yelled the prince Scragga at last. " We shall all perish in the dark," and animated by fear or fury, or by both, he lifted his spear and drove it with all his force at Sir Henry's breast. But he had forgotten the mail shirts that the king had given us, and which we wore beneath our clothing. The steel rebounded harmless, and before he could repeat the blow Curtis had snatched the spear from his hand and sent it straight through him. Scragga dropped dead.

At the sight, and driven mad with fear of the gathering darkness, and of the unholy shadow which, as they believed, was swallowing the moon, the companies of girls broke up in wild confusion, and ran screeching for the gateways. Nor did the panic stop there. The king himself, followed by his guards, some of the chiefs, and Gagool, who hobbled after them with marvellous alacrity, fled for the huts, so that in another minute we ourselves, the would-be victim Foulata, Infadoos, and most of the chiefs who had interviewed us on the previous night, were left alone upon the scene, together with the dead body of Scragga, Twala's son.

" Chiefs," I said, " we have given you the sign. If ye are satisfied let us fly swiftly to the place ye spoke of.   The charm cannot now be stopped. It will work for an hour and the half of an hour. Let us cover ourselves in the darkness."

" Come," said Infadoos, turning to go, an example which was followed by the awed captains, ourselves, and the girl Foulata, whom Good took by the arm.

Before we reached the gate of the kraal the moon went out utterly, and from every quarter of the firmament the stars rushed forth into the inky sky.

Holding each other by the hand we stumbled on through the darkness.

CHAPTER XII

BEFORE THE BATTLE

LUCKILY for us, Infadoos and the chiefs knew all the pathways of the great town perfectly, so that notwithstanding the gloom we made fair progress.

For an hour or more we journeyed on, till at length the eclipse began to pass, and that edge of the moon which had disappeared the first became again visible. Suddenly, as we watched, there burst from it a silver streak of light, accompanied by a wondrous ruddy glow, which hung upon the blackness of the sky like a celestial lamp, and a wild and lovely sight it was. In another five minutes the stars began to fade, and there was sufficient light to see our whereabouts. We then discovered that we were clear of the town of Loo and approaching a large flat-topped hill, measuring some two miles in circumference. This hill, which is of a formation common in South Africa, is not very high; indeed, its greatest elevation is not more than 200 feet, but it is shaped like a horseshoe, and its sides are rather precipitous and strewn with boulders. On the grass table-land at its summit is ample camping-ground, which had been utilized as a military cantonment of no mean strength. Its ordinary garrison was one regiment of three thousand men, but as we toiled up the steep side of the mountain in the returning moonlight we perceived that there were several of such regiments upon it.

Reaching the table-land at last, we found crowds of men roused from their sleep, shivering with fear and huddled up together in the utmost consternation at the natural phenomenon which they were witnessing. Passing through these without a word, we gained a hut in the centre of the ground, where we were astonished to find two men waiting, laden with our few goods and chattels, which of course we had been obliged to leave behind in our hasty flight.

" I sent for them," explained Infadoos; "also for these," and he lifted up Good's long-lost trousers.

With an exclamation of rapturous delight Good sprang at them, and instantly proceeded to put them on.

" Surely my lord will not hide his beautiful white legs ! " exclaimed Infadoos regretfully.

But Good persisted, and once only did the Kukuana people get the chance of seeing his beautiful legs again. Good is a very modest man. Henceforward they had to satisfy their æsthetic longings with his one whisker, his transparent eye, and his movable teeth.

Still gazing with fond remembrance at Good's trousers, Infadoos next informed us that he had commanded the regiments to muster so soon as the day broke, in order to explain to them fully the origin and circumstances of the rebellion which was decided on by the chiefs, and to introduce to them the rightful heir to the throne, Ignosi.

Accordingly, when the sun was up, the troops

—in all nearly twenty thousand men, and the flower of the Kukuana army—were mustered on a large open space, to which we went. The men were drawn up in three sides of a dense square, and presented a magnificent spectacle. We took our station on the open side of the square, and were speedily surrounded by all the principal chiefs and officers.

These, after silence had been proclaimed, Infadoos proceeded to address. He narrated to them in vigorous and graceful language—for, like most Kukuanas of high rank, he was a born orator—the history of Ignosi's father, and of how he had been basely murdered by Twala the king, and his wife and child driven out to starve. Then he pointed out that the people suffered and groaned under Twala's cruel rule, instancing the proceedings of the previous night, when under pretence of their being evil-doers, many of the noblest in the land had been dragged forth and wickedly done to death. Next he went on to say that the white lords from the Stars, looking down upon their country, had perceived its trouble, and determined, at great personal inconvenience, to alleviate its lot: That they had accordingly taken the real king of the Kukuanas, Ignosi, who was languishing in exile, by the hand, and led him over the mountains: That they had seen the wickedness of Twala's doings, and for a sign to the wavering, and to save the life of the girl Foulata actually, by the exercise of their high power, had put out the moon and slain the young fiend Scragga ; and that they were prepared to stand by them, and assist them to overthrow Twala, and set up the rightful king, Ignosi, in his place.

He finished his discourse amidst a murmur of approbation. Then Ignosi stepped forward and began to speak. Having reiterated all that Infadoos his uncle had said, he concluded a powerful speech in these words :—

" O chiefs, captains, soldiers, and people, ye have heard my words. Now must ye make choice between me and him who sits upon my throne, the uncle who killed his brother, and hunted his brother's child forth to die in the cold and the night. That I am indeed the king these "— pointing to the chiefs—" can tell you, for they have seen the snake about my middle. If I were not the king, would these white men be on my side with all their magic ? Tremble, chiefs, captains, soldiers, and people ! Is not the darkness they have brought upon the land to confound Twala and cover our flight, darkness even in the hour of the full moon, yet before your eyes ? "

" It is," answered the soldiers.

" I am the king ; I say to you, I am the king," went on Ignosi, drawing up his great stature to its full, and lifting his broad-bladed battle-axe above his head. " If there be any man among you who says that it is not so, let him stand forth and I will fight him now, and his blood shall be a red token that I tell you true. Let him stand forth, I say ; " and he shook the great axe till it flashed in the sunlight.

As nobody seemed inclined to respond to this heroic version of " Dilly, Dilly, come and be killed," our late henchman proceeded with his address.

" I am indeed the king, and should ye stand by my side in the battle, if I win the day, ye shall go with me to victory and honour. I will give you oxen and wives, and ye shall take place of all the regiments ; and if ye fall, I will fall with you.

"And, behold, I give you this promise, that when I sit upon the seat of my fathers, bloodshed shall cease in the land. No longer shall ye cry for justice to find slaughter, no longer shall the witch-finder hunt you out so that ye may be slain without a cause. No man shall die save he who offends against the laws. The 'eating up' of your kraals shall cease ; each one of you shall sleep secure in his own hut and fear naught, and justice shall walk blindfold throughout the land. Have ye chosen, chiefs, captains, soldiers, and people ? "

"We have chosen, O king," came back the answer.

"It is well. Turn your heads and see how Twala's messengers go forth from the great town, east and west, and north and south, to gather a mighty army to slay me and you, and these my friends and protectors. To-morrow, or perchance the next day, he will come against us with all who are faithful to him. Then I shall see the man who is indeed my man, the man who fears not to die for his cause ; and I tell you that he shall not be forgotten in the time of spoil. I have spoken, O chiefs, captains, soldiers, and people. Now go to your huts and make you ready for war."

There was a pause, till presently one of the chiefs lifted his hand, and out rolled the royal salute, "*Koom.*" It was a sign that the soldiers accepted Ignosi as their king. Then they marched off in battalions.

Half an hour afterwards we held a council of war, at which all the commanders of regiments were present. It was evident to us that before very long we should be attacked in overwhelming force. Indeed from our point of vantage on the hill we could see troops mustering, and messengers going forth from Loo in every direction, doubtless to summon soldiers to the king's assistance. We had on our side about twenty thousand men, composed of seven of the best regiments in the country. Twala, so Infadoos and the chiefs calculated, had at least thirty to thirty-five thousand on whom he could rely at present assembled in Loo, and they thought that by midday on the morrow he would be able to gather another five thousand or more to his aid. It was, of course, possible that some of his troops would desert and come over to us, but it was not a contingency which could be reckoned on. Meanwhile, it was clear that active preparations were being made to subdue us. Already strong bodies of armed men were patrolling round and round the foot of the hill, and there were other signs of coming assault.

Infadoos and the chiefs, however, were of opinion that no attack would take place that day, which would be devoted to preparation and to the removal by every available means of the moral effect produced upon the minds of the soldiery by the supposed magical darkening of the moon. The onslaught would be on the morrow, they said, and they proved to be right.

Meanwhile, we set to work to strengthen the position in all ways possible. Almost every man was turned out, and in the course of a day, which seemed far too short, much was done.

The paths up the hill—that was rather a sanatorium than a fortress, being used generally as the camping place of regiments suffering from recent service in unhealthy portions of the country—were carefully blocked with masses of stones, and every other approach was made as impregnable as time would allow. Piles of boulders were collected at various spots to be rolled down upon an advancing enemy, stations were appointed to the different regiments, and all preparation was made which our joint ingenuity could suggest.

Just before sundown, as we rested after our toil, we perceived a small company of men advancing towards us from the direction of Loo, one of whom bore a palm leaf in his hand for a sign that he came as a herald.

As he drew near, Ignosi, Infadoos, one or two chiefs and ourselves, went down to the foot of the mountain to meet him. He was a gallant-looking fellow, wearing the regulation leopard-skin cloak.

" Greeting ! " he cried, as he came ; " the king's greeting to those who make unholy war against the king ; the lion's greeting to the jackals that snarl around his heels."

" Speak," I said.

" These are the king's words. Surrender to the king's mercy ere a worse thing befall you. Already the shoulder has been torn from the black bull, and the king drives him bleeding about the camp."*

---

* This cruel custom is not confined to the Kukuanas, but is by no means uncommon amongst African tribes on the occasion of the outbreak of war or any other important public event.—A. Q.

" What are Twala's terms ? " I asked from curiosity.

" His terms are merciful, worthy of a great king. These are the words of Twala, the one-eyed, the mighty, the husband of a thousand wives, lord of the Kukuanas, keeper of the Great Road (Solomon's Road), beloved of the Strange Ones who sit in silence at the mountains yonder (the Three Witches), Calf of the black Cow, Elephant whose tread shakes the earth, Terror of the evil-doer, Ostrich whose feet devour the desert, huge One, black One, wise One, king from generation to generation ! these are the words of Twala : ' I will have mercy and be satisfied with a little blood. One in every ten shall die, the rest shall go free ; but the white man Incubu, who slew Scragga my son, and the black man his servant, who pretends to my throne, and Infadoos my brother, who brews rebellion against me, these shall die by torture as an offering to the Silent Ones.' Such are the merciful words of Twala."

After consulting with the others a little, I answered him in a loud voice, so that the soldiers might hear, thus—

" Go back, thou dog, to Twala, who sent thee, and say that we, Ignosi, veritable king of the Kukuanas, Incubu, Bougwan, and Macumazahn, the wise ones from the Stars, who make dark the moon, Infadoos, of the royal house, and the chiefs, captains, and people here gathered, make answer and say, ' That we will not surrender ; that before the sun has gone down twice, Twala's corpse shall stiffen at Twala's gate, and Ignosi, whose father Twala slew, shall reign in his stead.' Now go, ere we whip thee away, and beware how thou dost lift a hand against such as we are.''

The herald laughed loudly. '' Ye frighten not men with such swelling words,'' he cried out. '' Show yourselves as bold to-morrow, O ye who darken the moon. Be bold, fight, and be merry, before the crows pick your bones till they are whiter than your faces. Farewell ; perhaps we may meet in the fight ; fly not to the Stars but wait for me, I pray, white men.'' With this shaft of sarcasm he retired, and almost immediately the sun sank.

That night was a busy one, for weary as we were, so far as was possible by the moonlight all preparations for the morrow's fight were continued, and messengers were constantly coming and going from the place where we sat in council. At last about an hour after midnight, everything that could be done was done, and the camp, save for the occasional challenge of a sentry, sank into silence. Sir Henry and I, accompanied by Ignosi and one of the chiefs, descended the hill and made a round of the outposts. As we went, suddenly, from all sorts of unexpected places spears gleamed out in the moonlight, only to vanish again when we uttered the password. It was clear to us that none were sleeping at their posts. Then we returned, picking our way through thousands of sleeping warriors, many of whom were taking their last earthly rest.

The moonlight flickering along their spears played upon their features and made them ghastly ; the chilly night wind tossed their tall and hearse-like plumes. There they lay in wild confusion, with arms outstretched and twisted limbs ; their stern, stalwart forms looking weird and unhuman in the moonlight.

" How many of these do you suppose will be alive at this time to-morrow ? " asked Sir Henry.

I shook my head and looked again at the sleeping men, and to my tired and yet excited imagination it seemed as though Death had already touched them. My mind's eye singled out those who were sealed to slaughter, and there rushed in upon my heart a great sense of the mystery of human life, and an overwhelming sorrow at its futility and sadness. To-night these thousands slept their healthy sleep, to-morrow they, and many others with them, ourselves perhaps among them, would be stiffening in the cold ; their wives would be widows, their children fatherless, and their place know them no more for ever. Only the old moon would shine on serenely, the night wind would stir the grasses, and the wide earth would take its rest, even as it did æons before we were, and will do æons after we have been forgotten.

Yet man dies not whilst the world, at once his mother and his monument, remains. His name is lost, indeed, but the breath he breathed still stirs the pine-tops on the mountains, the sound of the words he spake yet echoes on through space ; the thoughts his brain gave birth to we have inherited to-day ; his passions are our cause of life ; the joys and sorrows that he knew are our familiar friends—the end from which he fled aghast will surely overtake us also !

Truly the universe is full of ghosts, not sheeted churchyard spectres, but the inextinguishable elements of individual life, which having once been, can never *die*, though they blend and change, and change again for ever.

All sorts of reflections of this nature passed through my mind—for as I grow older I regret to say that a detestable habit of thinking seems to be getting a hold of me—while I stood and stared at those grim yet fantastic lines of warriors, sleeping, as their saying goes, " upon their spears."

" Curtis," I said, " I am in a condition of pitiable fear."

Sir Henry stroked his yellow beard and laughed, as he answered—

" I have heard you make that sort of remark before, Quatermain."

" Well, I mean it now. Do you know, I very much doubt if one of us will be alive to-morrow night. We shall be attacked in overwhelming force, and it is quite a chance if we can hold this place."

" We'll give a good account of some of them, at any rate. Look here, Quatermain, this business is a nasty one, and one with which, properly speaking, we ought not to be mixed up, but we are in for it, so we must make the best of it. Speaking personally, I had rather be killed fighting than any other way, and now that there seems little chance of our finding my poor brother, it makes the idea easier to me. But fortune favours the brave, and we may succeed. Anyway, the battle will be awful, and having a reputation to keep up, we shall need to be in the thick of it."

He made this last remark in a mournful voice, but there was a gleam in his eye which belied its melancholy. I have an idea Sir Henry Curtis actually likes fighting.

After this we went to sleep for a couple of hours.

Just about dawn we were awakened by Infadoos, who came to say that great activity was to be observed in Loo, and that parties of the king's skirmishers were driving in our outposts.

We got up and dressed ourselves for the fray, each putting on his chain armour shirt, for which garments at the present juncture we felt exceedingly thankful. Sir Henry went the whole length about the matter, and dressed himself like a native warrior. " When you are in Kukuanaland, do as the Kukuanas do," he remarked, as he drew the shining steel over his broad breast, which it fitted like a glove. Nor did he stop there. At his request Infadoos had provided him with a complete set of native war uniform. Round his throat he fastened the leopard-skin cloak of a commanding officer, on his brows he bound the plume of black ostrich feathers worn only by generals of high rank, and about his middle a magnificent moocha of white ox-tails. A pair of sandals, a leglet of goat's hair, a heavy battle-axe, with a rhinoceros-horn handle, a round iron shield covered with white ox-hide, and the regulation number of *tollas*, or throwing knives, made up his equipment, to which, however, he added his revolver. The dress was, no doubt, a savage one, but I am bound to say that I seldom saw a finer sight than Sir Henry Curtis presented in this disguise. It showed off his magnificent physique to the greatest advantage, and when Ignosi arrived presently, arrayed in a similar costume, I thought to myself that I had never before seen two such splendid men.

As for Good and myself, the armour did not

suit us nearly so well. To begin with, Good insisted upon keeping on his new-found trousers, and a stout, short gentleman with an eyeglass, and one half of his face shaved, arrayed in a mail shirt, carefully tucked into a very seedy pair of corduroys, looks more remarkable than imposing. In my case, the chain shirt being too big for me, I put it on over all my clothes, which caused it to bulge in a somewhat ungainly fashion. I discarded my trousers, however, retaining only my veldtschoons, having determined to go into battle with bare legs in order to be the lighter for running, in case it became necessary to retire quickly. The mail coat, a spear, a shield, that I did not know how to use, a couple of *tollas*, a revolver, and a huge plume, which I pinned into the top of my shooting hat, in order to give a bloodthirsty finish to my appearance, completed my modest equipment. In addition to all these articles, of course we had our rifles, but as ammunition was scarce, and as they would be useless in case of a charge, we arranged that they should be carried behind us by bearers.

When at length we had equipped ourselves, we swallowed some food hastily, and then started out to see how things were going on. At one point in the table-land of the mountain, there was a little koppie of brown stone, which served the double purpose of headquarters and of a conning tower. Here we found Infadoos surrounded by his own regiment, the Greys, which was undoubtedly the finest in the Kukuana army, and the same that we had first seen at the outlying kraal. This regiment, now three thousand five hundred strong, was being held in reserve, and the men were lying down on the grass in companies, and watching the king's forces creep out of Loo in long ant-like columns. There seemed to be no end to the length of these columns— three in all, and each of them numbering at least eleven or twelve thousand men.

As soon as they were clear of the town the regiments formed up. Then one body marched off to the right, one to the left, and the third came on slowly towards us.

"Ah," said Infadoos, "they are going to attack us on three sides at once."

This seemed rather serious news, for our position on the top of the mountain, which measured a mile and a half in circumference, being an extended one, it was important to us to concentrate our comparatively small defending force as much as possible. But since it was impossible for us to dictate in what way we should be attacked, we had to make the best of it, and accordingly sent orders to the various regiments to prepare to receive the separate onslaughts.

CHAPTER XIII

THE ATTACK

SLOWLY, and without the slightest appearance of haste or excitement, the three columns crept on. When within about five hundred yards of us, the main or centre column halted at the root of a tongue of open plain which ran up into the hill, to give time to the other divisions to circumvent our position, which was shaped more or less in the form of a horseshoe, with its two points facing towards the town of Loo. The object of this manœuvre was that the threefold assault should be delivered simultaneously.

"Oh, for a gatling!" groaned Good, as he contemplated the serried phalanxes beneath us. "I would clear that plain in twenty minutes."

"We have not got one, so it is no use yearning for it; but suppose you try a shot, Quatermain," said Sir Henry. "See how near you can go to that tall fellow who appears to be in command. Two to one you miss him, and an even sovereign, to be honestly paid if ever we get out of this, that you don't drop the bullet within five yards."

This piqued me, so, loading the express with solid ball, I waited till my friend walked some ten yards out from his force, in order to get a better view of our position, accompanied only by an

orderly ; then, lying down and resting the express
upon a rock, I covered him. The rifle, like all
expresses, was only sighted to three hundred
and fifty yards, so to allow for the drop in tra-
jectory I took him half-way down the neck,
which ought, I calculated, to find him in the
chest. He stood quite still and gave me every
opportunity, but whether it was the excitement
or the wind, or the fact of the man being a long
shot, I don't know, but this was what happened.
Getting dead on, as I thought, a fine sight, I
pressed, and when the puff of smoke had cleared
away, to my disgust, I saw my man standing
unharmed, whilst his orderly, who was at least
three paces to the left, was stretched upon the
ground apparently dead. Turning swiftly, the
officer I had aimed at began to run towards his
men in evident alarm.

" Bravo, Quatermain ! " sang out Good ;
" you've frightened him."

This made me very angry, for, if possible to
avoid it, I hate to miss in public. When a man
is master of only one art he likes to keep up his
reputation in that art. Moved quite out of
myself at my failure, I did a rash thing. Rapidly
covering the general as he ran, I let drive with
the second barrel. Instantly the poor man
threw up his arms, and fell forward on to his face.
This time I had made no mistake ; and—I say it
as a proof of how little we think of others when
our own safety, pride, or reputation are in question—I was brute enough to feel delighted at
the sight.

The regiments who had seen the feat cheered
wildly at this exhibition of the white man's
magic, which they took as an omen of success,

while the force the general had belonged to—
which, indeed, as we ascertained afterwards, he
had commanded—fell back in confusion. Sir
Henry and Good now took up their rifles and
began to fire, the latter industriously " brown-
ing " the dense mass before him with a Winchester
repeater, and I also had another shot or two,
with the result, so far as we could judge, that we
put some six or eight men *hors de combat* before
they were out of range.

Just as we stopped firing there came an
ominous roar from our far right, then a similar
roar rose on our left. The two other divisions
were engaging us.

At the sound, the mass of men before us
opened out a little, and advanced towards the
hill and up the spit of bare grass land at a slow
trot, singing a deep-throated song as they ran.
We kept up a steady fire from our rifles as they
came, Ignosi joining in occasionally, and accounted for several men, but of course we produced no more effect upon that mighty rush of
armed humanity than he who throws pebbles
does on the breaking wave.

On they came, with a shout and the clashing
of spears ; now they were driving in the outposts
we had placed among the rocks at the foot of the
hill. After that the advance was a little slower,
for though as yet we had offered no serious op-
position, the attacking forces must climb up hill,
and they came slowly to save their breath.
Our first line of defence was about half-way down
the side of the slope, our second fifty yards
further back, while our third occupied the edge
of the plateau.

On they stormed, shouting their war-cry,

"*Twala! Twala! Chiele! Chiele!*" (Twala!
Twala! Smite! Smite!) "*Ignosi! Ignosi!
Chiele! Chiele!*" answered our people. They
were quite close now, and the *tollas*, or throwing-
knives, began to flash backwards and forwards,
and now with an awful yell the battle closed in.

To and fro swayed the mass of struggling
warriors, men falling fast as leaves in an autumn
wind ; but before long the superior weight of the
attacking force began to tell, and our first line of
defence was slowly pressed back, till it merged
into the second. Here the struggle was very
fierce, but again our people were driven back
and up, till at length, within twenty minutes of
the commencement of the fight, our third line
came into action.

But by this time the assailants were much
exhausted, and besides had lost many men killed
and wounded, and to break through that third
impenetrable hedge of spears proved beyond
their powers. For a while the seething lines of
savages swung backwards and forwards, in the
fierce ebb and flow of battle, and the issue was
doubtful. Sir Henry watched the desperate
struggle with a kindling eye, and then without a
word he rushed off, followed by Good, and flung
himself into the hottest of the fray. As for myself, I stopped where I was.

The soldiers caught sight of his tall form as he
plunged into the battle, and there rose a cry of—
"*Nanzia Incubu! Nanzia Unkungunklovo!*"
(Here is the Elephant !) "*Chiele! Chiele!*"

From that moment the end was no longer in
doubt. Inch by inch, fighting with splendid
gallantry, the attacking force was pressed back
down the hillside, till at last it retreated upon its

reserves in something like confusion. At that instant, too, a messenger arrived to say that the left attack had been repulsed ; and I was just beginning to congratulate myself, believing that the affair was over for the present, when, to our horror, we perceived our men who had been engaged in the right defence being driven towards us across the plain, followed by swarms of the enemy, who had evidently succeeded at this point.

Ignosi, who was standing by me, took in the situation at a glance, and issued a rapid order. Instantly the reserve regiment around us, the Greys, extended itself.

Again Ignosi gave a word of command, which was taken up and repeated by the captains, and in another second, to my intense disgust, I found myself involved in a furious onslaught upon the advancing foe. Getting as much as I could behind Ignosi's huge frame, I made the best of a bad job, and toddled along to be killed as though I liked it. In a minute or two—the time seemed all too short to me—we were plunging through the flying groups of our men, who at once began to re-form behind us, and then I am sure I do not know what happened. All I can remember is a dreadful noise of the meeting of shields, and the sudden apparition of a huge ruffian, whose eyes seemed literally to be starting out of his head, making straight at me with a bloody spear. But—I say it with pride—I rose —or rather sank—to the occasion. It was one before which most people would have collapsed once and for all. Seeing that if I stood where I was I must be killed, as the horrid apparition came I flung myself down in front of him so cleverly that, being unable to stop himself, he took a header right over my prostrate form. Before he could rise again, I had risen and settled the matter from behind with my revolver.

Shortly after this somebody knocked me down, and I remember no more of that charge.

When I came to I found myself back at the koppie, with Good bending over me holding some water in a gourd.

"How do you feel, old fellow?" he asked, anxiously.

I got up and shook myself before replying.

"Pretty well, thank you," I answered.

"Thank Heaven! When I saw them carry you in, I felt quite sick; I thought that you were done for."

"Not this time, my boy. I fancy I only got a rap on the head, which knocked me stupid. How has it ended?"

"They are repulsed at every point for a while. The loss is dreadfully heavy; we have quite two thousand killed and wounded, and they must have lost three. Look, there's a sight!" and he pointed to long lines of men advancing by fours.

In the centre of every group of four, and being borne by it, was a kind of hide tray, of which a Kukuana force always carries a quantity, with a loop for a handle at each corner. On these trays—and their number seemed endless—lay wounded men, who as they arrived were hastily examined by the medicine men, of whom ten were attached to the regiment. If the wound was not of a fatal character the sufferer was taken away and attended to as carefully as circumstances would allow. But if, on the other hand, the injured man's condition proved hopeless, what followed was very dreadful, though doubtless it may have been the truest mercy. One of the doctors, under pretence of carrying out an examination, swiftly opened an artery with a sharp knife, and in a minute or two the sufferer expired painlessly. There were many cases that day in which this was done. In fact, it was done in the majority of cases when the wound was in the body, for the gash made by the entry of the enormously broad spears used by the Kukuanas generally rendered recovery impossible. In most instances the poor sufferers were already unconscious, and in others the fatal " nick " of the artery was inflicted so swiftly and painlessly that they did not seem to notice it. Still it was a ghastly sight, and one from which we were glad to escape ; indeed, I never remember anything of the kind that affected me more than seeing those gallant soldiers thus put out of pain by the red-handed medicine men, except, indeed, on one occasion when, after an attack, I saw a force of Swazis burying their hopelessly wounded, *alive*.

Hurrying from this dreadful scene to the further side of the koppie, we found Sir Henry, who still held a battle-axe in his hand, Ignosi, Infadoos, and one or two of the chiefs in deep consultation.

" Thank Heaven, here you are, Quatermain ! I can't quite make out what Ignosi wants to do. It seems that though we have beaten off the attack, Twala is now receiving large reinforcements, and is showing a disposition to invest us, with the view of starving us out."

" That's awkward."

" Yes ; especially as Infadoos says that the water supply has given out."

" My lord, that is so," said Infadoos ; " the

spring cannot supply the wants of so great a
multitude, and it is failing rapidly. Before
night we shall all be thirsty. Listen, Macumazahn. Thou art wise, and hast doubtless
seen many wars in the lands from whence thou
camest—that is if indeed they make wars in the
Stars. Now tell us, what shall we do ? Twala
has brought up many fresh men to take the place
of those who have fallen. Yet Twala has learnt
his lesson ; the hawk did not think to find the
heron ready ; but our beak has pierced his
breast ; he fears to strike at us again. We too
are wounded, and he will wait for us to die ; he
will wind himself round us like a snake round a
buck, and fight the fight of ' sit down.' "

" I hear thee," I said.

" So, Macumazahn, thou seest we have no
water here, and but a little food, and we must
choose between these three things—to languish
like a starving lion in his den, or to strive to
break away towards the north, or "—and here
he rose and pointed towards the dense mass of
our foes—" to launch ourselves straight at
Twala's throat. Incubu, the great warrior—for
to-day he fought like a buffalo in a net, and
Twala's soldiers went down before his axe like
young corn before the hail ; with these eyes I saw
it—Incubu says ' Charge ' ; but the Elephant
is ever prone to charge. Now what says Macumazahn, the wily old fox, who has seen much,
and loves to bite his enemy from behind ? The
last word is in Ignosi the king, for it is a king's
right to speak of war ; but let us hear thy voice,
O Macumazahn, who watchest by night, and the
voice too of him of the transparent eye."

" What sayest thou, Ignosi ? " I asked.

" Nay, my father," answered our quondam servant, who now, clad as he was in the full panoply of savage war, looked every inch a warrior king, " do thou speak, and let me, who am but a child in wisdom beside thee, hearken to thy words."

Thus adjured, after taking hasty counsel with Good and Sir Henry, I delivered my opinion briefly to the effect that, being trapped, our better chance, especially in view of the failure of our water supply, was to initiate an attack upon Twala's forces. Then I recommended that the attack should be delivered at once, " before our wounds grew stiff," and also before the sight of Twala's overpowering force caused the hearts of our soldiers " to wax small like fat before a fire." Otherwise, I pointed out, some of the captains might change their minds, and, making peace with Twala, desert to him, or even betray us into his hands.

This expression of opinion seemed, on the whole, to be favourably received ; indeed, among the Kukuanas my utterances met with a respect which has never been accorded to them before or since. But the real decision as to our plans lay with Ignosi, who, since he had been recognized a rightful king, could exercise the almost unbounded rights of sovereignty, including, of course, the final decision on matters of generalship, and it was to him that all eyes were now turned.

At length, after a pause, during which he appeared to be thinking deeply, he spoke.

" Incubu, Macumazahn, and Bougwan, brave white men, and my friends ; Infadoos, my uncle, and chiefs ; my heart is fixed. I will strike at Twala this day, and set my fortunes on the blow,

ay, and my life—my life and your lives also.
Listen ; thus will I strike. Ye see how the hill
curves round like the half-moon, and how the
plain runs like a green tongue towards us within
the curve ? "

"We see," I answered.

"Good ; it is now mid-day, and the men
eat and rest after the toil of battle. When
the sun has turned and travelled a little way
towards the darkness, let thy regiment, my
uncle, advance with one other down to the
green tongue ; and it shall be that when Twala
sees it he will hurl his force at it to crush it.
But the spot is narrow, and the regiments can
come against thee one at a time only ; so may
they be destroyed one by one, and the eyes
of all Twala's army shall be fixed upon the
struggle the like of which has not been seen by
living man. And with thee, my uncle, shall
go Incubu my friend, that when Twala sees his
battle-axe flashing in the first rank of the Greys
his heart may grow faint. And I will come
with the second regiment, that which follows
thee, so that if ye are destroyed, as it might
happen, there may yet be a king left to fight
for ; and with me shall come Macumazahn the
wise."

"It is well, O king," said Infadoos, apparently
contemplating the certainty of the complete
annihilation of his regiment with perfect calm-
ness. Truly these Kukuanas are a wonderful
people. Death has no terrors for them when
it is incurred in the course of duty.

"And whilst the eyes of the multitude of
Twala's soldiers are thus fixed upon the fight,"
went on Ignosi, "behold, one-third of the men

who are left alive to us (*i.e.* about 6,000) shall
creep along the right horn of the hill and fall
upon the left flank of Twala's force. And
one-third shall creep along the left horn and
fall upon Twala's right flank. And when I
see that the horns are ready to toss Twala,
then will I, with the men who remain to me,
charge home in Twala's face, and if fortune
goes with us the day will be ours, and before
Night drives her black oxen from the mountains
to the mountains we shall sit in peace at Loo.
And now let us eat and make ready; and,
Infadoos, do thou prepare, that the plan be
carried out without fail; and stay, let my
white father Bougwan go with the right horn,
that his shining eye may give courage to the
captains."

The arrangements for attack thus briefly
indicated were set in motion with a rapidity
that spoke well for the perfection of the Kukuana
military system. Within little more than an
hour rations had been served out to the men
and devoured, the three divisions were formed,
the scheme of onslaught was explained to the
leaders, and the whole force, now numbering
about 18,000 men in all, was ready to be put
in motion, with the exception of a guard left in
charge of the wounded.

Presently Good came up to Sir Henry and
myself

"Good-bye, you fellows," he said; "I am
off with the right wing according to orders;
and so I have come to shake hands, in case we
should not meet again, you know," he added
significantly.

We shook hands in silence, and not without

the exhibition of as much emotion as Englishmen are wont to show.

"It is a queer business," said Sir Henry, his deep voice shaking a little, "and I confess I never expect to see to-morrow's sun. So far as I can make out, the Greys, with whom I am to go, are to fight until they are wiped out in order to enable the wings to slip round unawares and outflank Twala. Well, so be it; at any rate, it will be a man's death! Good-bye, old fellow. God bless you! I hope you will pull through and live to collar the diamonds; but if you do, take my advice and don't have anything more to do with Pretenders!"

In another second Good had wrung us both by the hand and gone; and then Infadoos came up and led off Sir Henry to his place in the forefront of the Greys, whilst, with many misgivings, I departed with Ignosi to my station in the second attacking regiment.

CHAPTER XIV

THE LAST STAND OF THE GREYS

IN a few more minutes the regiments destined to carry out the flanking movements had tramped off in silence, keeping carefully under the lee of the rising ground in order to conceal their advance from the keen eyes of Twala's scouts.

Half an hour or more was allowed to elapse between the setting out of the horns or wings of the army before any stir was made by the Greys and their supporting regiment, known as the Buffaloes, which formed its chest, and were destined to bear the brunt of the battle.

Both of these regiments were almost perfectly fresh, and full of strength, the Greys having been in reserve in the morning, and having lost but a small number of men in sweeping back that part of the attack which had proved successful in breaking the line of defence, on the occasion when I charged with them and was knocked silly for my pains. As for the Buffaloes, they had formed the third line of defence on the left, and since the attacking force at that point had not succeeded in breaking through the second, they had scarcely come into action at all.

Infadoos, who was a wary old general, and knew the absolute importance of keeping up the

spirits of his men on the eve of such a desperate
encounter, employed the pause in addressing his
own regiment, the Greys, in poetical language ;
explaining to them the honour that they were
receiving in being put thus in the forefront of
the battle, and having the great white warrior from
the Stars to fight with them in their ranks ; and
promising large rewards of cattle and pro-
motion to all who survived in the event of
Ignosi's arms being successful.

I looked down the long lines of waving black
plumes and stern faces beneath them, and
sighed to think that within one short hour
most, if not all, of those magnificent veteran
warriors, not a man who was under forty years
of age, would be laid dead or dying in the dust.
It could not be otherwise ; they were being
condemned, with that wise recklessness of
human life which marks the great general, and
often saves his forces and attains his ends, to
certain slaughter, in order to give their cause
and the remainder of the army a chance of
success. They were foredoomed to die, and
they knew it. It was to be their task to engage
regiment after regiment of Twala's army on
the narrow strip of green beneath us, till they
were exterminated, or till the wings found a
favourable opportunity for their onslaught. And
yet they never hesitated, nor could I detect a
sign of fear upon the face of a single warrior.
There they were—going to certain death, about
to quit the blessed light of day for ever, and
yet able to contemplate their doom without a
tremor. Even at that moment I could not
help contrasting their state of mind with my
own, which was far from comfortable, and

breathing a sigh of envy and admiration. Never before had I seen such an absolute devotion to the idea of duty, and such a complete indifference to its bitter fruits.

" Behold your king ! " ended old Infadoos, pointing to Ignosi; " go fight and fall for him, as is the duty of brave men, and cursed and shameful for ever be the name of him who shrinks from death for his king, or who turns his back from the foe. Behold your king, chiefs, captains, and soldiers ! Now do your homage to the sacred Snake, and then follow on, that Incubu and I may show you a road to the heart of Twala's forces."

There was a moment's pause, then suddenly a murmur arose from the serried phalanxes before us, a sound like the distant whisper of the sea, caused by the gentle tapping of the handles of six thousand spears against their holders' shields. Slowly it swelled, till its growing volume deepened and widened into a roar of rolling noise, that echoed like thunder against the mountains, and filled the air with heavy waves of sound. Then it decreased and by faint degrees died away into nothing and suddenly out crashed the royal salute.

Ignosi, I thought to myself, might well be a proud man that day, for no Roman emperor ever had such a salutation from gladiators " about to die."

Ignosi acknowledged this magnificent act of homage by lifting his battle-axe, and then the Greys filed off in a triple-line formation, each line containing about one thousand fighting men, exclusive of officers. When the last companies had advanced some five hundred yards, Ignosi put himself at the head of the Buffaloes, which regiment was drawn up in a similar threefold formation, and gave the word to march, and off we went, I, needless to say, uttering the most heartfelt prayers that I might come out of that job with a whole skin. Many a queer position have I found myself in, but never before in one quite so unpleasant as the present, or one in which my chance of coming off safe was smaller.

By the time that we reached the edge of the plateau the Greys were already half-way down the slope ending in the tongue of grass land that ran up into the bend of the mountain, something as the frog of a horse's foot runs up into the shoe. The excitement in Twala's camp on the plain beyond was very great, and regiment after regiment was starting forward at a long swinging trot in order to reach the root of the tongue of land before the attacking force could emerge into the plain of Loo.

This tongue, which was some three hundred yards in depth, even at its root or widest part was not more than four hundred and fifty paces across, while at its tip it scarcely measured ninety. The Greys, who, in passing down the side of the hill and on to the tip of the tongue had formed into column, on reaching the spot where it broadened out again, reassumed their triple-line formation and halted dead.

Then we—that is, the Buffaloes—moved down the tip of the tongue and took our stand in reserve, about one hundred yards behind the last line of the Greys, and on slightly higher ground. Meanwhile we had leisure to observe Twala's entire force, which evidently had been reinforced since the morning attack, and could not now, notwithstanding their losses, number less than forty thousand, moving swiftly up towards us. But as they drew near the root of the tongue they hesitated, having discovered that only one regiment could advance into the gorge at a time, and that there, some seventy yards from the mouth of it, unassailable except in front, on account of the high walls of boulder-strewn ground on each side, stood the famous regiment of Greys, the pride and glory of the Kukuana army, ready to hold the way against their forces as the three Romans once held the bridge against thousands.

They hesitated, and finally stopped their advance ; there was no eagerness to cross spears with these three grim ranks of warriors who stood so firm and ready. Presently, however, a tall general, wearing the customary head-dress of nodding ostrich plumes, appeared attended by a group of chiefs and orderlies, being, I thought, none other than Twala himself. He gave an order, and the first regiment, raising a shout, charged up towards the Greys, who remained perfectly still and silent till the attacking troops were within forty yards and a volley of *tollas*, or throwing-knives, came rattling among their ranks.

Then suddenly with a bound and a roar, they sprang forward with uplifted spears, and the regiments met in deadly strife. Next second the roll of the meeting shields came to our ears like the sound of thunder, and the plain seemed to be alive with flashes of light reflected from the shimmering spears. To and fro swung the surging mass of struggling, stabbing humanity, but not for long. Suddenly the attacking lines began to grow thinner, and then with a slow, long heave the Greys passed over them, just as a great wave heaves up its bulk and passes over a sunken ridge. It was done; that regiment was completely destroyed, but the Greys had but two lines left now; a third of their number were dead.

Closing up shoulder to shoulder, once more they halted in silence and awaited attack; and I was rejoiced to catch sight of Sir Henry's yellow beard as he moved to and fro arranging the ranks. So he was yet alive!

Meanwhile we moved on to the ground of the encounter, which was cumbered by about four thousand prostrate human beings, dead, dying, and wounded, and literally stained red with blood. Ignosi issued an order, which was rapidly passed down the ranks, to the effect that none of the enemy's wounded were to be killed, and so far as we could see this command was scrupulously carried out. It would have been a shocking sight, if we had found time to think of it.

But now a second regiment, distinguished by white plumes, kilts, and shields, was moving to the attack of the two thousand remaining Greys, who stood waiting in the same ominous silence as before, till the foe was within forty yards or so, when they hurled themselves with irresistible force upon them. Again there came the awful roll of the meeting shields, and as we watched the tragedy repeated itself.

But this time the issue was left longer in doubt; indeed, it seemed for a while almost impossible that the Greys should again prevail. The attacking regiment, which was formed of young men,

fought with the utmost fury, and at first seemed
by sheer weight to be driving the veterans back.
The slaughter was truly awful, hundreds falling
every minute ; and from among the shouts of
the warriors and the groans of the dying, set to
the music of clashing spears, came a continuous
hissing undertone of " *S'gee, s'gee,*" the note of
triumph of each victor as he passed his assegai
through and through the body of his fallen
foe.

But perfect discipline and steady and unchang-
ing valour can do wonders, and one veteran
soldier is worth two young ones, as soon became
apparent in the present case. For just when we
thought that it was all over with the Greys,
and were preparing to take their place so soon as
they made room by being destroyed, I heard Sir
Henry's deep voice ringing out through the din,
and caught a glimpse of his circling battle-axe
as he waved it high above his plumes. Then
came a change ; the Greys ceased to give ; they
stood still as a rock, against which the furious
waves of spearmen broke again and again,
only to recoil. Presently they began to move
once more—forward this time ; as they had no
firearms there was no smoke, so we could see it
all. Another minute and the onslaught grew
fainter.

" Ah, these are *men* indeed ; they will conquer
again," called out Ignosi, who was grinding his
teeth with excitement at my side. " See, it is
done ! "

Suddenly, like puffs of smoke from the mouth
of a cannon, the attacking regiment broke away
in flying groups, their white head-dresses streaming behind them in the wind, and left their

opponents victors, indeed, but, alas! no more a
regiment. Of the gallant triple line, which forty
minutes before had gone into action three thousand strong, there remained at most some six
hundred blood-bespattered men; the rest were
underfoot. And yet they cheered and waved
their spears in triumph, and then, instead of
falling back upon us as we expected, they ran
forward, for a hundred yards or so, after the
flying groups of foemen, took possession of a
rising knoll of ground, and, resuming their
triple formation, formed a threefold ring around
it. And there, thanks be to Heaven, standing
on the top of the mound for a minute, I saw
Sir Henry, apparently unharmed, and with him
our old friend Infadoos. Then Twala's regiments
rolled down upon the doomed band, and once
more the battle closed in.

As those who read this history will probably
long ago have gathered, I am, to be honest, a
bit of a coward, and certainly in no way given to
fighting, though somehow it has often been my
lot to get into unpleasant positions, and to be
obliged to shed a man's blood. But I have
always hated it, and kept my own blood as
undiminished in quantity as possible, sometimes
by a judicious use of my heels. At this moment,
however, for the first time in my life, I felt my
bosom burn with martial ardour. Warlike fragments from the " Ingoldsby Legends," together
with numbers of sanguinary verses in the Old
Testament, sprang up in my brain like mush-
rooms in the dark; my blood, which hitherto
had been half-frozen with horror, went beating
through my veins, and there came upon me a
savage desire to kill and spare not. I glanced

round at the serried ranks of warriors behind us, and somehow, all in an instant, I began to wonder if my face looked like theirs. There they stood, their heads craned forward over their shields, the hands twitching, the lips apart, the fierce features instinct with the hungry lust of battle, and in the eyes a look like the glare of a bloodhound when he sights his quarry.

Only Ignosi's heart, to judge from his comparative self-possession, seemed, to all appearance, to beat as calmly as ever beneath his leopard-skin cloak, though even *he* still ground his teeth. I could bear it no longer.

" Are we to stand here till we put out roots, Umbopa—Ignosi, I mean—while Twala swallows our brothers yonder ? " I asked.

" Nay, Macumazahn," was the answer ; " see now is the ripe moment : let us pluck it."

As he spoke a fresh regiment rushed past the ring upon the little mound, and wheeling round, attacked it from the hither side.

Then, lifting his battle-axe, Ignosi gave the signal to advance, and, raising the Kukuana war-cry, the Buffaloes charged home with a rush like the rush of the sea.

What followed immediately on this it is out of my power to tell. All I can remember is a wild yet ordered advance, that seemed to shake the ground ; a sudden change of front and forming up on the part of the regiment against which the charge was directed ; then an awful shock, a dull roar of voices, and a continuous flashing of spears, seen through a red mist of blood.

When my mind cleared I found myself standing inside the remnant of the Greys near the top of

the mound, and just behind no less a person than
Sir Henry himself. How I got there I had at
the moment no idea, but Sir Henry afterwards
told me that I was borne up by the first furious
charge of the Buffaloes almost to his feet, and then
left, as they in turn were pressed back. Thereon
he dashed out of the circle and dragged me into
it.

As for the fight that followed, who can describe
it ? Again and again the multitudes surged
against our momentarily lessening circle, and
again and again we beat them back.

> " The stubborn spearmen still made good
>   The dark impenetrable wood,
> Each stepping where his comrade stood
>   The instant that he fell,"

as some one or other beautifully puts it.

It was a splendid thing to see those brave
battalions come on time after time over the
barriers of their dead, sometimes holding corpses
before them to receive our spear thrusts, only
to leave their own corpses to swell the rising
piles. It was a gallant sight to see that sturdy
old warrior, Infadoos, as cool as though he were
on parade, shouting out orders, taunts, and even
jests, to keep up the spirit of his few remaining
men, and then, as each charge rolled on, stepping
forward to wherever the fighting was thickest,
to bear his share in repelling it. And yet more
gallant was the vision of Sir Henry, whose ostrich
plumes had been shorn off by a spear stroke,
so that his long yellow hair streamed out in the
breeze behind him. There he stood, the great
Dane, for he was nothing else, his hands, his
axe, and his armour, all red with blood, and none

could live before his stroke. Time after time
I saw it sweeping down, as some great warrior
ventured to give him battle, and as he struck
he shouted " *O-hoy! O-hoy!* " like his Berserkir
forefathers, and the blow went crashing through
shield and spear, through head-dress, hair, and
skull, till at last none would of their own will
come near the great white " *umtagati*," the wizard,
who killed and failed not.

But suddenly there rose a cry of " *Twala, y'*
Twala," and out of the press sprang forward
none other than the gigantic one-eyed king
himself, also armed with battle-axe and shield,
and clad in chain armour.

" Where art thou, Incubu, thou white man,
who slewest Scragga my son—see if thou canst
slay me ! " he shouted, and at the same time
hurled a *tolla* straight at Sir Henry, who fortunately saw it coming, and caught it on his shield,
which it transfixed, remaining wedged in the
iron plate behind the hide.

Then, with a cry, Twala sprang forward straight
at him, and with his battle-axe struck him such
a blow upon the shield that the mere force and
shock of it brought Sir Henry, strong man as
he is, down upon his knees.

But at this time the matter went no further,
for that instant there rose from the regiments
pressing round us something like a shout
of dismay, and on looking up I saw the
cause.

To the right and to the left the plain was alive
with the plumes of charging warriors. The outflanking squadrons had come to our relief. The
time could not have been better chosen. All
Twala's army, as Ignosi predicted would be the

case, had fixed their attention on the bloody
struggle which was raging round the remnant
of the Greys and that of the Buffaloes, who were
now carrying on a battle of their own at a little
distance, which two regiments had formed the
chest of our army. It was not until our horns
were about to close upon them that they had
dreamed of their approach. And now, before
they could even assume a proper formation for
defence, the outflanking *Impis* had leapt, like
greyhounds, on their flanks.

In five minutes the fate of the battle was
decided. Taken on both flanks, and dismayed
at the awful slaughter inflicted upon them by
the Greys and Buffaloes, Twala's regiments
broke into flight, and soon the whole plain
between us and Loo was scattered with groups
of running soldiers making good their retreat.
As for the forces that had so recently surrounded
us and the Buffaloes, they melted away as though
by magic, and presently we were left standing
there like a rock from which the sea has retreated.
But what a sight it was ! Around us the dead
and dying lay in heaped-up masses, and of the
gallant Greys there remained but ninety-five
men upon their feet. More than three thousand
four hundred had fallen in this one regiment,
most of them never to rise again.

" Men," said Infadoos calmly, as between the
intervals of binding a wound in his arm he surveyed what remained to him of his corps, " ye
have kept up the reputation of your regiment,
and this day's fighting will be well spoken of
by your children's children." Then he turned
round and shook Sir Henry Curtis by the hand.
' Thou art a great man, Incubu," he said simply ;

" I have lived a long life among warriors, and known many a brave one, yet have I never seen a man like unto thee."

At this moment the Buffaloes began to march past our position on the road to Loo, and as they went a message was brought to us from Ignosi requesting Infadoos, Sir Henry, and myself to join him. Accordingly, orders having been issued to the remaining ninety men of the Greys to employ themselves in collecting the wounded, we joined Ignosi, who informed us that he was pressing on to Loo to complete the victory by capturing Twala, if that should be possible. Before we had gone far suddenly we discovered the figure of Good sitting on an ant-heap about one hundred paces from us. Close beside him was the body of a Kukuana.

" He must be wounded," said Sir Henry anxiously. As he made the remark, an untoward thing happened. The dead body of the Kukuana soldier, or rather what had appeared to be his dead body, suddenly sprang up, knocked Good head over heels off the ant-heap, and began to spear him. We rushed forward in terror, and as we drew near we saw the brawny warrior making dig after dig at the prostrate Good, who at each prod jerked all his limbs into the air. Seeing us coming, the Kukuana gave one final and most vicious dig, and with a shout of " Take that, wizard ! " bolted away. Good did not move, and we concluded that our poor comrade was done for. Sadly we came towards him, and were astonished to find him pale and faint indeed, but with a serene smile upon his face, and his eyeglass still fixed in his eye.

" Capital armour this," he murmured, on

catching sight of our faces bending over him.
"How sold that beggar must have been," and
then he fainted. On examination we discovered
that he had been seriously wounded in the leg
by a *tolla* in the course of the pursuit, but that
the chain armour had prevented his last assailant's spear from doing anything more than
bruise him badly. It was a merciful escape.
As nothing could be done for him at the
moment, he was placed on one of the wicker
shields used for the wounded, and carried along
with us.

On arriving before the nearest gate of Loo
we found one of our regiments watching it in
obedience to orders received from Ignosi. The
other regiments were in the same way guarding
the different exits to the town. The officer in
command of this regiment saluted Ignosi as king,
and informed him that Twala's army had taken
refuge in the town, whither Twala himself had
also escaped, but he thought that they were
thoroughly demoralized, and would surrender.
Thereupon Ignosi, after taking counsel with us,
sent forward heralds to each gate ordering the
defenders to open, and promising on his royal
word life and forgiveness to every soldier who
laid down his arms. This message was not without its effect. Presently, amid the shouts and
cheers of the Buffaloes, the bridge was dropped
across the fosse, and the gates upon the further
side were flung open.

Taking due precautions against treachery,
we marched on into the town. All along the
roadways stood dejected warriors, their heads
drooping, and their shields and spears at their
feet, who, as Ignosi passed, saluted him as king.

On we marched, straight to Twala's kraal. When we reached the great space, where a day or two previously we had seen the review and the witch hunt, we found it deserted. No, not quite deserted, for there, on the further side, in front of his hut, sat Twala himself, with but one attendant—Gagool.

It was a melancholy sight to see him seated, his battle-axe and shield by his side, his chin upon his mailed breast, with but one old crone for companion, and notwithstanding his cruelties and misdeeds, a pang of compassion shot through me as I looked upon Twala thus " fallen from his high estate." Not a soldier of all his armies, not a courtier out of the hundreds who had cringed round him, not even a solitary wife, remained to share his fate or halve the bitterness of his fall. Poor savage ! he was learning the lesson which Fate teaches to most of us who live long enough, that the eyes of mankind are blind to the discredited, and that he who is defenceless and fallen finds few friends and little mercy. Nor, indeed, in this case did he deserve any.

Filing through the kraal gate, we marched across the open space to where the ex-king sat. When within about fifty yards of him the regiment was halted, and accompanied only by a small guard we advanced towards him, Gagool reviling us bitterly as we came. As we drew near, Twala, for the first time, lifted his plumed head, and fixed his one eye, which seemed to flash with suppressed fury almost as brightly as the great diamond bound round his forehead, upon his successful rival—Ignosi.

" Hail, O king ! " he said, with bitter mockery ;

" thou who hast eaten of my bread, and now by the aid of the white men's magic hast seduced my regiments and defeated mine army, hail! What fate hast thou for me, O king ? "

" The fate thou gavest to my father, whose throne thou hast sat on these many years ! " was the stern answer.

" It is good. I will show thee how to die, that thou mayest remember it against thine own time. See, the sun sinks in blood," and he pointed with his battle-axe towards the setting orb ; " it is well that my sun should go down with it. And now, O king ! I am ready to die, but I crave the boon of the Kukuana royal House* to die fighting. Thou canst not refuse it, or even those cowards who fled to-day will hold thee shamed."

" It is granted. Choose—with whom wilt thou fight ? Myself I cannot fight with thee, for the king fights not except in war."

Twala's sombre eye ran up and down our ranks, and I felt, as for a moment it rested on myself, that the position had developed a new horror. What if he chose to begin by fighting *me ?* What chance should I have against a desperate savage six feet five high, and broad in proportion ? I might as well commit suicide at once. Hastily I made up my mind to decline the combat, even if I were hooted out of Kukuana-land as a consequence. It is, I think, better

---

* It is a law amongst the Kukuanas that no man of the royal blood can be put to death unless by his own consent, which is, however, never refused. He is allowed to choose a succession of antagonists, to be approved by the king, with whom he fights, till one of them kills him.—A Q.

to be hooted than to be quartered with a battle-axe.

Presently Twala spoke.

" Incubu, what sayest thou, shall we end what we began to-day, or shall I call thee coward, white—even to the liver ? "

" Nay," interposed Ignosi hastily ; " thou shalt not fight with Incubu."

" Not if he is afraid," said Twala.

Unfortunately Sir Henry understood this remark, and the blood flamed up into his cheeks.

" I will fight him," he said ; " he shall see if I am afraid."

" For Heaven's sake," I entreated, " don't risk your life against that of a desperate man. Anybody who saw you to-day will know that you are not a coward."

" I will fight him," was the sullen answer. " No living man shall call me a coward. I am ready now ! " and he stepped forward and lifted his axe.

I wrung my hands over this absurd piece of Quixotism ; but if he was determined on fighting, of course I could not stop him.

" Fight not, my white brother," said Ignosi, laying his hand affectionately on Sir Henry's arm ; " thou hast fought enough, and if aught befell thee at his hands it would cut my heart in twain."

" I will fight, Ignosi," was Sir Henry's answer.

" It is well, Incubu ; thou art a brave man. It will be a good fight. Behold, Twala, the Elephant is ready for thee."

The ex-king laughed savagely, and stepping forward faced Curtis. For a moment they stood thus, and the light of the sinking sun caught their stalwart frames and clothed them both in fire. They were a well-matched pair.

Then they began to circle round each other, their battle-axes raised.

Suddenly Sir Henry sprang forward and struck a fearful blow at Twala, who stepped to one side. So heavy was the stroke that the striker half overbalanced himself, a circumstance of which his antagonist took a prompt advantage. Circling his massive battle-axe round his head, he brought it down with tremendous force. My heart jumped into my mouth; I thought that the affair was already finished. But no; with a quick upward movement of the left arm Sir Henry interposed his shield between himself and the axe, with the result that its outer edge was shorn away, the axe falling on his left shoulder, but not heavily enough to do any serious damage. In another moment Sir Henry got in a second blow, which was also received by Twala upon his shield. Then followed blow upon blow, that were, in turn, either received upon the shields or avoided. The excitement grew intense; the regiment which was watching the encounter forgot its discipline, and, drawing near, shouted and groaned at every stroke. Just at this time, too, Good, who had been laid upon the ground by me, recovered from his faint, and, sitting up, perceived what was going on. In an instant he was up, and catching hold of my arm, hopped about from place to place on one leg, dragging me after him, and yelling encouragements to Sir Henry—

" Go it, old fellow ! " he hallooed. " That was a good one ! Give it him amidships," and so on.

Presently Sir Henry, having caught a fresh stroke upon his shield, hit out with all his force. The blow cut through Twala's shield and through the tough chain armour behind it, gashing him in the shoulder. With a yell of pain and fury Twala returned the blow with interest, and, such was his strength, shore right through the rhinoceros' horn handle of his antagonist's battle-axe, strengthened as it was with bands of steel, wounding Curtis in the face.

A cry of dismay rose from the Buffaloes as our hero's broad axe-head fell to the ground; and Twala, again raising his weapon, flew at him with a shout. I shut my eyes. When I opened them again it was to see Sir Henry's shield lying on the ground, and Sir Henry himself with his great arms twined round Twala's middle. To and fro they swung, hugging each other like bears, straining with all their mighty muscles for dear life, and dearer honour. With a supreme effort Twala swung the Englishman clean off his feet, and down they came together, rolling over and over on the lime paving, Twala striking out at Curtis's head with the battle-axe, and Sir Henry trying to drive the *tolla* he had drawn from his belt through Twala's armour.

It was a mighty struggle, and an awful thing to see.

" Get his axe ! " yelled Good ; and perhaps our champion heard him.

At any rate, dropping the *tolla*, he snatched at the axe, which was fastened to Twala's wrist by a strip of buffalo hide, and still rolling over and over, they fought for it like wild cats, drawing their breath in heavy gasps. Suddenly the hide string burst, and then, with a great effort, Sir

Henry freed himself, the weapon remaining in his hand. Another second and he was upon his feet, the red blood streaming from the wound in his face, and so was Twala. Drawing the heavy *tolla* from his belt, he reeled straight at Curtis and struck him upon the breast. The stab came home true and strong, but whoever it was who made that chain armour, he understood his art, for it withstood the steel. Again Twala struck out with a savage yell, and again the sharp knife rebounded, and Sir Henry went staggering back. Once more Twala came on, and as he came our great Englishman gathered himself together, and swinging the big axe round his head, hit at him with all his force. There was a shriek of excitement from a thousand throats, and, behold! Twala's head seemed to spring from his shoulders; then it fell and came rolling and bounding along the ground towards Ignosi, stopping just at his feet. For a second the corpse stood upright; then with a dull crash it came to the earth, and the gold torque from its neck rolled away across the pavement. As it did so Sir Henry, overpowered by faintness and loss of blood, fell heavily across the body of the dead king.

In a second he was lifted up, and eager hands were pouring water on his face. Another minute, and the grey eyes opened wide.

He was not dead.

Then I, just as the sun sank, stepping to where Twala's head lay in the dust, unloosed the diamond from the dead brows, and handed it to Ignosi.

" Take it," I said, " lawful king of the Kukuanas —king by birth and victory."

Ignosi bound the diadem upon his brows.

Then advancing, he placed his foot upon the broad chest of his headless foe and broke out into a chant, or rather a pæan of triumph, so beautiful, and yet so utterly savage, that I despair of being able to give an adequate idea of it. Once I heard a scholar with a fine voice read aloud from the Greek poet Homer, and I remember that the sound of the rolling lines seemed to make my blood stand still. Ignosi's chant, uttered as it was in a language as beautiful and sonorous as the old Greek, produced exactly the same effect on me, although I was exhausted with toil and many emotions.

" *Now,*" he began, " *now is our rebellion swallowed up in victory, and our evil-doing is justified by strength.*

" *In the morning the oppressors arose and shook themselves ; they bound on their plumes and made them ready to war.*

" *They rose up and grasped their spears : the soldiers called to the captains, ' Come, lead us '— and the captains cried to the king, ' Direct thou the battle.'*

" *They arose in their pride, twenty thousand men, and yet a twenty thousand.*

" *Their plumes covered the earth as the plumes of a bird cover her nest ; they shook their spears and shouted, yea, they hurled their spears into the sunlight ; they lusted for the battle and were glad.*

" *They came up against me ; their strong ones ran swiftly to slay me ; they cried, ' Ha! ha! he is as one already dead.'*

" *Then breathed I on them, and my breath was as the breath of a storm, and lo! they were not.*

" *My lightnings pierced them ; I licked up their strength with the lightning of my spears ; I shook them to the earth with the thunder of my shouting.*

" *They broke—they scattered—they were gone as the mists of the morning.*

" *They are food for the crows and the foxes, and the place of battle is fat with their blood.*

" *Where are the mighty ones who rose up in the morning ?*

" *Where are the proud ones who tossed their plumes and cried, ' He is as one already dead ' ?*

" *They bow their heads, but not in sleep ; they are stretched out, but not in sleep.*

" *They are forgotten ; they have gone into the blackness, and will not return ; yea, others shall lead away their wives, and their children shall remember them no more.*

" *And I—I ! the king—like an eagle I have found my eyrie.*

" *Behold ! far have I wandered in the night time, yet have I returned to my young at the daybreak.*

" *Creep ye under the shadow of my wings, O people, and I will comfort you, and ye shall not be dismayed.*

" *Now is the good time, the time of spoil.*

" *Mine are the cattle in the valleys, mine also are the virgins in the kraals.*

" *The winter is overpast, the summer is come.*

" *Now shall Evil cover up her face, and Mercy and Joy shall dwell in the land.*

" *Rejoice, rejoice, my people !*

" *Let all the world rejoice in that the tyranny is trodden down, in that I am the king.*"

Ignosi ceased, and out of the gathering gloom came back the deep reply—

" *Thou art the king !* "

Thus was my prophecy to the herald fulfilled, and within the forty-eight hours Twala's headless corpse was stiffening at Twala's gate.

CHAPTER XV

GOOD FALLS SICK

AFTER the fight was ended, Sir Henry and Good were carried into Twala's hut, where I joined them. They were both utterly exhausted by exertion and loss of blood, and, indeed, my own condition was little better. I am very wiry, and can stand more fatigue than most men, probably on account of my light weight and long training ; but that night I was fairly done up, and, as is always the case with me when exhausted, that old wound which the lion gave me began to pain me. Also my head was aching violently from the blow I had received in the morning, when I was knocked senseless. Altogether, a more miserable trio than we were that evening it would have been difficult to discover ; and our only comfort lay in the reflection that we were exceedingly fortunate to be there to feel miserable, instead of being stretched dead upon the plain, as so many thousands of brave men were that night, who had risen well and strong in the morning.

Somehow, with the assistance of the beautiful Foulata, who, since we had been the means of saving her life, had constituted herself our handmaiden, and especially Good's, we managed to get off the chain shirts, which had certainly saved the lives of two of us that day. As I expected, we found that the flesh underneath was terribly contused, for though the steel links had kept the weapons from entering, they had not prevented them from bruising. Both Sir Henry and Good were a mass of contusions, and I was by no means free. As a remedy Foulata brought us some pounded green leaves, with an aromatic odour, which, when applied as a plaster, gave us considerable relief.

But though the bruises were painful, they did not give us such anxiety as Sir Henry's and Good's wounds. Good had a hole right through the fleshy part of his " beautiful white leg," from which he had lost a great deal of blood ; and Sir Henry, with other hurts, had a deep cut over the jaw, inflicted by Twala's battle-axe. Luckily Good is a very decent surgeon, and so soon as his small box of medicines was forthcoming, having thoroughly cleansed the wounds, he managed to stitch up first Sir Henry's and then his own pretty satisfactorily, considering the imperfect light given by the primitive Kukuana lamp in the hut. Afterwards he plentifully smeared the injured places with some antiseptic ointment, of which there was a pot in the little box, and we covered them with the remains of a pocket-handkerchief which we possessed.

Meanwhile Foulata had prepared us some strong broth, for we were too weary to eat. This we swallowed, and then threw ourselves down on the piles of magnificent karrosses, or fur rugs, which were scattered about the dead king's great hut. By a very strange instance of the irony of fate, it was on Twala's own couch, and wrapped in Twala's own particular karross, that Sir

Henry, the man who had slain him, slept that night.

I say slept; but after that day's work sleep was indeed difficult. To begin with, in very truth the air was full

> " Of farewells to the dying
> And mournings for the dead.[1]

From every direction came the sound of the wailing of women whose husbands, sons, and brothers had perished in the fight. No wonder that they wailed, for over twelve thousand men, or nearly a fifth of the Kukuana army, had been destroyed in that awful struggle. It was heart-rending to lie and listen to their cries for those who would never return; and it made me understand the full horror of the work done that day to further man's ambition. Towards midnight, however, the ceaseless crying of the women grew less frequent, till at length the silence was only broken at intervals of a few minutes by a long piercing howl that came from a hut in our immediate rear, which, as I afterwards discovered, proceeded from Gagool " keening " over the dead king Twala.

After that I got a little fitful sleep, only to wake from time to time with a start, thinking that I was once more an actor in the terrible events of the last twenty-four hours. Now I seemed to see that warrior whom my hand had sent to his last account charging at me on the mountain-top; now I was once more in that glorious ring of Greys, which made its immortal stand against all Twala's regiments upon the little mound; and now again I saw Twala's plumed and gory head roll past my feet with gnashing teeth and glaring eye.

At last, somehow or other, the night passed
away ; but when dawn broke I found that my
companions had slept no better than myself.
Good, indeed, was in a high fever, and very soon
afterwards began to grow light-headed, and also,
to my alarm, to spit blood, the result, no doubt,
of some internal injury, inflicted by the desperate
efforts made by the Kukuana warrior on the
previous day to force his big spear through the
chain armour. Sir Henry, however, seemed
pretty fresh, notwithstanding his wound on the
face, which made eating difficult and laughter an
impossibility, though he was so sore and stiff
that he could scarcely stir.

About eight o'clock we had a visit from Infadoos, who appeared but little the worse—tough
old warrior that he was—for his exertions in the
battle, although he informed us that he had been
up all night. He was delighted to see us, but
much grieved at Good's condition, and shook our
hands cordially. I noticed, however, that he
addressed Sir Henry with a kind of reverence, as
though he were something more than man ; and,
indeed, as we afterwards found out, the great
Englishman was looked on throughout Kukuanaland as a supernatural being. No man, the
soldiers said, could have fought as he fought,
or, at the end of a day of such toil and bloodshed,
could have slain Twala, who, in addition to being
the king, was supposed to be the strongest warrior
in the country, in single combat, shearing through
his bull-neck at a stroke. Indeed, that stroke
became proverbial in Kukuanaland, and any
extraordinary blow or feat of strength was henceforth known as " Incubu's blow."

Infadoos told us also that all Twala's regiments

had submitted to Ignosi, and that like submissions were beginning to arrive from chiefs in the outlying country. Twala's death at the hands of Sir Henry had put an end to all further chance of disturbance; for Scragga had been his only son, and there was no rival claimant to the throne left alive.

I remarked that Ignosi had swum to power through blood. The old chief shrugged his shoulders. " Yes," he answered; " but the Kukuana people can only be kept cool by letting their blood flow sometimes. Many were killed, indeed, but the women were left, and others would soon grow up to take the places of the fallen. After this the land would be quiet for a while."

Afterwards, in the course of the morning we had a short visit from Ignosi, on whose brows the royal diadem was now bound. As I contemplated him advancing with kingly dignity, an obsequious guard following his steps, I could not help recalling to my mind the tall Zulu who had presented himself to us at Durban some few months back, asking to be taken into our service, and reflecting on the strange revolutions of the wheel of fortune.

" Hail, O king ! " I said, rising.

" Yes, Macumazahn. King at last, by the might of your three right hands," was the ready answer.

All was, he said, going on well ; and he hoped to arrange a great feast in two weeks' time in order to show himself to the people.

I asked him what he had settled to do with Gagool.

" She is the evil genius of the land," he answered, " and I shall kill her, and all the witch-doctors with her ! She has lived so long that none can remember when she was not old, and she it is who has always trained the witch-hunters, and made the land wicked in the sight of the heavens above."

"Yet she knows much," I replied; "it is easier to destroy knowledge, Ignosi, than to gather it."

"That is so," he said thoughtfully. "She, and she only, knows the secret of the 'Three Witches,' yonder, whither the great road runs, where the kings are buried, and the Silent Ones sit."

"Yes, and the diamonds are. Forget not thy promise, Ignosi; thou must lead us to the mines, even, if thou hast to spare Gagool alive to show the way."

"I will not forget, Macumazahn, and I will think on what thou sayest."

After Ignosi's visit I went to see Good, and found him quite delirious. The fever set up by his wound seemed to have taken a firm hold of his system, and to be complicated with an internal injury. For four or five days his condition was most critical; indeed, I believe firmly that had it not been for Foulata's indefatigable nursing he must have died.

Women are women, all the world over, whatever their colour. Yet somehow it seemed curious to watch this dusky beauty bending night and day over the fevered man's couch and performing all the merciful errands of a sick-room swiftly, gently, and with as fine an instinct as that of a trained hospital nurse. For the first night or two I tried to help her, and so did Sir Henry as soon as his stiffness allowed him to move, but Foulata bore our interference with impatience, and finally insisted upon our leaving him to her, saying that our movements made him restless, which I think was true. Day and night she watched him and tended him, giving him his only medicine, a native cooling drink made of milk, in which was infused juice from the bulb of a species of tulip, and keeping the flies from settling on him. I can see the whole picture now as it appeared night after night by the light of our primitive lamp ; Good tossing to and fro, his features emaciated, his eyes shining large and luminous, and jabbering nonsense by the yard ; and seated on the ground by his side, her back resting against the wall of the hut, the soft-eyed, shapely Kukuana beauty, her face, weary as it was, animated by a look of infinite compassion—or was it something more than compassion ?

For two days we thought that he must die, and crept about with heavy hearts.

Only Foulata would not believe it.

" He will live," she said.

For three hundred yards or more around Twala's chief hut, where the sufferer lay, there was silence ; for by the king's order all who lived in the habitations behind it, except Sir Henry and myself, had been removed, lest any noise should come to the sick man's ears. One night, it was the fifth of Good's illness, as was my habit, I went across to see how he was getting on before turning in for a few hours.

I entered the hut carefully. The lamp placed upon the floor showed the figure of Good, tossing no more, but lying quite still.

So it had come at last ! In the bitterness of my heart I gave something like a sob.

" Hush—h—h ! " came from the patch of dark shadow behind Good's head.

Then, creeping closer, I saw that he was not dead, but sleeping soundly, with Foulata's taper fingers clasped tightly in his poor white hand. The crisis had passed, and he would live. He slept like that for eighteen hours ; and I scarcely like to say it, for fear I should not be believed, but during the entire period did this devoted girl sit by him, fearing that if she moved and drew away her hand it would wake him. What she must have suffered from cramp and weariness, to say nothing of want of food, nobody will ever know ; but it is the fact that, when at last he woke, she had to be carried away—her limbs were so stiff that she could not move them.

After the turn had once been taken, Good's recovery was rapid and complete. It was not till he was nearly well that Sir Henry told him of all he owed to Foulata ; and when he came to the story of how she sat by his side for eighteen hours, fearing lest by moving she should wake him, the honest sailor's eyes filled with tears. He turned and went straight to the hut where Foulata was preparing the mid-day meal, for we were back in our old quarters now, taking me with him to interpret in case he could not make his meaning clear to her, though I am bound to say that she understood him marvellously as a rule, considering how extremely limited was his foreign vocabulary.

" Tell her," said Good, " that I owe her my life, and that I will never forget her kindness."

I interpreted, and under her dark skin she actually seemed to blush.

Turning to him with one of those swift and graceful motions that in her always reminded me

of the flight of a wild bird, Foulata answered
softly, glancing at him with her large brown eyes—

" Nay, my lord ; my lord forgets ! Did he not
save *my* life, and am I not my lord's handmaiden ? "

It will be observed that the young lady appeared
entirely to have forgotten the share which Sir
Henry and myself had taken in her preservation
from Twala's clutches. But that is the way of
women ! I remember my dear wife was just the
same. Well, I retired from that little interview
sad at heart. I did not like Miss Foulata's soft
glances, for I knew the fatal amorous propensities
of sailors in general, and of Good in particular.

There are two things in the world, as I have
found it, which cannot be prevented ; you cannot
keep a Zulu from fighting, or a sailor from falling
in love upon the slightest provocation !

It was a few days after this last occurrence that
Ignosi held his great " indaba," or council, and
was formally recognized as king by the "indunas,"
or head men, of Kukuanaland. The spectacle
was a most imposing one, including as it did a
grand review of troops. On this day the remaining fragments of the Greys were formally paraded,
and in the face of the army thanked for their
splendid conduct in the great battle. To each
man the king made a large present of cattle,
promoting them one and all to the rank of officers
in the new corps of Greys which was in process
of formation. An order was also promulgated
throughout the length and breadth of Kukuanaland that, whilst we honoured the country by our
presence, we three were to be greeted with the
royal salute, and to be treated with the same
ceremony and respect that was by custom

accorded to the king. Also the power of life and death was publicly conferred upon us. Ignosi, too, in the presence of his people, reaffirmed the promises which he had made, to the effect that no man's blood should be shed without trial, and that witch-hunting should cease in the land.

When the ceremony was over we waited upon Ignosi, and informed him that we were now anxious to investigate the mystery of the mines to which Solomon's Road ran, asking him if he had discovered anything about them.

" My friends," he answered, " I have discovered this. It is there that the three great figures sit, who here are called the ' Silent Ones,' and to whom Twala would have offered the girl Foulata as a sacrifice. It is there, too, in a great cave deep in the mountain, that the kings of the land are buried ; there ye shall find Twala's body, sitting with those who went before him. There, also, is a deep pit, which, at some time, long-dead men dug out, mayhap for the stones ye speak of, such as I have heard men in Natal tell of at Kimberley. There, too, in the Place of Death is a secret chamber, known to none but the king and Gagool. But Twala who knew it, is dead, and I know it not, nor know I what is in it. Yet there is a legend in the land that once, many generations gone, a white man crossed the mountains, and was led by a woman to the secret chamber, and shown the wealth hidden in it. But before he could take it, she betrayed him, and he was driven by the king of that day back to the mountains, and since then no man has entered the place."

" The story is surely true, Ignosi, for on the mountains we found the white man," I said.

"Yes, we found him. And now I have promised you that if ye can come to that chamber, and the stones are there——"

"The gem upon thy forehead proves that they are there," I put in, pointing to the great diamond I had taken from Twala's dead brows.

"Mayhap; if they are there," he said, "ye shall have as many as ye can take hence—if indeed ye would leave me, my brothers."

"First we must find the chamber," said I.

"There is but one who can show it to thee—Gagool."

"And if she will not?"

"Then she must die," said Ignosi sternly. "I have saved her alive but for this. Stay, she shall choose," and calling to a messenger he ordered Gagool to be brought before him.

In a few minutes she came, hurried along by two guards, whom she was cursing as she walked.

"Leave her," said the king to the guards.

So soon as their support was withdrawn, the withered old bundle—for she looked more like a bundle than anything else, out of which her two bright and wicked eyes gleamed like those of a snake—sank in a heap on to the floor.

"What will ye with me, Ignosi?" she piped. "Ye dare not touch me. If ye touch me I will slay you as ye sit. Beware of my magic."

"Thy magic could not save Twala, old she-wolf, and it cannot hurt me," was the answer. "Listen; I will this of thee, that thou reveal to us the chamber where are the shining stones."

"Ha! ha!" she piped, "none know its secret but I, and I will never tell thee. The white devils shall go hence empty-handed."

"Thou shalt tell me. I will make thee tell me."

"How, O king? Thou art great, but can thy power wring the truth from a woman?"

"It is difficult, yet will I do it."

"How, O king?"

"Nay, thus; if thou tellest not thou shalt slowly die."

"Die!" she shrieked, in terror and fury; "ye dare not touch me—man, ye know not who I am. How old think ye am I? I knew your fathers, and your fathers' fathers' fathers. When the country was young I was here; when the country grows old I shall still be here. I cannot die unless I be killed by chance, for none dare slay me."

"Yet will I slay thee. See, Gagool, mother of evil, thou art so old that thou canst no longer love thy life. What can life be to such a hag as thou, who hast no shape, nor form, nor hair, nor teeth—hast naught, save wickedness and evil eyes? It will be mercy to make an end of thee, Gagool."

"Thou fool," shrieked the old fiend, "thou accursed fool, deemest thou that life is sweet only to the young? It is not so, and naught thou knowest of the heart of man to think it. To the young, indeed, death is sometimes welcome, for the young can feel. They love and suffer, and it wrings them to see their beloved pass to the land of shadows. But the old feel not, they love not, and, *ha! ha!* they laugh to see another go out into the dark; *ha! ha!* they laugh to see the evil that is done under the sun. All they love is life, the warm, warm sun, and the sweet, sweet air. They are afraid of the cold, afraid of the cold and the dark, *ha! ha! ha!*" and the old hag writhed in ghastly merriment on the ground.

"Cease thine evil talk and answer me," said Ignosi angrily. "Wilt thou show the place where the stones are, or wilt thou not ? If thou wilt not thou diest, even now," and he seized a spear and held it over her.

"I will not show it ; thou darest not kill me, darest not ! He who slays me will be accursed for ever."

Slowly Ignosi brought down the spear till it pricked the prostrate heap of rags.

With a wild yell Gagool sprang to her feet, then fell again and rolled upon the floor.

"Nay, I will show it. Only let me live, let me sit in the sun and have a bit of meat to suck, and I will show thee."

"It is well. I thought that I should find a way to reason with thee. To-morrow shalt thou go with Infadoos and my white brothers to the place, and beware how thou failest, for if thou showest it not, then thou shalt slowly die. I have spoken."

"I will not fail, Ignosi. I always keep my word—*ha! ha! ha!* Once before a woman showed the chamber to a white man, and, behold ! evil befell him," and here her wicked eyes glinted. "Her name was Gagool also. Perchance I was that woman."

"Thou liest," I said, "that was ten generations gone."

"Mayhap, mayhap ; when one lives long one forgets. Perhaps it was my mother's mother who told me, surely her name was Gagool also. But mark, ye will find in the place where the bright playthings are a bag of hide full of stones. The man filled that bag, but he never took it away. Evil befell him, I say, evil befell him ! Perhaps it was my mother's mother who told me. It will be a merry journey—we can see the bodies of those who died in the battle as we go. Their eyes will be gone by now, and their ribs will be hollow. *Ha! ha! ha!"*

CHAPTER XVI

THE PLACE OF DEATH

IT was already dark on the third day after the scene described in the previous chapter when we camped in some huts at the foot of the " Three Witches," as the triangle of mountains were called to which Solomon's Great Road ran. Our party consisted of our three selves and Foulata, who waited on us—especially on Good—Infadoos, Gagool, who was borne along in a litter, inside which she could be heard muttering and cursing all day long, and a party of guards and attendants. The mountains, or rather the three peaks of the mountain, for the mass was evidently the result of a solitary upheaval, were, as I have said, in the form of a triangle, of which the base was towards us, one peak being on our right, one on our left, and one straight in front of us. Never shall I forget the sight afforded by those three towering peaks in the early sunlight of the following morning. High, high above us, up into the blue air, soared their twisted snow-wreaths. Beneath the snow-line the peaks were purple with heaths, and so were the wild moors that ran up the slopes towards them. Straight before us the white ribbon of Solomon's Great Road stretched away uphill to the foot of the centre peak, about five miles from us, and there stopped. It was its terminus.

I had better leave the feelings of intense excitement with which we set out on our march that morning to the imagination of those who read this history. At last we were drawing near to the wonderful mines that had been the cause of the miserable death of the old Portuguese Dom three centuries ago, of my poor friend, his ill-starred descendant, and also, as we feared, of George Curtis, Sir Henry's brother. Were we destined, after all that we have gone through, to fare any better? Evil befell them, as that old fiend Gagool said; would it also befall us? Somehow, as we were marching up that last stretch of beautiful road, I could not help feeling a little superstitious about the matter, and so I think did Good and Sir Henry.

For an hour and a half or more we tramped on up the heather-fringed way, going so fast in our excitement that the bearers of Gagool's hammock could scarcely keep pace with us, and its occupant piped out to us to stop.

" Walk more slowly, white men," she said, projecting her hideous shrivelled countenance between the grass curtains, and fixing her gleaming eyes upon us; " why will ye run to meet the evil that shall befall you, ye seekers after treasure ? " and she laughed that horrible laugh which always sent a cold shiver down my back, and for a while quite took the enthusiasm out of us.

However, on we went, till we saw before us, and between ourselves and the peak, a vast circular hole with sloping sides, three hundred feet or more in depth, and quite half a mile round.

" Can't you guess what this is ? " I said to Sir

Henry and Good, who were staring in astonishment at the awful pit before us.

They shook their heads.

" Then it is clear that you have never seen the diamond diggings at Kimberley. You may depend on it that this is Solomon's Diamond Mine. Look there," I said, pointing to the strata of stiff blue clay which were yet to be seen among the grass and bushes that clothed the sides of the pit, " the formation is the same. I'll be bound that if we went down there we should find ' pipes ' of soapy brecciated rock. Look, too," and I pointed to a series of worn flat slabs of stone that were placed on a gentle slope below the level of a watercourse which in some past age had been cut out of the solid rock ; " if those are not tables once used to wash the ' stuff,' I'm a Dutchman."

At the edge of this vast hole, which was none other than the pit marked on the old Dom's map, the Great Road branched into two and circumvented it. In many places, by the way, this surrounding road was built entirely of blocks of stone, apparently with the object of supporting the edges of the pit and preventing falls of reef. Along this path we pressed, driven by curiosity to see what the three towering objects were which we could discern from the hither side of the great gulf. As we drew nearer we perceived that they were Colossi of some sort or another, and rightly conjectured that before us sat the three " Silent Ones " that are held in such awe by the Kukuana people. But it was not until we were quite close to them that we recognized the full majesty of these " Silent Ones."

There. upon huge pedestals of dark rock,

sculptured with rude emblems of the Phallic worship, separated from each other by a distance of twenty paces, and looking down the road which crossed some sixty miles of plain to Loo, were three colossal seated forms—two male and one female—each measuring about eighteen feet from the crown of its head to the pedestal.

The female form, which was nude, was of great though severe beauty, but unfortunately the features had been injured by centuries of exposure to the weather. Rising from either side of her head were the points of a crescent. The two male Colossi, on the contrary, were draped, and presented a terrifying cast of features, especially the one to our right, which had the face of a devil. That to our left was serene in countenance, but the calm upon it was dreadful. It was the calm of that inhuman cruelty, Sir Henry remarked, which the ancients attributed to beings potent for good, who could yet watch the sufferings of humanity, if not with rejoicing, at least without sorrow. These three statues form a most awe-inspiring trinity, as they sit there in their solitude, and gaze out across the plain for ever.

Contemplating these " Silent Ones," as the Kukuanas call them, an intense curiosity again seized us to know whose were the hands which had shaped them, who it was that had dug the pit and made the road. Whilst I was gazing and wondering, suddenly it occurred to me— being familiar with the Old Testament—that Solomon went astray after strange gods, the names of three of whom I remembered—" Ashtoreth, the goddess of the Zidonians, Chemosh, the god of the Moabites, and Milcom, the god of the children of Ammon "—and I suggested to my

companions that the figures before us might
represent these false and exploded divinities.

" Hum," said Sir Henry, who is a scholar,
having taken a high degree in classics at college,
" there may be something in that ; Ashtoreth
of the Hebrews was the Astarte of the Phœnicians,
who were the great traders of Solomon's time.
Astarte, who afterwards became the Aphrodite
of the Greeks, was represented with horns like
the half-moon, and there on the brow of the female
figure are distinct horns. Perhaps these Colossi
were designed by some Phœnician official who
managed the mines. Who can say ? "*

Before we had finished examining these extraordinary relics of remote antiquity, Infadoos came
up, and having saluted the " Silent Ones " by
lifting his spear, asked us if we intended entering
the " Place of Death " at once, or if we would
wait till after we had taken food at mid-day.
If we were ready to go at once, Gagool had
announced her willingness to guide us. As it
was not later than eleven o'clock—driven to it
by a burning curiosity—we announced our
intention of proceeding instantly, and I suggested
that, in case we should be detained in the cave,
we should take some food with us. Accordingly
Gagool's litter was brought up, and that lady
herself assisted out of it. Meanwhile Foulata,
at my request, stored some " biltong," or dried
game-flesh, together with a couple of gourds of

---

* Compare Milton, " Paradise Lost," Book 1. :—

> " With these in troop
> Came Ashtoreth, whom the Phœnicians called
> Astarté, Queen of Heaven, with crescent horns;
> To whose bright image nightly by the moon
> Sidonian virgins paid their vows and songs."

water, in a reed basket. Straight in front of us, at a distance of some fifty paces from the backs of the Colossi, rose a sheer wall of rock, eighty feet or more in height, that gradually sloped upwards till it formed the base of the lofty snow-wreathed peak, which soared into the air three thousand feet above us. As soon as she was clear of her hammock Gagool cast one evil grin upon us, and then, leaning on a stick, hobbled off towards the face of this wall. We followed her till we came to a narrow portal solidly arched that looked like the opening of a gallery of a mine.

Here Gagool was waiting for us, still with that evil grin upon her horrid face.

" Now, white men from the Stars," she piped ; " great warriors, Incubu, Bougwan, and Macumazahn the wise, are ye ready ? Behold, I am here to do the bidding of my lord the king, and to show you the store of bright stones. *Ha! ha! ha!* "

" We are ready," I said.

" Good ! good ! Make strong your hearts to bear what ye shall see. Comest thou too, Infadoos, thou who didst betray thy master ? "

Infadoos frowned as he answered—

" Nay, I come not ; it is not for me to enter there. But thou, Gagool, curb thy tongue, and beware how thou dealest with my lords. At thy hands will I require them, and if a hair of them be hurt, Gagool, be'st thou fifty times a witch, thou shalt die. Hearest thou ? "

" I hear, Infadoos ; I know thee, thou didst ever love big words ; when thou wast a babe I remember thou didst threaten thine own mother. That was but the other day. But fear not, fear not, I live only to do the bidding of the king. I have done the bidding of many kings, Infadoos, till in the end they did mine. *Ha! ha!* I go to look upon their faces once more, and Twala's also! Come on, come on, here is the lamp," and she drew a large gourd full of oil, and fitted with a rush wick, from under her fur cloak.

" Art thou coming, Foulata? " asked Good in his villainous kitchen Kukuana, in which he had been improving himself under that young lady's tuition.

" I fear, my lord," the girl answered timidly.

" Then give me the basket."

" Nay, my lord, whither thou goest there will I go also."

" The deuce you will! " thought I to myself; " that may be rather awkward if ever we get out of this."

Without further ado Gagool plunged into the passage, which was wide enough to admit of two walking abreast, and quite dark. We followed the sound of her voice as she piped to us to come on, in some fear and trembling, which was not allayed by the flutter of a sudden rush of wings.

" Hullo! what's that? " halloed Good; " somebody hit me in the face."

" Bats," said I; " on you go."

When, so far as we could judge, we had gone some fifty paces, we perceived that the passage was growing faintly light. Another minute, and we were in perhaps the most wonderful place that the eyes of living man have beheld.

Let the reader picture to himself the hall of the vastest cathedral he ever stood in, windowless indeed, but dimly lighted from above, presumably by shafts connected with the outer air and driven in the roof, which arched away a hundred feet above our heads, and he will get some idea of the size of the enormous cave in which we found ourselves, with the difference that this cathedral designed by nature was loftier and wider than any built by man. But its stupendous size was the least of the wonders of the place, for running in rows adown its length were gigantic pillars of what looked like ice, but were, in reality, huge stalactites. It is impossible for me to convey any idea of the overpowering beauty and grandeur of these pillars of white spar, some of which were not less than twenty feet in diameter at the base, and sprang up in lofty and yet delicate beauty sheer to the distant roof. Others again were in process of formation. On the rock floor there was in these cases what looked, Sir Henry said, exactly like a broken column in an old Grecian temple, whilst high above, depending from the roof, the point of a huge icicle could be dimly seen.

Even as we gazed we could hear the process going on, for presently with a tiny splash a drop of water would fall from the far-off icicle on to the column below. On some columns the drops only fell once in two or three minutes, and in these cases it would be an interesting calculation to discover how long, at that rate of dripping, it would take to form a pillar, say eighty feet high by ten in diameter. That the process, in at least one instance, was incalculably slow, the following example will suffice to show. Cut on one of these pillars we discovered the rude likeness of a mummy, by the head of which sat what appeared to be the figure of an Egyptian god, doubtless the handiwork of some old-world labourer in the mine. This work of art was

executed at the natural height at which an idle
fellow, be he Phœnician workman or British
cad, is in the habit of trying to immortalize
himself at the expense of nature's masterpieces,
namely, about five feet from the ground. Yet
at the time that we saw it, which *must* have been
nearly three thousand years after the date of
the execution of the carving, the column was only
eight feet high, and was still in process of formation, which gives a rate of growth of a foot to
a thousand years, or an inch and a fraction to a
century. This we knew because, as we were
standing by it, we heard a drop of water fall.

Sometimes the stalagmites took strange forms,
presumably where the dropping of the water had
not always been on the same spot. Thus, one
huge mass, which must have weighed a hundred
tons or so, was in the shape of a pulpit, beautifully
fretted over outside with a design that looked
like lace. Others resembled strange beasts, and
on the sides of the cave were fan-like ivory
tracings, such as the frost leaves upon a pane.

Out of the vast main aisle there opened here
and there smaller caves, exactly, Sir Henry said,
as chapels open out of great cathedrals. Some
were large, but one or two—and this is a wonderful
instance of how nature carries out her handiwork by the same unvarying laws, utterly
irrespective of size—were tiny. One little nook,
for instance, was no larger than an unusually
big doll's house, and yet it might have been a
model of the whole place, for the water dropped,
tiny icicles hung, and spar columns were forming
in just the same way.

We had not, however, enough time to examine
this beautiful cavern so thoroughly as we should

have liked to do, for unfortunately Gagool seemed
to be indifferent to stalactites, and only anxious
to get her business over. This annoyed me the
more, as I was particularly anxious to discover,
if possible, by what system the light was admitted
into the cave, and whether it was by the hand
of man or by that of nature that this was done,
also if the place had been used in any way in
ancient times, as seemed probable. However, we
consoled ourselves with the idea that we would
investigate it thoroughly on our return, and
followed on after our uncanny guide.

On she led us, straight to the top of the vast
and silent cave, where we found another doorway,
not arched as the first was, but square at the
top, something like the doorways of Egyptian
temples.

"Are ye prepared to enter the Place of Death,
White Men?" asked Gagool, evidently with a
view to making us feel uncomfortable.

"Lead on, Macduff," said Good solemnly,
trying to look as though he was not at all alarmed,
as indeed we all did except Foulata, who caught
Good by the arm for protection.

"This is getting rather ghastly," said Sir
Henry, peeping into the dark doorway. "Come
on, Quatermain—*seniores priores*. Don't keep
the old lady waiting!" and he politely made
way for me to lead the van, for which inwardly I
did not bless him.

Tap, tap, went old Gagool's stick down the
passage, as she trotted along, chuckling hideously;
and still overcome by some unaccountable pre-
sentiment of evil, I hung back.

"Come, get on, old fellow," said Good, " or
we shall lose our fair guide."

Thus adjured, I started down the passage, and
after about twenty paces found myself in a gloomy
apartment some forty feet long, by thirty broad,
and thirty high, which in some past age evidently
had been hollowed, by hand labour, out of the
mountain.   This apartment was not nearly so well
lighted as the vast stalactite ante-cave, and at
the first glance all I could discern was a massive
stone table running down its length, with a colossal
white figure at its head, and life-sized white
figures all round it.   Next I discovered a brown
thing, seated on the table in the centre, and in
another moment my eyes grew accustomed to
the light, and I saw what all these things were,
and was tailing out of the place as hard as my
legs would carry me.

I am not a nervous man in a general way, and
very little troubled with superstitions, of which
I have lived to see the folly ; but I am free to own
that this sight quite upset me, and had it not
been that Sir Henry caught me by the collar
and held me, I do honestly believe that in another
five minutes I should have been outside the
stalactite cave, and that a promise of all the
diamonds in Kimberley would not have induced
me to enter it again.   But he held me tight, so
I stopped because I could not help myself.   Next
second, however, *his* eyes became focused to
the light, and he let go of me, and began to mop
the perspiration off his forehead.   As for Good, he
swore feebly, while Foulata threw her arms round
his neck and shrieked.

Only Gagool chuckled loud and long.

It *was* a ghastly sight.   There at the end of
the long stone table, holding in his skeleton
fingers a great white spear, sat *Death* himself,

shaped in the form of a colossal human skeleton, fifteen feet or more in height. High above his head he held the spear, as though in the act to strike; one bony hand rested on the stone table before him, in the position a man assumes on rising from his seat, whilst his frame was bent forward so that the vertebræ of the neck and the grinning, gleaming skull projected towards us, and fixed its hollow eye-places upon us, the jaws a little open, as though it were about to speak.

"Great heavens!" said I faintly, at last, "what can it be?"

"And what are *those things?*" asked Good, pointing to the white company round the table.

"And what on earth is *that thing?*" said Sir Henry, pointing to the brown creature seated on the table.

"*Hee! hee! hee!*" laughed Gagool. "To those who enter the Hall of the Dead, evil comes. *Hee! hee! hee! ha! ha!*"

"Come, Incubu, brave in battle, come and see him thou slewest;" and the old creature caught Curtis's coat in her skinny fingers, and led him away towards the table. We followed.

Presently she stopped and pointed at the brown object seated on the table. Sir Henry looked, and started back with an exclamation; and no wonder, for there, quite naked, seated on the table, the head which Curtis's battle-axe had shorn from the body resting on its knees, was the gaunt corpse of Twala, the last king of the Kukuanas. Yes, there, the head perched upon the knees, it sat in all its ugliness, the vertebræ projecting a full inch above the level of the shrunken flesh of the neck, for all the world

like a black double of Hamilton Tighe.* Over
the surface of the corpse there was gathered
a thin glassy film, that made its appearance yet
more appalling, for which we were, at the moment,
quite unable to account, till presently we observed
that from the roof of the chamber the water
fell steadily, *drip! drip! drip!* on to the neck
of the corpse, whence it ran down over the
entire surface, and finally escaped into the rock
through a tiny hole in the table. Then I guessed
what the film was—*Twala's body was being
transformed into a stalactite.*

A look at the white forms seated on the stone
bench which ran round that ghastly board
confirmed this view. They were human bodies
indeed, or rather they had been human ; now they
were *stalactites*. This was the way in which
the Kukuana people had from time immemorial
preserved their royal dead. They petrified them.
What the exact system might be, if there was any,
beyond the placing of them for a long period
of years under the drip, I never discovered, but
there they sat, iced over and preserved for ever
by the silicious fluid.

Anything more awe-inspiring than the spectacle
of this long line of departed royalties (there were
twenty-seven of them, the last being Ignosi's
father), wrapped, each of them, in a shroud of
ice-like spar, through which the features could
be dimly made out and seated round that in-
hospitable board, with Death himself for a host,
it is impossible to imagine. That the practice
of thus preserving their kings must have been
an ancient one is evident from the number,

---

* " Now haste ye, my handmaidens, haste and see
    How he sits there and glowers with his head on his knee."

which, allowing for an average reign of fifteen years, supposing that every king who reigned was placed here—an improbable thing, as some are sure to have perished in battle far from home—would fix the date of its commencement at four and a quarter centuries back.

But the colossal Death, who sits at the head of the board, is far older than that, and, unless I am much mistaken, owes his origin to the same artist who designed the three Colossi. He is hewn out of a single stalactite, and, looked at as a work of art, is most admirably conceived and executed. Good, who understands anatomy, declared that, so far as he could see, the anatomical design of the skeleton is perfect down to the smallest bones.

My own idea is, that this terrific object was a freak of fancy on the part of some old-world sculptor, and that its presence had suggested to the Kukuanas the idea of placing their royal dead under its awful presidency. Or perhaps it was set there to frighten away any marauders who might have designs upon the treasure chamber beyond. I cannot say. All I can do is to describe it as it is, and the reader must form his own conclusion.

Such, at any rate, was the White Death and such were the White Dead!

CHAPTER XVII

SOLOMON'S TREASURE CHAMBER

WHILE we were engaged in recovering from our fright, and in examining the grisly wonders of the Place of Death, Gagool had been differently occupied. Somehow or other—for she was marvellously active when she chose—she had scrambled on to the great table, and made her way to where our departed friend Twala was placed, under the drip, to see, suggested Good, how he was " pickling," or for some dark purpose of her own. Then she hobbled back, stopping now and again to address a remark, the tenor of which I could not catch, to one or other of the shrouded forms, just as you or I might greet an old acquaintance. Having gone through this mysterious and hòrrible ceremony, she squatted herself down on the table immediately under the White Death, and began, so far as I could make out, to offer up prayers to it. The spectacle of this wicked old creature pouring out supplications, evil ones, no doubt, to the arch enemy of mankind, was so uncanny that it caused us to hasten our inspection.

" Now, Gagool," said I, in a low voice—somehow one did not dare to speak above a whisper in that place—" lead us to the chamber."

The old creature promptly scrambled down off the table.

"My lords are not afraid?" she said, leering up into my face.

"Lead on."

"Good, my lords;" and she hobbled round to the back of the great Death. "Here is the chamber; let my lords light the lamp, and enter," and she placed the gourd full of oil upon the floor, and leaned herself against the side of the cave. I took out a match, of which we had still a few in a box, and lit a rush wick, and then looked for the doorway, but there was nothing before us except the solid rock. Gagool grinned. "The way is there, my lords. *Ha! ha! ha!*"

"Do not jest with us," I said sternly.

"I jest not, my lords. See!" and she pointed at the rock.

As she did so, on holding up the lamp we perceived that a mass of stone was rising slowly from the floor and vanishing into the rock above, where doubtless there is a cavity prepared to receive it. The mass was of the width of a good-sized door, about ten feet high and not less than five feet thick. It must have weighed at least twenty or thirty tons, and was clearly moved upon some simple balance principle of counter-weights, probably the same as that by which the opening and shutting of an ordinary modern window is arranged. How the principle was set in motion, of course none of us saw; Gagool was careful to avoid this; but I have little doubt that there was some very simple lever, which was moved ever so little by pressure on a secret spot, thereby throwing additional weight on to the hidden counterbalances, and

causing the whole mass to be lifted from the
ground.

Very slowly and gently the great stone raised
itself, until at last it had vanished altogether,
and a dark hole presented itself to us in the place
which the door had filled.

Our excitement was so intense, as we saw the
way to Solomon's treasure chamber thrown open
at last, that I for one began to tremble and shake.
Would it prove a hoax after all, I wondered, or
was old Da Silvestra right ? and were there
vast hoards of wealth stored in that dark place,
hoards which would make us the richest men in
the whole world ? We should know in a minute
or two.

" Enter, white men from the Stars," said
Gagool, advancing into the doorway ; " but
first hear your servant, Gagool the old. The
bright stones that ye will see were dug out of the
pit over which the Silent Ones are set, and
stored here, I know not by whom. But once has
this place been entered since the time that those
who stored the stones departed in haste, leaving
them behind. The report of the treasure went
down indeed among the people who lived in the
country from age to age, but none knew where the
chamber was, nor the secret of the door. But it
happened that a white man reached this country
from over the mountains—perchance he too
came ' from the Stars '—and was well received
by the king of that day. He it is who sits yonder,"
and she pointed to the fifth king at the table of
the Dead. " And it came to pass that he and
a woman of the country who was with him
journeyed to this place, and that by chance the
woman learnt the secret of the door—a thousand

years might ye search, but ye should never find it. Then the white man entered with the woman and found the stones, and filled with stones the skin of a small goat, which the woman had with her to hold food. And as he was going from the chamber he took up one more stone, a large one, and held it in his hand." Here she paused.

" Well," I asked, breathless with interest as we all were, " what happened to Da Silvestra ? "

The old hag started at the mention of the name.

" How knowest thou the dead man's name ? " she asked sharply ; and then, without waiting for an answer, went on—

" None know what happened ; but it came about that the white man was frightened, for he flung down the goat-skin, with the stones, and fled out with only the one stone in his hand, and that the king took, and it is the stone which thou, Macumazahn, didst take from Twala's brow."

" Have none entered here since ? " I asked, peering again down the dark passage.

" None, my lords. Only the secret of the door has been kept, and every king has opened it, though he has not entered. There is a saying, that those who enter there will die within a moon, even as the white man died in the cave upon the mountain, where ye found him, Macumazahn, and therefore the kings do not enter. *Ha ! ha !* mine are true words."

Our eyes met as she said it, and I turned sick and cold. How did the old hag know all these things ?

" Enter, my lords. If I speak truth, the goat-skin with the stones will lie upon the floor ; and if there is truth as to whether it is death to enter here, that will ye learn afterwards. *Ha ! ha ! ha !*"

and she hobbled through the doorway, bearing
the light with her ; but I confess that once
more I hesitated about following.

" Oh, confound it all ! " said Good ; " here
goes. I am not going to be frightened by that
old devil ; " and followed by Foulata, who,
however, evidently did not at all like the business,
for she was shivering with fear, he plunged into
the passage after Gagool—an example which we
quickly followed.

A few yards down the passage, in the narrow
way hewn out of the living rock, Gagool had
paused, and was waiting for us.

" See, my lords," she said, holding the light
before her, " those who stored the treasure here
fled in haste, and bethought them to guard against
any who should find the secret of the door, but
had not the time," and she pointed to large
square blocks of stone, which, to the height of
two courses (about two feet three), had been
placed across the passage with a view to walling
it up. Along the side of the passage were similar
blocks ready for use, and, most curious of all,
a heap of mortar and a couple of trowels, which
tools, so far as we had time to examine them,
appeared to be of a similar shape and make to
those used by workmen to this day.

Here Foulata, who had been in a state of great
fear and agitation throughout, said that she felt
faint and could go no farther, but would wait there.
Accordingly we set her down on the unfinished
wall, placing the basket of provisions by her side,
and left her to recover.

Following the passage for about fifteen paces
farther, we came suddenly to an elaborately
painted wooden door. It was standing wide open.

Whoever was last there had either not found the time, or had forgotten, to shut it.

Across the threshold of this door lay a skin bag, formed of a goat-skin, that appeared to be full of pebbles.

" *Hee ! hee !* white men," sniggered Gagool, as the light from the lamp fell upon it. " What did I tell you, that the white man who came here fled in haste, and dropped the woman's bag—behold it ! "

Good stooped down and lifted it. It was heavy and jingled.

" By Jove ! I belive it's full of diamonds," he said, in an awed whisper ; and, indeed, the idea of a small goat-skin full of diamonds is enough to awe anybody.

" Go on," said Henry impatiently. " Here, old lady, give me the lamp," and taking it from Gagool's hand, he stepped through the doorway and held it high above his head.

We pressed in after him, forgetful for the moment of the bag of diamonds, and found ourselves in Solomon's treasure chamber.

At first, all that the somewhat faint light given by the lamp revealed was a room hewn out of the living rock, and apparently not more than ten feet square. Next there came into sight, stored one on the other to the arch of the roof, a splendid collection of elephant-tusks. How many of them there were we did not know, for of course we could not see to what depth they went back, but there could not have been less than the ends of four or five hundred tusks of the first quality visible to our eyes. There, alone, was enough ivory before us to make a man wealthy for life. Perhaps, 1 thought, it was from this very store that Solomon drew the raw material for his " great throne of ivory," of which " there was not the like made in any kingdom."

On the opposite side of the chamber were about a score of wooden boxes, something like Martini-Henry ammunition boxes, only rather larger, and painted red.

" There are the diamonds," cried I; " bring the light."

Sir Henry did so, holding it close to the top box, of which the lid, rendered rotten by time even in that dry place, appeared to have been smashed in, probably by Da Silvestra himself. Pushing my hand through the hole in the lid I drew it out full, not of diamonds, but of gold pieces, of a shape that none of us had seen before, and with what looked like Hebrew characters stamped upon them.

" Ah ! " I said, replacing the coin, " we sha'n't go back empty-handed, anyhow. There must be a couple of thousand pieces in each box, and there are eighteen boxes. I suppose this was the money to pay the workmen and merchants."

" Well," put in Good, " I think that is the lot ; I don't see any diamonds, unless the old Portuguee put them all into his bag."

" Let my lords look yonder where it is darkest, if they would find the stones," said Gagool, interpreting our looks. " There my lords will find a nook, and three stone chests in the nook, two sealed and one open."

Before translating this to Sir Henry, who carried the light, I could not resist asking how she knew these things, if no one had entered the place since the white man, generations ago.

" Ah, Macumazahn, the watcher by night,"

was the mocking answer, " ye who live in the stars, do ye not know that some have eyes which can see through rock ? *Ha! ha! ha!*"

" Look in that corner, Curtis," I said, indicating the spot Gagool had pointed out.

" Hullo, you fellows," he cried, " here's a recess. Great heavens ! see here."

We hurried up to where he was standing in a nook, shaped something like a small bow window. Against the wall of this recess were placed three stone chests, each about two feet square. Two were fitted with stone lids, the lid of the third rested against the side of the chest, which was open.

" *See!*" he repeated hoarsely, holding a lamp over the open chest. We looked, and for a moment could make nothing out, on account of a silvery sheen that dazzled us. When our eyes grew used to it we saw that the chest was three parts full of uncut diamonds, most of them of considerable size. Stooping, I picked some up. Yes, there was no doubt of it, there was the unmistakable soapy feel about them.

I fairly gasped as I dropped them.

" We are the richest men in the whole world," I said. " Monte Cristo was a fool to us."

" We shall flood the market with diamonds," said Good.

" Got to get them there first," suggested Sir Henry.

We stood still with pale faces and stared at each other, the lantern in the middle and the glimmering gems below, as though we were conspirators about to commit a crime, instead of being, as we thought, the most fortunate men on earth.

" Hee! hee! hee!" cackled old Gagool behind us, as she flitted about like a vampire bat. "There are the bright stones ye love, white men, as many as ye will; take them, run them through your fingers, *eat* of them, hee! hee; *drink* of them, *ha! ha!*"

At that moment there was something so ridiculous to my mind in the idea of eating and drinking diamonds, that I began to laugh outrageously, an example which the others followed, without knowing why. There we stood and shrieked with laughter over the gems that were ours, which had been found for *us* thousands of years ago by the patient delvers in the great hole yonder, and stored for *us* by Solomon's long-dead overseer, whose name, perchance, was written in the characters stamped on the faded wax that yet adhered to the lids of the chests. Solomon never got them, nor David, nor Da Silvestra, nor anybody else. *We* had got them: there before us were millions of pounds' worth of diamonds, and thousands of pounds' worth of gold and ivory only waiting to be taken away.

Suddenly the fit passed off, and we stopped laughing.

"Open the other chests, white men," croaked Gagool, "there are surely more therein. Take your fill, white lords! *Ha! ha!* take your fill."

Thus adjured, we set to work to pull up the stone lids on the other two, first—not without a feeling of sacrilege—breaking the seals that fastened them.

Hoorah! they were full too, full to the brim; at least, the second one was; no wretched Da Silvestra had been filling goat-skins out of that. As for the third chest, it was only about a fourth full, but the stones were all picked ones ; none less than twenty carats, and some of them as large as pigeon-eggs. A good many of these bigger ones, however, we could see by holding them up to the light, were a little yellow, " off coloured," as they call it at Kimberley.

What we did *not* see, however, was the look of fearful malevolence that old Gagool favoured us with as she crept, crept like a snake, out of the treasure chamber and down the passage towards the door of solid rock.

* * * * *

Hark ! Cry upon cry comes ringing up the vaulted path. It is Foulata's voice !

" *Oh, Bougwan ! help ! help ! the stone falls !* "

" Leave go, girl ! Then— —"

" *Help ! help ! she has stabbed me !* "

By now we are running down the passage, and this is what the light from the lamp shows us. The door of rock is closing down slowly ; it is not three feet from the floor. Near it struggle Foulata and Gagool. The red blood of the former runs to her knee, but still the brave girl holds the old witch, who fights like a wild cat. Ah ! she is free ! Foulata falls, and Gagool throws herself on the ground, to twist like a snake through the crack of the closing stone. She is under—ah ! God ! too late ! too late ! The stone nips her, and she yells in agony. Down, down, it comes, all the thirty tons of it, slowly pressing her old body against the rock below. Shriek upon shriek, such as we never heard, then a long sickening *crunch*, and the door was shut just as, rushing down the passage, we hurled ourselves against it.

It was all done in four seconds.

Then we turned to Foulata. The poor girl was stabbed in the body, and I saw that she could not live long.

" Ah ! Bougwan, I die ! " gasped the beautiful creature. " She crept out—Gagool ; I did not see her, I was faint—and the door began to fall ; then she came back, and was looking up the path —I saw her come in through the slowly falling door, and caught her and held her, and she stabbed me, and I *die*, Bougwan ! "

" Poor girl ! poor girl ! " Good cried ; and then, as he could do nothing else, he fell to kissing her.

" Bougwan," she said, after a pause, " is Macumazahn there ? It grows so dark, I cannot see."

" Here I am, Foulata."

" Macumazahn, be my tongue for a moment, I pray thee, for Bougwan cannot understand me, and before I go into the darkness I would speak a word."

" Say on, Foulata, I will render it."

" Say to my lord, Bougwan, that—I love him, and that I am glad to die because I know that he cannot cumber his life with such as I am, for the sun may not mate with the darkness, nor the white with the black.

" Say that, since I saw him, at times I have felt as though there were a bird in my bosom, which would one day fly hence and sing elsewhere. Even now, though I cannot lift my hand, and my brain grows cold, I do not feel as though my heart were dying ; it is so full of love that it could live a thousand years, and yet be young. Say that if I live again, mayhap I shall see him

in the Stars, and that—I will search them all,
though perchance there I should still be black
and he would—still be white. Say—nay,
Macumazahn, say no more, save that I love—
Oh, hold me closer, Bougwan, I cannot feel thine
arms—*oh! oh!*"

"She is dead—she is dead!" exclaimed Good,
rising in grief, the tears running down his honest
face.

"You need not let that trouble you, old fellow,"
said Sir Henry.

"Eh!" said Good; "what do you mean?"

"I mean that you will soon be in a position
to join her. *Man, don't you see that we are buried
alive?*"

Until Sir Henry uttered these words I do not
think that the full horror of what had happened
had come home to us, pre-occupied as we were
with the sight of poor Foulata's end. But now
we understood. The ponderous mass of rock
had closed, probably for ever, for the only brain
which knew its secret was crushed to powder
beneath it. This was a door that none could hope
to force with anything short of dynamite in large
quantities. And we were the wrong side of it!

For a few minutes we stood horrified there
over the corpse of Foulata. All the manhood
seemed to have gone out of us. The first shock
of this idea of the slow and miserable end that
awaited us was overpowering. We saw it all
now; that fiend Gagool had planned this snare
for us from the first. It must have been just the
jest that her evil mind would have rejoiced in,
the idea of the three white men, whom, for some
reason of her own, she had always hated, slowly
perishing of thirst and hunger in the company

of the treasure they had coveted. Now I saw the point of that sneer of hers about eating and drinking the diamonds. Perhaps somebody had tried to serve the poor old Dom in the same way, when he abandoned the skin full of jewels.

" This will never do," said Sir Henry hoarsely ; " the lamp will soon go out. Let us see if we can't find the spring that works the rock."

We sprang forward with desperate energy, and, standing in a bloody ooze, began to feel up and down the door and the sides of the passage. But no knob or spring could we discover.

" Depend on it," I said, " it does not work from the inside ; if it did Gagool would not have risked trying to crawl underneath the stone. It was the knowledge of this that made her try to escape at all hazards, curse her."

" At all events," said Sir Henry with a hard little laugh, " retribution was swift ; hers was almost as awful an end as ours is likely to be. We can do nothing with the door ; let us go back to the treasure room."

We turned and went, and as we passed it I perceived by the unfinished wall across the passage the basket of food which poor Foulata had carried. I took it up, and brought it with me to the accursed treasure chamber that was to be our grave. Then we returned and reverently bore in Foulata's corpse, laying it on the floor by the boxes of coins.

Next we seated ourselves, leaning our backs against the three stone chests of priceless treasure.

" Let us divide the food," said Sir Henry, " so as to make it last as long as possible." Accordingly we did so. It would, we reckoned, make four infinitesimally small meals for each of us, enough, say, to support life for a couple of days. Besides the " biltong," or dried game-flesh, there were two gourds of water, each holding about a quart.

" Now," said Sir Henry grimly, " let us eat and drink, for to-morrow we die."

We each ate a small portion of the " biltong," and drank a sip of water. Needless to say, we had but little appetite, though we were sadly in need of food, and felt better after swallowing it. Then we got up and made a systematic examination of the walls of our prison-house, in the faint hope of finding some means of exit, sounding them and the floor carefully.

There was none. It was not probable that there would be any to a treasure chamber.

The lamp began to burn dim. The fat was nearly exhausted.

" Quatermain," said Sir Henry, " what is the time—your watch goes ? "

I drew it out and looked at it. It was six o'clock ; we had entered the cave at eleven.

" Infadoos will miss us," I suggested. " If we do not return to-night he will search for us in the morning, Curtis."

" He may search in vain. He does not know the secret of the door nor even where it is. No living person knew it yesterday, except Gagool. To-day no one knows it. Even if he found the door he could not break it down. All the Kukuana army could not break through five feet of living rock. My friends, I see nothing for it but to bow ourselves to the will of the Almighty. The search for treasure has brought many to a bad end ; we shall go to swell their number."

The lamp grew dimmer yet.

Presently it flared up and showed the whole scene in strong relief, the great mass of white tusks, the boxes of gold, the corpse of poor Foulata stretched before them, the goat-skin full of treasure, the dim glimmer of the diamonds, and the wild, wan faces of us three white men seated there awaiting death by starvation.

Then the flame sank and expired.

CHAPTER XVIII

WE ABANDON HOPE

I CAN give no adequate description of the horrors of the night which followed. Mercifully they were to some extent mitigated by sleep, for even in such a position as ours wearied nature will sometimes assert itself. But I, at any rate found it impossible to sleep much. Putting aside the terrifying thought of our impending doom—for the bravest man on earth might well quail from such a fate as awaited us, and I never made any pretensions to be brave—the *silence* itself was too great to allow of it. Reader, you may have lain awake at night and thought the silence oppressive, but I say with confidence that you can have no idea what a vivid, tangible thing is perfect silence. On the surface of the earth there is always some sound or motion, and though it may in itself be imperceptible, yet it deadens the sharp edge of absolute silence. But here there was none. We were buried in the bowels of a huge snow-clad peak. Thousands of feet above us the fresh air rushed over the white snow, but no sound of it reached us. We were separated by a long tunnel and five feet of rock even from the awful chamber of the Dead ; and the dead make no noise. The crashing of all the artillery of earth and heaven could not have come to our ears in our living tomb. We were cut off from every echo of the world—we were as men already dead.

And then the irony of the situation forced itself upon me. There around us lay treasures enough to pay off a moderate national debt, or to build a fleet of ironclads, and yet we would have bartered them all gladly for the faintest chance of escape. Soon, doubtless, we should be rejoiced to exchange them for a bit of food or a cup of water, and, after that, even for the privilege of a speedy close to our sufferings. Truly wealth, which men spend their lives in acquiring, is a valueless thing at the last.

And so the night wore on.

"Good," said Sir Henry's voice at last, and it sounded awful in the intense stillness, "how many matches have you in the box?"

"Eight, Curtis."

"Strike one and let us see the time."

He did so, and in contrast to the dense darkness the flame nearly blinded us. It was five o'clock by my watch. The beautiful dawn was now blushing on the snow-wreaths far over our heads, and the breeze would be stirring the night mists in the hollows.

"We had better eat something and keep up our strength," I suggested.

"What is the good of eating?" answered Good; "the sooner we die and get it over the better."

"While there is life there is hope," said Sir Henry.

Accordingly we ate and sipped some water, and another period of time passed. Then Sir Henry suggested that it might be well to get as near the door as possible and halloa, on the faint chance of somebody catching a sound outside. Accordingly Good, who, from long practice at sea, has a fine piercing note, groped his way down the passage and began. I must say that he made a most diabolical noise. I never heard such yells ; but it might have been a mosquito buzzing for all the effect they produced.

After a while he gave it up and came back very thirsty, and had to drink some water. Then we stopped yelling, as it encroached on the supply of water.

So we sat down once more against the chests of useless diamonds in that dreadful inaction, which was one of the hardest circumstances of our fate ; and I am bound to say that, for my part, I gave way in despair. Laying my head against Sir Henry's broad shoulder I burst into tears ; and I think that I heard Good gulping away on the other side, and swearing hoarsely at himself for doing so.

Ah, how good and brave that great man was ! Had we been two frightened children, and he our nurse, he could not have treated us more tenderly. Forgetting his own share of miseries, he did all he could to soothe our broken nerves, telling stories of men who had been in somewhat similar circumstances, and miraculously escaped ; and when these failed to cheer us, pointing out how, after all, it was only anticipating an end which must come to us all, that it would soon be over, and that death from exhaustion was a merciful one (which is not true). Then, in a diffident sort of way, as once before I had heard him do, he suggested that we should throw ourselves on the mercy of a higher power, which for my part I did with great vigour.

His is a beautiful character, very quiet, but very strong.

And so somehow the day went as the night had gone, if, indeed, one can use these terms where all was densest night, and when I lit a match to see the time it was seven o'clock.

Once more we ate and drank, and as we did so an idea occurred to me.

"How is it," said I, "that the air in this place keeps fresh? It is thick and heavy, but it is perfectly fresh."

"Great heavens!" said Good, starting up, "I never thought of that. It can't come through the stone door, for it's air-tight, if ever a door was. It must come from somewhere. If there were no current of air in the place we should have been stifled when we first came in. Let us have a look."

It was wonderful what a change this mere spark of hope wrought in us. In a moment we were all three groping about on our hands and knees, feeling for the slightest indication of a draught. Presently my ardour received a check. I put my hand on something cold. It was poor Foulata's dead face.

For an hour or more we went on feeling about, till at last Sir Henry and I gave it up in despair, having been considerably hurt by constantly knocking our heads against tusks, chests, and the sides of the chamber. But Good still persevered, saying, with an approach to cheerfulness, that it was better than doing nothing.

" I say, you fellows," he said presently, in a constrained sort of voice, " come here."

Needless to say we scrambled towards him quickly enough.

" Quatermain, put your hand here where mine is. Now, do you feel anything ? "

" I *think* I feel air coming up."

" Now listen." He rose and stamped upon the place, and a flame of hope shot up in our hearts. *It rang hollow.*

With trembling hands I lit a match. I had only three left, and we saw that we were in the angle of the far corner of the chamber, a fact that accounted for our not having noticed the hollow sound of the place during our former exhaustive examination. As the match burnt we scrutinized the spot. There was a join in the solid rock floor, and, great heavens ! there, let in level with the rock, was a stone ring. We said no word, we were too excited, and our hearts beat too wildly with hope to allow us to speak. Good had a knife, at the back of which was one of those hooks that are made to extract stones from horses' hoofs. He opened it, and scratched round the ring with it. Finally he worked it under, and levered away gently for fear of breaking the hook. The ring began to move. Being of stone it had not got set fast in all the centuries it had lain there, as would have been the case had it been of iron. Presently it was upright. Then he thrust his hands into it and tugged with all his force, but nothing budged.

" Let me try," I said impatiently, for the situation of the stone, right in the angle of the corner, was such that it was impossible for two to pull at once. I took hold and strained away, but no results.

Then Sir Henry tried and failed.

Taking the hook again, Good scratched all round the crack where we felt the air coming up.

" Now, Curtis," he said, " tackle on, and put your back into it ; you are as strong as two. Stop," and he took off a stout black silk handkerchief, which, true to his habits of neatness, he still wore, and ran it through the ring. " Quatermain, get Curtis round the middle and pull for dear life when I give the word. *Now.*"

Sir Henry put out all his enormous strength, and Good and I did the same, with such power as nature had given us.

" Heave ! heave ! it's giving," gasped Sir Henry ; and I heard the muscles of his great back cracking. Suddenly there was a grating sound, then a rush of air, and we were all on our backs on the floor with a heavy flag-stone upon the top of us. Sir Henry's strength had done it, and never did muscular power stand a man in better stead.

" Light a match, Quatermain," he said, so soon as we had picked ourselves up and got our breath ; " carefully, now."

I did so, and there before us, Heaven be praised ! was the *first step of a stone stair.*

" Now what is to be done ? " asked Good.

" Follow the stair, of course, and trust to Providence."

" Stop ! " said Sir Henry ; " Quatermain, get the bit of biltong and the water that are left ; we may want them."

I went, creeping back to our place by the chests for that purpose, and as I was coming away an

idea struck me. We had not thought much of
the diamonds for the last twenty-four hours or
so; indeed, the very idea of diamonds was
nauseous, seeing what they entailed upon us;
but, reflected I, I may as well pocket a few in
case we ever should get out of this ghastly hole.
So I just put my fist into the first chest and filled
all the available pockets of my old shooting
coat, topping up—this was a happy thought
—with a couple of handfuls of big ones out of
the third chest.

"I say, you fellows," I sang out, "won't you
take some diamonds with you? I've filled my
pockets."

"Oh! hang the diamonds!" said Sir Henry.
"I hope that I may never see another."

As for Good, he made no answer. He was,
I think, taking his last farewell of all that was
left of the poor girl who had loved him so well.
And curious as it may seem to you, my reader,
sitting at home at ease, and reflecting on the
vast, indeed the immeasurable, wealth which
we were thus abandoning, I can assure you that
if you had passed some twenty-eight hours with
next to nothing to eat and drink in that place,
you would not have cared to cumber yourself
with diamonds whilst plunging down into the
unknown bowels of the earth, in the wild hope
of escape from an agonizing death. If from
the habits of a lifetime, it had not become a sort
of second nature with me never to leave anything worth having behind if there was the
slightest chance of my being able to carry it
away, I am sure that I should not have bothered
to fill my pockets.

"Come on, Quatermain," said Sir Henry

who was already standing on the first step of
the stone stair. "Steady, I will go first."

"Mind where you put your feet, there may
be some awful hole underneath," I answered.

"Much more likely to be another room,"
said Sir Henry, while he descended slowly, counting the steps as he went.

When he got to "fifteen" he stopped.
"Here's the bottom," he said. "Thank good-
ness! I think it's a passage. Come on down."

Good went next, and I followed last, and on
reaching the bottom lit one of the two remaining
matches. By its light we could just see that
we were standing in a narrow tunnel, which
ran right and left at right angles to the staircase
we had descended. Before we could make out
any more, the match burnt my fingers and went
out. Then arose the delicate question of which
way to go. Of course, it was impossible to
know what the tunnel was, or where it ran to,
and yet to turn one way, might lead us to safety,
and the other to destruction. We were utterly
perplexed, till suddenly it struck Good that
when I had lit the match the draught of the
passage blew the flame to the left.

"Let us go against the draught," he said;
" air draws inwards, not outwards."

We took this suggestion, and feeling along the
wall with the hand, whilst trying the ground
before us at every step, we departed from that
accursed treasure chamber on our terrible quest
for life. If ever it should be entered again by
living man, which I do not think probable, he
will find tokens of our visit in the open chests
of jewels, the empty lamp, and the white bones
of poor Foulata.

When we had groped our way for about a
quarter of an hour along the passage, suddenly
it took a sharp turn, or else was bisected by
another, which we followed, only in course of
time to be led into a third. And so it went on
for some hours. We seemed to be in a stone
labyrinth which led nowhere. What all these
passages are, of course I cannot say, but we
thought that they must be the ancient workings
of a mine, of which the various shafts and adits
travelled hither and thither as the ore led them.
This is the only way in which we could account
for such a multitude of galleries.

At length we halted, thoroughly worn out
with fatigue and with that hope deferred which
maketh the heart sick, and ate up our poor
remaining piece of biltong and drank our last
sup of water, for our throats were like lime-
kilns. It seemed to us that we had escaped
death in the darkness of the chamber only to meet
him in the darkness of the tunnels. As we stood,
once more utterly depressed, I thought that
I caught a sound, to which I called the attention
of the others. It was very faint and very far
off, but it *was* a sound, a faint, murmuring sound,
for the others heard it too, and no words can
describe the blessedness of it after all those
hours of utter, awful stillness.

" By heaven ! it's running water," said Good.
" Come on."

Off we started again in the direction from which
the faint murmur seemed to come, groping our
way as before along the rocky walls. As we
went it became more and more audible, till at
last it seemed quite loud in the quiet. On,
yet on ; now we could distinctly make out the

unmistakable swirl of rushing water. And yet
how could there be running water in the bowels
of the earth ? Now we were quite near to it,
and Good, who was leading, swore that he could
smell it.

" Go gently, Good," said Sir Henry, " we
must be close." *Splash !* and a cry from Good.

He had fallen in.

" Good ! Good ! where are you ? " we shouted,
in terrified distress. To our intense relief an
answer came back in a choky voice.

" All right ; I've got hold of a rock. Strike
a light to show me where you are."

Hastily I lit the last remaining match. Its
faint gleam discovered to us a dark mass of
water running at our feet. How wide it was
we could not see, but there, some way out, was
the dark form of our companion hanging on to
a projecting rock.

" Stand clear to catch me," sung out Good.
" I must swim for it."

Then we heard a splash, and a great struggle.
Another minute and he had grabbed at and
caught Sir Henry's outstretched hand, and we
had pulled him up high and dry into the
tunnel.

" My word ! " he said, between his gasps,
" that was touch and go. If I hadn't caught that
rock, and known how to swim, I should have
been done. It runs like a mill-race, and I could
feel no bottom."

We dared not follow the banks of the subterranean river for fear lest we should fall into
it again in the darkness. So after Good had
rested a while, and we had drunk our fill of the
water, which was sweet and fresh, and washed

our faces, that needed it sadly, as well as we could, we started from the banks of this African Styx, and began to retrace our steps along the tunnel, Good dripping unpleasantly in front of us. At length we came to another gallery leading to our right.

" We may as well take it," said Sir Henry wearily ; " all roads are alike here ; we can only go on till we drop."

Slowly, for a long, long while, we stumbled, utterly exhausted, along this new tunnel, Sir Henry now leading the way.

Suddenly he stopped, and we bumped up against him.

" Look ! " he whispered, " is my brain going, or is that light ? "

We stared with all our eyes, and there, yes, there, far ahead of us, was a faint, glimmering spot, no larger than a cottage window pane. It was so faint, that I doubt if any eyes, except those which, like ours, had for days seen nothing but blackness, could have perceived it at all.

With a gasp of hope we pushed on. In five minutes there was no longer any doubt ; it *was* a patch of faint light. A minute more and a breath of real live air was fanning us. On we struggled. All at once the tunnel narrowed. Sir Henry went on his knees. Smaller yet it grew, till it was only the size of a large fox's earth—it was *earth* now, mind you ; the rock had ceased.

A squeeze, a struggle, and Sir Henry was out, and so was Good, and so was I, and there above us were the blessed stars, and in our nostrils was the sweet air. Then suddenly something gave, and we were all rolling over and over and over through grass and bushes and soft wet soil.

I caught at something and stopped. Sitting up I hallooed lustily. An answering shout came from just below, where Sir Henry's wild career had been stopped by some level ground. I scrambled to him, and found him unhurt, though breathless. Then we looked for Good. A little way off we discovered him also, jammed in a forked root. He was a good deal knocked about, but soon came to himself.

We sat down together there on the grass, and the revulsion of feeling was so great that really I think we cried for joy. We had escaped from that awful dungeon, which was so near to becoming our grave. Surely some merciful Power guided our footsteps to the jackal hole, for that is what it must have been, at the termination of the tunnel. And see, yonder on the mountains the dawn we had never thought to look upon again was blushing rosy red.

Presently the grey light stole down the slopes, and we saw that we were at the bottom, or rather, nearly at the bottom, of the vast pit in front of the entrance to the cave. Now we could make out the dim forms of the three Colossi who sat upon its verge. Doubtless those awful passages, along which we had wandered the livelong night, had been originally in some way connected with the great diamond mine. As for the subterranean river in the bowels of the mountain, Heaven only knows what it is, or whence it flows, or whither it goes. I, for one, have no anxiety to trace its course.

Lighter it grew, and lighter yet. We could see each other now, and such a spectacle as we presented I have never set eyes on before or since. Gaunt-cheeked, hollow-eyed wretches, smeared all over with dust and mud, bruised, bleeding, the long fear of imminent death yet written on our countenances, we were, indeed, a sight to frighten the daylight. And yet it is a solemn fact that Good's eye-glass was still fixed in Good's eye. I doubt whether he had ever taken it out at all. Neither the darkness, nor the plunge in the subterranean river, nor the roll down the slope, had been able to separate Good and his eye-glass.

Presently we rose, fearing that our limbs would stiffen if we stopped there longer, and commenced with slow and painful steps to struggle up the sloping sides of the great pit. For an hour or more we toiled steadfastly up the blue clay, dragging ourselves on by the help of the roots and grasses with which it was clothed.

At last it was done, and we stood by the great road, on the side of the pit opposite to the Colossi.

At the side of the road, a hundred yards off, a fire was burning in front of some huts, and round the fire were figures. We staggered towards them, supporting one another, and halting every few paces. Presently one of the figures rose, saw us and fell on to the ground, crying out for fear.

"Infadoos, Infadoos! it is we, thy friends."

He rose; he ran to us, staring wildly, and still shaking with fear.

"Oh, my lords, my lords, it is indeed you

come back from the dead !—come back from the dead ! "

And the old warrior flung himself down before us, and clasping Sir Henry's knees, he wept aloud for joy.

CHAPTER XIX

IGNOSI'S FAREWELL

TEN days from that eventful morning found us once more in our old quarters at Loo ; and, strange to say, but little the worse for our terrible experience, except that my stubbly hair came out of the treasure cave about three shades greyer than it went in, and that Good never was quite the same after Foulata's death, which seemed to move him very greatly. I am bound to say, looking at the thing from the point of view of an oldish man of the world, that I consider her removal was a fortunate occurrence, since, otherwise, complications would have been sure to ensue. The poor creature was no ordinary native girl, but a person of great, I had almost said stately, beauty, and of considerable refinement of mind. But no amount of beauty or refinement could have made an entanglement between Good and herself a desirable occurrence ; for, as she herself put it, " Can the sun mate with the darkness, or the white with the black ? "

I need hardly state that we never again penetrated into Solomon's treasure chamber. After we had recovered from our fatigues, a process which took us forty-eight hours, we descended into the great pit in the hope of finding the hole by which we had crept out of the mountain,

but with no success. To begin with, rain had
fallen, and obliterated our spoor ; and what
is more, the sides of the vast pit were full of
ant-bear and other holes. It was impossible to
say to which of these we owed our salvation.
Also, on the day before we started back to
Loo, we made a further examination of the
wonders of the stalactite cave, and, drawn by
a kind of restless feeling, even penetrated once
more into the Chamber of the Dead. Passing
beneath the spear of the White Death we gazed,
with sensations which it would be quite impossible
for me to describe, at the mass of rock that
had shut us off from escape, thinking the while
of the priceless treasures beyond, of the mysterious
old hag whose flattened fragments lay crushed
beneath it, and of the fair girl of whose tomb
it was the portal. I say gazed at the " rock,"
for, examine as we would, we could find no
traces of the join of the sliding door ; nor, indeed,
could we hit upon the secret, now utterly lost,
that worked it, though we tried for an hour or
more. It is certainly a marvellous bit of mechan-
ism, characteristic, in its massive and yet inscrut-
able simplicity, of the age which produced it ; and
I doubt if the world has such another to show.

At last we gave it up in disgust ; though, if
the mass had suddenly risen before our eyes, I
doubt if we should have screwed up courage
to step over Gagool's mangled remains, and once
more enter the treasure chamber, even in the
sure and certain hope of unlimited diamonds.
And yet I could have cried at the idea of leaving
all that treasure, the biggest treasure probably
that in the world's history has ever been accumulated in one spot. But there was no help

for it. Only dynamite could force its way through five feet of solid rock. And so we left it. Perhaps, in some remote unborn century, a more fortunate explorer may hit upon the " Open Sesame," and flood the world with gems. But, myself, I doubt it. Somehow, I seem to feel that the millions of pounds' worth of jewels that lie in the three stone coffers will never shine round the neck of an earthly beauty. They and Foulata's bones will keep cold company till the end of all things.

With a sigh of disappointment we made our way back, and next day started for Loo. And yet it was really very ungrateful of us to be disappointed ; for, as the reader will remember, by a lucky thought, I had taken the precaution to fill the pockets of my old shooting coat with gems before we left our prison house. A good many of these fell out in the course of our roll down the side of the pit, including most of the big ones, which I had crammed in on the top. But, comparatively speaking, an enormous quantity still remained, including eighteen large stones ranging from about one hundred to thirty carats in weight. My old shooting coat still held sufficient treasure to make us all, if not millionaires, at least exceedingly wealthy men, and yet to keep enough stones each to make the three finest sets of gems in Europe. So we had not done so badly.

On arriving at Loo we were most cordially received by Ignosi, whom we found well, and busily engaged in consolidating his power, and reorganizing the regiments which had suffered most in the great struggle with Twala.

He listened with intense interest to our wonderful story ; but when we told him of old Gagool's frightful end he grew thoughtful.

"Come hither," he called, to a very old Induna or councillor, who was sitting with others in a circle round the king, but out of ear-shot. The ancient man rose, approached, saluted, and seated himself.

"Thou art aged," said Ignosi.

"Ay, my lord the king! Thy father's father and I were born on the same day."

"Tell me, when thou wast little, didst thou know Gagaoola the witch doctress ? "

"Ay, my lord the king ! "

"How was she then—young, like thee ? "

"Not so, my lord the king! She was even as she is now and as she was in the days of my grandfather before me ; old and dried, very ugly, and full of wickedness."

"She is no more ; she is dead."

"So, O king! then is an ancient curse taken from the land."

"Go ! "

"*Koom !* I go, black Puppy, who tore out the old dog's throat. *Koom !* "

"Ye see, my brothers," said Ignosi, " this was a strange woman, and I rejoice that she is dead. She would have let you die in the dark place, and mayhap afterwards she had found a way to slay me, as she found a way to slay my father, and set up Twala, whom her heart loved, in his place. Now go on with the tale ; surely there never was its like ! "

After I had narrated all the story of our escape, as we had agreed between ourselves that I should, I took the opportunity to address Ignosi as to our departure from Kukuanaland.

" And now, Ignosi," I said, " the time has
come for us to bid thee farewell, and start to
see our own land once more. Behold, Ignosi,
thou camest with us a servant, and now we
leave thee a mighty king. If thou art grateful
to us, remember to do even as thou didst promise ;
to rule justly, to respect the law, and to put none
to death without a cause. So shalt thou prosper.
To-morrow, at break of day, Ignosi, thou wilt
give us an escort who shall lead us across the
mountains. Is it not so, O king ? "

Ignosi covered his face with his hands for a
while before answering.

" My heart is sore," he said at last ; " your
words split my heart in twain. What have I
done to you, Incubu, Macumazahn, and Bougwan,
that ye should leave me desolate ? Ye who
stood by me in rebellion and in battle, will ye
leave me in the day of peace and victory ?
What will ye—wives ? Choose from among the
maidens ! A place to live in ? Behold, the
land is yours as far as ye can see. The white
man's houses ? Ye shall teach my people how
to build them. Cattle for beef and milk ?
Every married man shall bring you an ox or
a cow. Wild game to hunt ? Does not the
elephant walk through my forests, and the
river-horse sleep in the reeds ? Would ye make
war ? My Impis wait your word. If there is
anything more which I can give, that will I
give you."

" Nay, Ignosi, we want none of these things,"
I answered ; " we would seek our own place."

" Now do I learn," said Ignosi bitterly, and
with flashing eyes, " that ye love the bright stones
more than me, your friend. Ye have the stones ;

now ye would go to Natal and across the moving
black water and sell them, and be rich, as it is
the desire of a white man's heart to be. Cursed
for your sake be the white stones, and cursed he
who seeks them. Death shall it be to him who
sets foot in the Place of Death to find them. I
have spoken. White men, ye can go."

I laid my hand upon his arm. "Ignosi," I
said, "tell us, when thou didst wander in Zululand, and among the white people in Natal,
did not thine heart turn to the land thy mother
told thee of, thy native land, where thou didst
see the light, and play when thou wast little,
the land where thy place was ? "

" It was even so, Macumazahn."

" In like manner, Ignosi, do our hearts turn
to our land and to our own place."

Then came a silence. When Ignosi broke it,
it was in a different voice.

" I do perceive that now as ever thy words
are wise and full of reason, Macumazahn ; that
which flies in the air loves not to run along the
ground ; the white man loves not to live on the
level of the black. Well, ye must go, and leave
my heart sore, because ye will be as dead to me,
since from where ye are no tidings can come
to me.

" But listen, and let all the white men know
my words. No other white man shall cross the
mountains, even if any man live to come so far.
I will see no traders with their guns and rum.
My people shall fight with the spear, and drink
water, like their forefathers before them. I will
have no praying-men to put a fear of death into
men's hearts, to stir them up against the law
of the king, and make a path for the white men

who follow to run on. If a white man comes to my gates I will send him back ; if a hundred come I will push them back ; if armies come, I will make war on them with all my strength, and they shall not prevail against me. None shall ever seek for the shining stones : no, not an army, for if they come I will send a regiment and fill up the pit, and break down the white columns in the caves and choke them with rocks, so that none can reach even to that door of which you speak, and whereof the way to move it is lost. But for you three, Incubu, Macumazahn, and Bougwan, the path is always open ; for behold ye are dearer to me than aught that breathes.

" And ye would go. Infadoos, my uncle, and my Induna, shall take you by the hand and guide you with a regiment. There is, as I have learned, another way across the mountains that he shall show you. Farewell, my brothers, brave white men. See me no more, for I have no heart to bear it. Behold, I make a decree, and it shall be published from the mountains to the mountains ; your names, Incubu, Macumazahn, and Bougwan, shall be ' hlonipa ' even as the names of dead kings, and he who speaks them shall die.* So shall your memory be preserved in the land for ever.

" Go now, ere my eyes rain tears like a woman's. At times as ye look back down the path of life,

* This extraordinary and negative way of showing intense respect is by no means unknown among African people, and the result is that if, as is usual, the name in question has a significance, the meaning must be expressed by an idiom or another word. In this way a memory is preserved for generations, or until the new word utterly supplants the old one.—A. Q.

or when ye are old and gather yourselves together
to crouch before the fire, because for you the
sun has no more heat, ye will think of how we
stood shoulder to shoulder in that great battle
which thy wise words planned, Macumazahn ;
of how thou wast the point of the horn that
galled Twala's flank, Bougwan ; whilst thou
stoodst in the ring of the Greys, Incubu, and
men went down before thine axe like corn before
a sickle ; ay, and of how thou didst break that
wild bull Twala's strength, and bring his pride
to dust. Fare ye well for ever, Incubu, Macumazahn, and Bougwan, my lords and my friends."

Ignosi rose and looked earnestly at us for a
few seconds. Then he threw the corner of his
karross over his head, so as to cover his face
from us.

We went in silence.

Next day at dawn we left Loo, escorted by our
old friend Infadoos, who was heart-broken at
our departure, and by the regiment of Buffaloes.
Early as was the hour, all the main street of the
town was lined with multitudes of people, who
gave us the royal salute as we passed at the
head of the regiment, while the women blessed
us for having rid the land of Twala, throwing
flowers before us as we went. It was really
very affecting, and not the sort of thing one is
accustomed to meet with from natives.

One ludicrous incident occurred, however,
which I rather welcomed, as it gave us something
to laugh at.

Just before we reached the confines of the town,
a pretty young girl, with some lovely lilies in
her hand, ran forward and presented them to

Good—somehow they all seemed to like Good; I think his eye-glass and solitary whisker gave him a fictitious value—and then said that she had a boon to ask.

" Speak on," he answered.

" Let my lord show his servant his beautiful white legs, that his servant may look on them, and remember them all her days, and tell of them to her children; his servant has travelled four days' journey to see them, for the fame of them has gone throughout the land."

" I'll be hanged if I do ! " exclaimed Good excitedly.

" Come, come, my dear fellow," said Sir Henry, " you can't refuse to oblige a lady."

" I won't," replied Good obstinately; " it is positively indecent."

However, in the end he consented to draw up his trousers to the knee, amidst notes of rapturous admiration from all the women present, especially the gratified young lady, and in this guise he had to walk till we got clear of the town.

Good's legs, I fear, will never be so greatly admired again. Of his melting teeth, and even of his " transparent eye," the Kukuanas wearied more or less, but of his legs never.

As we travelled, Infadoos told us that there was another pass over the mountains to the north of the one followed by Solomon's Great Road, or rather that there was a place where it is possible to climb down the wall of cliff which separates Kukuanaland from the desert, and is broken by the towering shapes of Sheba's Breasts. It appeared, too, that rather more than two years previously a party of Kukuana hunters had descended this path into the desert in search of ostriches, whose plumes are much prized among them for war head-dresses, and that in the course of their hunt they had been led far from the mountains and were much troubled by thirst. Seeing trees on the horizon, however, they walked towards them, and discovered a large and fertile oasis some miles in extent, and plentifully watered. It was by way of this oasis that Infadoos suggested that we should return, and the idea seemed to us a good one, for it appeared that we should thus escape the rigours of the mountain pass. Also some of the hunters were in attendance to guide us to the oasis, from which, they stated, they could perceive other fertile spots far away in the desert.*

Travelling easily, on the night of the fourth day's journey we found ourselves once more on the crest of the mountains that separate Kukuanaland from the desert, which rolled away in sandy billows at our feet, and about twenty-five miles to the north of Sheba's Breasts.

At dawn on the following day, we were led to the edge of a very precipitous chasm, by which we were to descend the precipice, and gain the plain two thousand and more feet below.

---

* It often puzzled all of us to understand how it was possible that Ignosi's mother, bearing the child with her, should have survived the dangers of her journey across the mountains and the desert, dangers which so nearly proved fatal to ourselves. It has since occurred to me, and I give the idea to the reader for what it is worth, that she must have taken this second route, and wandered out like Hagar into the wilderness. If she did so, there is no longer anything inexplicable about the story, since, as Ignosi himself related, she may well have been picked up by some ostrich hunters before she or the child was exhausted, and led by them to the oasis, and thence by stages to the fertile country, and so on by slow degrees southwards to Zululand.—A. Q.

Here we bade farewell to that true friend and
sturdy old warrior, Infadoos, who solemnly
wished all good upon us, and nearly wept with
grief. " Never, my lords," he said, " shall mine
old eyes see the like of you again. Ah! the
way that Incubu cut his men down in the battle!
Ah! for the sight of that stroke with which he
swept off my brother Twala's head! It was
beautiful—beautiful! I may never hope to
see such another, except perchance in happy
dreams."

We were very sorry to part from him ; indeed,
Good was so moved that he gave him as a sou-
venir—what do you think ?—an *eye-glass ;* afterwards we discovered that it was a spare one.
Infadoos was delighted, foreseeing that the
possession of such an article would increase his
prestige enormously, and after several vain
attempts he actually succeeded in screwing it
into his own eye. Anything more incongruous
than the old warrior looked with an eye-glass
I never saw. Eye-glasses do not go well with
leopard-skin cloaks and black ostrich plumes.

Then, after seeing that our guides were well
laden with water and provisions, and having
received a thundering farewell salute from the
Buffaloes, we wrung Infadoos by the hand, and
began our downward climb. A very arduous
business it proved to be, but somehow that
evening we found ourselves at the bottom without
accident.

" Do you know," said Sir Henry that night,
as we sat by our fire and gazed up at the beetling
cliffs above us, " I think that there are worse
places than Kukuanaland in the world, and that
I have known unhappier times than the last

month or two, though I have never spent such queer ones. Eh! you fellows?"

"I almost wish I were back," said Good, with a sigh.

As for myself, I reflected that all's well that ends well; but in the course of a long life of shaves, I never had such shaves as those which I had recently experienced. The thought of that battle still makes me feel cold all over, and as for our experience in the treasure chamber——!

Next morning we started on a toilsome trudge across the desert, having with us a good supply of water carried by our five guides, and camped that night in the open, marching again at dawn on the morrow.

By noon of the third day's journey we could see the trees of the oasis of which the guides spoke, and within an hour of sundown we were walking once more upon grass and listening to the sound of running water.

CHAPTER XX

FOUND

A ND now I come to perhaps the strangest adventure that happened to us in all this strange business, and one which shows how wonderfully things are brought about.

I was walking along quietly, some way in front of the other two, down the banks of the stream which runs from the oasis till it is swallowed up in the hungry desert sands, when suddenly I stopped and rubbed my eyes, as well I might. There, not twenty yards in front of me, placed in a charming situation, under the shade of a species of fig-tree, and facing to the stream, was a cosy hut, built more or less on the Kafir principle with grass and withes, but having a full-length door instead of a bee-hole.

"What the dickens," said I to myself, "can a hut be doing here?" Even as I said it the door of the hut opened, and there limped out of it a *white man* clothed in skins, and with an enormous black beard. I thought that I must have got a touch of the sun. It was impossible. No hunter ever came to such a place as this. Certainly no hunter would ever settle in it. I stared and stared, and so did the other man, and just at that juncture Sir Henry and Good walked up.

"Look here, you fellows," I said, "is that a white man, or am I mad?"

Sir Henry looked, and Good looked, and then all of a sudden the lame white man with a black beard uttered a great cry, and began hobbling towards us. When he was close he fell down in a sort of faint.

With a spring Sir Henry was by his side.

"Great Powers!" he cried, "*it is my brother George!*"

At the sound of the disturbance, another figure, also clad in skins, emerged from the hut, a gun in his hand, and ran towards us. On seeing me he too gave a cry.

"Macumazahn," he halloed, "don't you know me, Baas? I'm Jim the hunter. I lost the note you gave me to give to the Baas, and we have been here nearly two years." And the fellow fell at my feet, and rolled over and over, weeping for joy.

"You careless scoundrel!" I said; "you ought to be well hided."

Meanwhile the man with the black beard had recovered and risen, and he and Sir Henry were pump-handling away at each other, apparently without a word to say. But whatever they had quarrelled about in the past—I suspect it was a lady, though I never asked—it was evidently forgotten now.

"My dear old fellow," burst out Sir Henry at last, "I thought that you were dead. I have been over Solomon's Mountains to find you, and now I come across you perched in the desert, like an old *aasvögel*."*

"I tried to go over Solomon's Mountains nearly

* Vulture.

two years ago," was the answer, spoken in the
hesitating voice of a man who has had little recent
opportunity of using his tongue, " but when I
got here a boulder fell on my leg and crushed it,
and I have been able to go neither forward nor
back."

Then I came up. " How do you do, Mr.
Neville ? " I said ; " do you remember me ? "

" Why," he said, " isn't it Quatermain, eh,
and Good too ? Hold on a minute, you fellows,
I am getting dizzy again. It is all so very
strange, and, when a man has ceased to hope,
so very happy ! "

That evening, over the camp fire, George Curtis
told us his story, which, in its way, was almost
as eventful as our own, and, put shortly, amounted
to this. A little less than two years before,
he had started from Sitanda's Kraal, to try to
reach Suliman's Berg. As for the note I had
sent him by Jim, that worthy had lost it, and he
had never heard of it till to-day. But, acting
upon information he received from the natives,
he headed not for Sheba's Breasts, but for the
ladder-like descent of the mountains down which
we had just come, which is clearly a better route
than that marked out in old Dom Silvestra's
plan. In the desert he and Jim suffered great
hardships, but finally they reached this oasis,
where a terrible accident befell George Curtis.
On the day of their arrival he was sitting by the
stream, and Jim was extracting the honey from
the nest of a stingless bee which is to be found in
the desert, on the top of a bank immediately
above him. In so doing he loosened a great
boulder of rock, which fell upon George Curtis's
right leg, crushing it frightfully. From that day

he had been so lame that he found it impossible to go either forward or back, and had preferred to take the chances of dying on the oasis to the certainty of perishing in the desert.

As for food, however, they got on pretty well, for they had a good supply of ammunition, and the oasis was frequented, especially at night, by large quantities of game, which came thither for water. These they shot, or trapped in pitfalls, using the flesh for food, and, after their clothes wore out, the hides for clothing.

" And so," George Curtis ended, " we have lived for nearly two years, like a second Robinson Crusoe and his man Friday, hoping against hope that some natives might come here to help us away, but none have come. Only last night we settled that Jim should leave me, and try to reach Sitanda's Kraal to get assistance. He was to go to-morrow, but I had little hope of ever seeing him back again. And now *you*, of all people in the world, *you*, who as I fancied had long ago forgotten all about me, and were living comfortably in old England, turn up in a promiscuous way and find me where you least expected. It is the most wonderful thing that I ever heard of, and the most merciful too."

Then Sir Henry set to work and told him the main facts of our adventures, sitting till late into the night to do it.

" By Jove ! " he said, when I showed him some of the diamonds : " well, at least you have got something for your pains, besides my worthless self."

Sir Henry laughed. " They belong to Quatermain and Good. It was a part of the bargain that they should divide any spoils there might be."

This remark set me thinking, and having spoken to Good, I told Sir Henry that it was our joint wish that he should take a third portion of the diamonds, or, if he would not, that his share should be handed to his brother, who had suffered even more than ourselves on the chance of getting them. Finally we prevailed upon him to consent to this arrangement, but George Curtis did not know of it until some time afterwards.

* * * * *

And here, at this point, I think that I shall end my history. Our journey across the desert back to Sitanda's Kraal was most arduous, especially as we had to support George Curtis, whose right leg was very weak indeed, and continually threw out splinters of bone. But we did accomplish it somehow, and to give its details would only be to reproduce much of what happened to us on the former occasion.

Six months from the date of our re-arrival at Sitanda's, where we found our guns and other goods quite safe, though the old scoundrel in charge was much disgusted at our surviving to claim them, saw us all once more safe and sound at my little place on the Berea, near Durban, where I am now writing. Thence I bid farewell to all who have accompanied me throughout the strangest trip I ever made in the course of a long and varied experience.

P.S.—Just as I had written the last word, a Kafir came up my avenue of orange trees, carrying a letter in a cleft stick, which he had brought from the post. It turned out to be from Sir Henry, and as it speaks for itself I give it in full.

" *October 1st, 1884.*
" *Brayley Hall, Yorkshire.*

" *My dear Quatermain,*
　　" *I sent you a line a few mails back to say that the three of us, George, Good and myself, fetched up all right in England. We got off the boat at Southampton, and went up to town. You should have seen what a swell Good turned out the very next day, beautifully shaved, frock coat fitting like a glove, brand new eye-glass, etc., etc. I went and walked in the park with him, where I met some people I know, and at once told them the story of his ' beautiful white legs.'*

" *He is furious, especially as some ill-natured person has printed it in a society paper.*

" *To come to business, Good and I took the diamonds to Streeter's to be valued, as we arranged, and really I am afraid to tell you what they put them at, it seems so enormous. They say that of course it is more or less guesswork, as such stones have never to their knowledge been put on the market in anything like such quantities. It appears that (with the exception of one or two of the largest) they are of the finest water, and equal in every way to the best Brazilian stones. I asked them if they would buy them, but they said that it was beyond their power to do so, and recommended us to sell by degrees, for fear lest we should flood the market. They offer, however, a hundred and eighty thousand for a small portion of them.*

" *You must come home, Quatermain, and see about these things, especially if you insist upon making the magnificent present of the third share, which does not belong to me, to my brother George. As for Good, he is no good. His time is too much* occupied in shaving and other matters connected with the vain adorning of the body. But I think he is still down on his luck about Foulata. He told me that since he had been home, he hadn't seen a woman to touch her, either as regards her figure or the sweetness of her expression.

" I want you to come home, my dear old comrade, and to buy a house near here. You have done your day's work, and have lots of money now, and there is a place for sale quite close which would suit you admirably. Do come; the sooner the better; you can finish writing the story of our adventures on board ship. We have refused to tell the tale till it is written by you, for fear lest we shall not be believed. If you start on receipt of this you will reach here by Christmas, and I book you to stay with me for that. Good is coming, and George; and so, by the way, is your boy Harry (there's a bribe for you). I have had him down for a week's shooting, and like him. He is a cool young hand; he shot me in the leg, cut out the pellets, and then remarked upon the advantages of having a medical student with every shooting party.

" Good-bye, old boy; I can't say any more, but I know that you will come, if it is only to oblige

" Your sincere friend,

" Henry Curtis.

" P.S.—The tusks of the great bull that killed poor Khiva have now been put up in the hall here, over a pair of buffalo horns you gave me, and look magnificent; and the axe with which I chopped off Twala's head is fixed above my writing-table. I wish that we could have managed to bring away the coats of chain armour.

" H.C."

To-day is Tuesday. There is a steamer going on Friday, and I really think that I must take Curtis at his word, and sail by her for England, if it is only to see you, Harry, my boy, and to look after the printing of this history, which is a task that I do not like to trust to anybody else.

ALLAN QUATERMAIN.

THE STORY OF PENGUIN CLASSICS

Before 1946 ... 'Classics' are mainly the domain of academics and students, without readable editions for everyone else. This all changes when a little-known classicist, E. V. Rieu, presents Penguin founder Allen Lane with the translation of Homer's *Odyssey* that he has been working on and reading to his wife Nelly in his spare time.

1946 *The Odyssey* becomes the first Penguin Classic published, and promptly sells three million copies. Suddenly, classic books are no longer for the privileged few.

1950s Rieu, now series editor, turns to professional writers for the best modern, readable translations, including Dorothy L. Sayers's *Inferno* and Robert Graves's *The Twelve Caesars*, which revives the salacious original.

1960s 1961 sees the arrival of the Penguin Modern Classics, showcasing the best twentieth-century writers from around the world. Rieu retires in 1964, hailing the Penguin Classics list as 'the greatest educative force of the 20th century'.

1970s A new generation of translators arrives to swell the Penguin Classics ranks, and the list grows to encompass more philosophy, religion, science, history and politics.

1980s The Penguin American Library joins the Classics stable, with titles such as *The Last of the Mohicans* safeguarded. Penguin Classics now offers the most comprehensive library of world literature available.

1990s Penguin Popular Classics are launched, offering readers budget editions of the greatest works of literature. Penguin Audiobooks brings the classics to a listening audience for the first time, and in 1999 the launch of the Penguin Classics website takes them online to an ever larger global readership.

The 21st Century Penguin Classics are rejacketed for the first time in nearly twenty years. This world famous series now consists of more than 1,300 titles, making the widest range of the best books ever written available to millions – and constantly redefining the meaning of what makes a 'classic'.

The Odyssey continues ...

The best books ever written

PENGUIN (Ⓟ) CLASSICS

SINCE 1946

Find out more at www.penguinclassics.com